CRUEL PARADISE

J.T. GEISSINGER

Published by J.T. Geissinger, Inc.

www.jtgeissinger.com

ISBN: 978-1-7338243-7-8

Cover design by Letitia Hasser, RBA Designs

Printed in the United States of America

For Jay, my partner in crime.

For never was a story of more woe
than this of Juliet and her Romeo.

~ Romeo and Juliet, Act V, Scene III

JULES

"This is literally the worst idea you've ever had."

"I think it's genius."

Watching me with pursed lips and her arms folded over her chest in disapproval as I clumsily attempt to pick the lock, Fin snorts. "Yes, but you were dropped on your head a lot as a baby."

"Will you be quiet? I'm almost in."

"In jail, you mean. Incarcerated. Because in ten more seconds, I'm going to call the cops on you myself. You're completely inept at breaking and entering. Especially the breaking part. I could die of old age before you're finished."

Standing six feet tall, with blonde hair that hangs halfway to her waist and a figure that stops men dead in their tracks, my best friend is as pretty as she is impatient. She's also funny, whip smart, and an excellent thief, which is why I brought her with me tonight.

One needs a trusted accomplice when stealing two thousand boxes of diapers.

For moral support, if nothing else.

Not that she's giving it to me.

Sighing, she says, "You're a hot mess, girlfriend. I've seen better Dumpster fires."

"If you'd shut up a minute, I could concentrate!"

She checks her watch, pressing a dial to illuminate the face, and impatiently starts counting seconds. "Ten. Nine. Eight. Seven."

"It's a friggin' padlock, and I'm using a friggin' bobby pin! Gimme a break!"

"No excuses. I could've had it open a year ago. Six. Five. Four. Three."

I give up, stand straight, and glare at her through the shadows. "Fine. You win. Tyrant."

She slings the backpack off her shoulders, unzips it, removes a bolt cutter, and hands it to me with a smile. "Do you think you can cut through the chain yourself, princess, or will you need help with that, too?"

"Remind me to put hair remover in your shampoo bottle when we get home."

I turn back to the lock. The bolt cutters efficiently snap through the metal links of the chain, and the chain slithers to the ground with the lock still attached at one end.

Fin holds out her hand. I pass her the bolt cutters. Back into her pack they go, then she pulls open the heavy door of the warehouse. We slip inside silently, take a moment to let our eyes adjust to the gloom, then locate what we came for.

Fully loaded and ready for tomorrow's trip to the distribution center, the delivery truck sits at the far end of the loading dock's bay.

We head toward it at an unhurried trot, our footsteps echoing off the high ceiling's exposed rafters.

I say, "You're sure you can get that thing started?"

She scoffs. "How dare you."

"And you're sure Max disabled the cameras and silent alarm?"

I'm not looking at Fin, but I swear I hear her eyes roll. "Yes, grandma. I'm positive. I should've made you pop a Xanax before we left."

"But then I wouldn't have been able to drive."

"I hate to break it to you, but I'm driving."

"You drive as well as you cook. *I'm* driving."

"Excuse me, Martha Stewart, but not everyone has the cooking gene."

"There's no such thing as a cooking gene."

"There totally is. You're Italian. It's in your DNA."

"Ha! Maybe if you tried using the stove instead of a blow-torch to heat your food, you wouldn't have so many problems."

Fin waves a dismissive hand in the air, ending the conversation. She hates to be reminded of that time she set fire to the kitchen cooking stir fry with a metalworking tool.

When we get to the truck, we encounter the minor issue of the doors being locked. Fin uses the bolt cutters to smash the driver's window, and the problem is solved. We climb inside.

She takes all of five seconds to hotwire it, the showoff.

When the engine roars to life with a satisfying belch from the tailpipe, I say, "Wait!"

Startled, she glances at me. "What?"

"I'm supposed to be driving."

"Too bad, so sad, possession is nine-tenths of the law."

"How is that cliché applicable in this situation?"

She smiles. "My butt is already in possession of the driver's seat. Besides, someone needs to roll up that…" She pauses, then says, "Oh."

Her deflated tone makes my spinal nerves tingle. "Oh? What *oh*?"

"*That* oh." She points beyond the windshield to the huge rolling metal door through which the delivery trucks enter and exit the bay.

That it's closed isn't the problem. The problem is the big

steel locks anchored to the cement floor on either side at the bottom.

I stare at the locks, flabbergasted. "Shit!"

She says drily, "Well put, Shakespeare."

"I thought Max took care of security?"

"Those locks must be brand new. That door was supposed to be able to be manually opened from the inside when the security system went down."

"So what do we do? There's no way the bolt cutters can get through metal that thick."

Fin peers at the door for a moment. "Pray for a miracle?"

I throw my hands in the air. "*Pray?* Criminal masterminds don't rely on a supreme being to get them out of tight spots! They go to plan B!" I pause. "What's plan B?"

At least she has the decency to look sheepish. "We don't have one."

I groan. "No backup plan again? We're *terrible* at this!"

She says defensively, "We're not that bad." Then, under her breath: "At least I know how to hotwire a vehicle."

I stare at the door in frustration for several seconds, then pronounce, "Oh, screw it. We'll improvise."

She hoots. "Improvise? The last time you used that word, I ended up dangling from a sixth story hotel window."

"You lived."

"You do recall that the building was engulfed in flames at the time? And I was naked?"

I ignore her. "Just floor it. Pedal to the metal. We'll probably be able to smash through."

She turns to me with arched brows. "*Probably?*"

I try to make my nod look firm and convincing. "This is a class seven rig with almost five hundred horse power. She'll get it done." I think for a moment. "Or we'll die in a fiery explosion. Either way, it'll be awesome."

Fin stares at me like I've got horns growing out of my head. Then she grins. "And this is why we're best friends, Thelma."

I grin back. "I love you, too, Louise."

She stomps her foot onto the gas pedal.

The truck lurches forward, diesel engine bellowing, tires pluming smoke.

We scream in unison at the top of our lungs as we rocket toward the metal roll up door.

KILLIAN

Fascinated, I watch the security video on my computer's screen over and over, replaying it so many times that Declan starts to fidget in impatience.

I glance up at him, standing beside the desk, six-plus feet of killing power with linebacker's shoulders and eyes the color of a frozen arctic lake that never thaws.

"Diapers."

"Aye." He shrugs, like he can't understand it, either.

"What kind of thief steals a truck full of diapers and leaves the safe with three hundred grand in cash in it untouched?"

"One with a death wish, apparently."

I rewind the video again, shaking my head in disbelief as the truck plows through the steel door at top speed.

It's like a scene from an action movie.

There's no sound, but I can imagine the deafening racket it must've made as metal met metal. First, the massive door bows in the middle, warping out of shape. Then it rips clean off from the building at the top, slamming forward onto the ground with a billowing cloud of dust and sparks.

The bottom of the door stays bolted to the cement, forcing the truck to fly into the air as it careens over a pile of crumpled metal.

As it lands, the truck swerves wildly. It appears about to topple over onto its side, but the driver regains control, straightens the vehicle, and speeds off through the empty parking lot, vanishing from the camera's sight.

"The cameras at the warehouse were disabled, but I got this from the clothing manufacturer across the street. We tapped into their security system to see if they caught anything, and Bob's your uncle. Unfortunately, this is the only angle that caught our diaper pincher on film."

"Any prints at the scene?"

"No. They must've worn gloves."

I sit back into the large captain's chair, wondering which of my many enemies is both dumb and suicidal enough to have attempted this bizarre theft.

Diapers. What the bloody hell?

We're in the office in Liam's penthouse. No—*my* penthouse. Even after a year of living here, it doesn't feel like mine. Probably because my twin brother's taste in interior décor would make Count Dracula feel right at home.

Everything is black. Glossy, cold, and black. It's like living inside a very modern coffin.

Unfortunately, when you're impersonating someone, you need to leave their uninspired choices in clothing, art, and furniture alone.

Bypassing the question of why the hell my brother owns a diaper factory, I say, "How much is a truckload of diapers worth?"

Declan lifts a muscular shoulder. "Maybe ninety grand."

"That's hardly worth the effort."

"Agreed."

7

"Especially considering there isn't exactly a hot market for stolen nappies. How is this thief planning to get his money from the take? Garage sales? eBay?"

"Maybe he's got a lot of kids."

I have to admit, I enjoy Declan's dry sense of humor.

The rest of his personality, however, I could do without.

"The diapers are low priority, but I'm concerned about the hacking of the security system. Someone's got some smarts, even if it wasn't the driver."

"If you're thinking it's a crew, it's not likely to be one from around here. The locals know that company belongs to Liam." He pauses. "Sorry. You."

I wave it off. I'm used to people calling me by my brother's name by now. "See what you can find out. But keep it quiet."

"You don't want me to call O'Malley at the precinct and let him handle it?"

"No. I can't have word getting out that the head of the Irish mafia had two thousand diapers snatched from under his nose. My reputation would be shot."

Declan nods solemnly. "Next thing you know, old ladies will be holding up your convenience stores for Bingo money, and the Girl Scouts will challenge you to a turf war."

He turns and leaves before I can tell him to piss off, the smart ass.

I've forgotten about the purloined diapers until Declan strolls back into my office at six that evening.

I'm still sitting in the captain's chair. Stacks of reports, statements, and contracts requiring my signature crowd the large mahogany desk in front of me.

Had I known there was so much paperwork involved in

running an international criminal empire, I might not have volunteered for the job. And don't get me started on the employee problems. You'd think grown men wouldn't need so much supervision. I feel like I'm running a daycare center.

I look up to find Declan approaching. He's carrying a laptop. His expression is solemn, but there's a mischievous twinkle in his eyes.

I gesture to the chair across from my desk to indicate he should sit.

After he lowers his considerable bulk into the chair and gets settled, he strums his fingers thoughtfully on the closed lid of the Mac in his lap. "You believe in astrology?"

I say drily, "Sure. That and Big Foot, too."

"Big Foot could be a real thing. I saw a show on the telly once—"

"Declan."

"Sorry. Where was I?"

"About to get your block knocked off."

"Oh, right. Astrology." He pauses to look at me meaningfully. "Mercury is in retrograde."

I gaze at him steadily from under lowered brows. "You're aware, I assume, that I'm in possession of an extremely short temper and a large collection of guns? Several of which are within reach?"

Ignoring my threat, Declan continues. "The thing about Mercury is that it can be a trickster. Especially when in retrograde. Everything gets fucked up. Computers crash, flights get cancelled, contracts fall through."

He takes another meaningful pause. "Things are backward."

"You have three seconds to make your point before I put a bullet between your eyes."

Declan smiles. "What would be the most backward thing you could think of about a man who'd steal a truckload of diapers?"

Honestly, if Liam didn't like him so much, Declan would already be bleeding out on the Turkish rug.

Before I can riddle his body with bullet holes, he pronounces, "If the man were a woman."

I take a moment to gauge if he's joking. "A woman?"

Looking inexplicably pleased, he nods. "And not only one of them."

When he doesn't continue, I say, "If it takes you more than a single word to tell me how many women stole a goddamn truck full of goddamn diapers from me, I'll separate your head from your body."

"Two."

"Thank you."

"You're welcome."

We stare at each other. Finally, I say, "You enjoy annoying me, don't you?"

He shrugs. "Aye. Don't take it personally. I just like to poke bears."

My tone bone dry, I say, "Lucky me."

"It took Liam about a decade to get used to me, so." He shrugs again.

"A word of advice, Declan: my brother has all the patience in the family. I'm the one with the hair-trigger temper."

He makes a face and shakes his head. "That's what you want people to think. From what I've seen, you're extremely methodical and precise. When you kill someone, you've been planning it for a long time."

I resist the urge to sigh. Instead, I lean back in my chair, fold my hands over my stomach, and gaze at him.

After a while, he says, "Okay, so I'm thinking that look means you've already figured out how you're going to kill me, and the next time I irritate you, I'll find myself swinging from the rafters."

"And the noose will be made of your own bowels."

Picturing it, he grimaces. "Wow. You're going full Hannibal Lecter on me."

I allow my lips to curve into a faint, evil smile. "Aye. In several more minutes, I might be wearing your face as a mask. Tell me about the women."

With a grudging grunt, he sits forward, sets the laptop on my desk, and opens it. He types on the keyboard for a moment, then turns the screen toward me.

I'm looking at a closeup of a large delivery truck. The shot is from the front. It's grainy, but visible through the windshield are the driver and passenger of the truck.

The driver is a blonde. The passenger is a brunette. They're not gazing out the windshield, but instead are looking at each other.

Looking at each other and laughing.

Hard.

I glance up at Declan. He puts his hands in the air, like, *I've got nothin'.*

I turn my attention back to the screen. It's hard to discern their features, but it's obvious both women are young.

And, judging by their uproarious laughter, probably high on drugs.

"*These* are the diaper thieves."

"Aye."

"Do you recognize either one of them?"

"Nope. No hits in any database on their faces, either, though that could be due to the angle. Hit the right arrow key."

When I do, another still shot appears. This time I'm looking at the same truck, but from the rear. It's parked in the middle of a grassy field, tailgate lowered, back doors wide open.

It's empty.

Declan says, "They offloaded the haul in a rural area about thirty minutes outside the city and abandoned the truck. Tire tracks coming into and going out of the field suggest multiple smaller vehicles were involved."

I don't have to ask to know that he tracked the truck to the field by hacking into streetlight cameras near the warehouse, but I do have another question.

"Where did those smaller vehicles go from there?"

"No idea."

Surprised, I look up at him. He says, "They cut the feed to all the traffic cameras within miles of that field."

He sounds impressed, which irks me. "So hack a satellite to find out where they went."

He blinks.

Looks like I'll have to do the heavy lifting myself. "Forget it. I still don't understand the diaper angle. If they wanted to steal something from me, there are far more valuable hauls they could've gone after."

"Assuming they even knew you owned that factory." His cell phone dings. He digs it from his pocket, looks at it, and frowns.

"What is it?"

Instead of answering, he stands and walks to the coffee table in front of the sofa across the room. He picks up the TV remote and hits a button. The television comes on to the local news station.

Standing outside the front of an institutional-looking red brick building, a cheerful blonde reporter beams at the screen.

"In other news tonight, we have a heartwarming story about the generosity of the human spirit. As we reported last month, a fire destroyed the storage facility of the headquarters of Newborns in Need here in Boston. NIN provides care necessities free of charge to agencies and hospitals serving premature, ill, or impoverished newborns throughout the United States.

"As this location is the main distribution hub for those critically needed supplies, the fire was particularly devastating. But today, an anonymous donor gifted *two thousand* boxes of diapers to the organization to replenish their losses.

"In addition to the diapers, large quantities of formula, clothing, blankets, and toys were also donated. No word on who the anonymous philanthropist might be, but Meryl Hopkins, president of the charity, has called him an angel. Back to you in the studio, John."

Declan clicks off the TV and looks at me in disbelief. "A philanthropist thief? I don't get it."

"Neither do I. By any chance, does Liam own other companies serving the newborn market?"

"No."

I mull it over for a moment, equal parts confused and intrigued.

A pair of female thieves breaks into a warehouse and steals a truckload of diapers. If caught, they'd be facing first degree grand theft charges with a possible maximum sentence of thirty years in prison, charitable donation notwithstanding.

So why risk it?

And what about the other items, the clothing, food, and toys? If those were stolen, too, that means the diaper theft was part of a larger, organized operation. One that must've taken weeks or months to plan.

All with a final payout of nothing?

It doesn't make sense.

No one in their right mind takes such risk with zero reward. If it wasn't money the thieves were after, it was definitely something else.

Because if there's one thing I know for sure about human nature, it's that a person who isn't motivated by greed is usually motivated by something much darker.

Like amassing power, for instance.

Like taking revenge.

Things I myself am all too familiar with.

When I start to type fast and hard on my computer's keyboard, Declan says, "What're you doing?"

"Going hunting." The Department of Defense website loads, and I quickly get to work.

Ready or not, thieves, here I come.

3

JULES

*W*hen I glance over my shoulder again, Fin sighs in exasperation.

"Will you quit doing that? You're making me jumpy."

I mumble an apology and take another sip of my margarita, but can't shake the sensation that I'm being stared at intently.

Considering I grew up under the constant, watchful gaze of several dozen bodyguards, tutors, and nannies, I know the feeling well.

Which is why I'm on edge when I should be celebrating.

Sitting on either side of me at the high-top table in La Fiesta's noisy, crowded bar, Fin and Max don't share my jitters. They're all smiles and easy laughs, flirting with the cute bartender who keeps sending over free drinks.

As usual, I'm the lucky beneficiary of the incandescent glow my friends produce—hence the free drinks—but if I were here alone, I'd be paying.

Not because I'm a dog or anything. Though compared to the curvy, creamy beauty of Fin and the edgy, tough-girl sex appeal of Max, I'm as interesting as the sole of a shoe.

It's for the same reason I wear baggy clothes and no makeup

and go by a fake last name: to blend in. To disappear into the background.

Attention is the last thing I want.

Attention means questions, and questions mean answers, and answers—especially truthful ones—are something I never give.

For a girl like me, attention can be dangerous.

It can be deadly.

So I keep my head down and my mouth shut and stay as cool and detached as possible, even as these two yahoos on either side of me cause spontaneous erections all around.

I wish Fin didn't have such a fondness for low-cut blouses.

"Could you put those things away?" I say crossly, waving a hand at her boobs. "They're almost in my salsa."

I grab the dish of salsa out from under her hovering breasts, take a tortilla chip from a basket in the center of the table, and dunk the chip into the sauce. Then I pop it into my mouth, enjoying the spicy, satisfying crunch.

Fin smiles serenely at me. "I know this is hard for you to understand, B Cups, but the girls need air."

"What they need is scaffolding."

She arches her brows. "Are you suggesting my glorious cleavage is sagging?"

"No. I'm suggesting you invest in some undergarments that don't provide the male population of Boston with an anatomical drawing of your chest. It's like you're wearing tracing paper for a bra. That man over there is about to have a heart attack."

Fin turns her green-eyed gaze to the person in question, an elderly gentleman sitting a few tables away. He promptly chokes on his taco when he notices her looking at him.

She says fondly, "The poor things. They don't stand a chance."

"Speaking of poor things," says Max under her breath, "that guy at the end of the bar is *fire*. My panties are melting."

She's staring over my left shoulder. When I start to turn my head in that direction, she hisses, "Don't look!"

"How am I supposed to judge if he's fire if I can't look?"

"I mean don't look *now*." She casually pretends to inspect her manicure. "I'll let you know as soon as he's not burning holes into the back of your head."

So someone *is* staring at me.

A man.

Not good.

"What does he look like?"

Max glances up, then quickly back down to her nails. A flush of red creeps over her cheeks. She mutters, "Like he could impregnate a woman through osmosis. Jesus, those eyes. That face. That *body*."

After a surreptitious glance in his direction that she tries to disguise by tossing her hair, Fin pipes in, "He looks like a cross between James Bond and Wolverine. Only bigger. And hotter."

Max nods. "And way more dangerous."

Dangerous? My heart skips a beat. All the little hairs on my arms stand on end.

My tone as stiff as my spine, I say to Fin, "Give me your compact."

She shares a worried look with Max, then digs into the handbag hanging off the side of her chair and produces the small mirrored compact she never goes anywhere without.

She hands it to me silently.

I flick it open, take a steadying breath, and lift it to my face.

Pretending to check my non-existent lipstick, I check out the guy at the end of the bar behind me instead.

Reflected in the mirror, a pair of blistering dark eyes meet mine.

Sweet Jesus. I feel a jolt like someone plugged me into a socket.

Max was wrong. He isn't fire.

He's a fucking volcano.

Big, dark haired, and utterly masculine, he's got a jaw covered in scruff and a wide, sensuous mouth. His black Armani suit is molded to his frame, showcasing bulging biceps and thick thighs. When he rubs a hand over his jaw, I catch a glimpse of the array of tattoos on his knuckles.

As if he knows my stomach dropped to the floor at the sight of him, his full lips curve into a small, mocking smile.

Horrified, I whisper, "Clean up on aisle five."

It's one of our many code phrases. Translated, it means: everything's fucked, create a diversion, and run away as fast as you can.

Fin freezes.

Max does too, then sighs. "Well, shit."

As for me, I snap shut the compact, hand it back to Fin, then guzzle the rest of my margarita. I touch the knife in my coat pocket, wishing it were a gun. Then I look back and forth between my friends.

My heart hammers against my breastbone. My blood is molten lava in my veins.

"Ready?"

Fin says indignantly, "I'm *not* losing another pair of Louboutins."

Max says, "This is why you should always wear biker boots like me, dummy. Those spiky things you like aren't meant for running."

"If I wanted to look like a homeless circus performer, I would definitely dress like you, Maxima."

"Up yours, Finley."

Scowling because she hates to be called by her full name, Max stands abruptly and stalks off, pushing through a swinging door that leads to a back corridor of the restaurant where the restrooms are.

Five seconds later, we hear a muffled *boom*, then screaming. Moments later, the fire alarms screech to life.

The restaurant erupts into chaos.

Panicked men and women stream out from the corridor Max disappeared into, shoving each other and tripping over their own feet in their haste. All the patrons at the tables around us jump to their feet, exclaiming, and stampede toward the front door.

Emergency lights flash red and blue.

The sprinkler system kicks on, spitting freezing water from the ceiling.

Above the opening to the corridor, gray plumes of smoke billow up the wall.

Fin grabs my hand. We start running.

Pushing against the flow of bodies, we head toward the kitchen, dodging toppled chairs and trying not to slip on the slick tile floor. As soon as we burst through the kitchen doors, I drop Fin's hand and we go in opposite directions.

She makes a hard left toward the employee break room. I run toward the exit at the back. We'll hook up again at the apartment later after everyone has left the all-clear code on a designated voicemail.

If one of us fails to call, the other two won't go back to the apartment.

Ever.

Outside, the cold evening air is a stinging slap on my heated cheeks. I'm in the parking lot behind the restaurant. Overflowing Dumpsters flank me, reeking of trash.

I run as fast as I can to the street, not looking behind me. Once there, I make a sharp right and head to the next street, a busy boulevard with four lanes of traffic zooming past at top speed.

I don't hear footsteps pounding behind me. All I hear is the wild thunder of my heartbeat and my panting, panicked breaths.

When I hit the corner of the boulevard, I glance over my shoulder, but no one's there.

He isn't following me.

I escaped.

Gulping air, I slow my pace but keep going, headed to the bright lights of the building ahead. It's an old-fashioned movie theater, the kind with a tiny box office near the sidewalk and a gilded Art Deco marquee. A small crowd mills in front, waiting for the doors to open.

Like a gift from the universe, a taxi pulls to a stop at the curb right outside.

I break into a run again.

Beating out a young couple just about to open the back door of the cab, I dive inside, slam the door shut, and slide low in the seat, peering out the window for any sign of danger.

I tell the driver breathlessly, "Beacon Hill, please."

A low voice to my left says, "Fifty-nine Mount Vernon Street, if I'm not mistaken."

The voice has an Irish accent. My blood freezes to ice in my veins.

I turn my head, and there he is on the seat beside me, smiling like some testosterone-jacked version of the Cheshire Cat.

The volcano.

AKA Liam Black.

AKA the biggest, baddest, most ruthless mobster on both sides of the Atlantic.

The man I stole a truckload of diapers from.

Shit.

4

JULES

*W*hen I merely sit and gape at him in horror, he says, "Swanky neighborhood you live in."

His smile grows wider. Light from the theater marquee glints off his perfect white teeth. "I guess that old saying 'crime doesn't pay' is wrong."

The cab pulls away from the curb into traffic. I manage to detach my tongue from the roof of my mouth and sit up straight in my seat. Then I level him with a look that attempts withering disdain, but probably falls miles short of it considering how many of my body functions are on the verge of complete failure.

I say tartly, "You should know."

"Ah. Sass." He chuckles. "I wondered what you'd go with. Most people in your situation choose denial. Then the bargaining starts." He pauses, smile fading. His voice drops an octave. "Then the tears."

"You won't get tears out of me. And if you think you intimidate me, think again."

He arches his brows. "Have you had a recent head injury? Because that's the only logical reason you wouldn't be intimidated. I have to assume you know who I am, considering the dramatic exit you and your friends made from the restaurant."

He waits, watching me with those laser beam eyes and that small, smug smile, radiating danger and masculinity in equal doses.

I hate him.

I've known men like him my entire life, and I hate them all.

Holding his gaze, I say, "I don't have a head injury. And I know exactly who you are. And *you* should know that no matter what you do to me, how much you hurt me or how long you make it last, I won't tell you anything."

A strange look crosses his face. Disgust or disappointment, I can't tell which. But then the cab goes over a bump in the road and the look disappears, as if it were never there in the first place.

"Are you so eager to meet your maker?" he murmurs, dark eyes glittering.

"I'm eager to get away from you," I snap back. "So hurry up and shoot me or strangle me or whatever it is you've got in mind, so we can be done with it already."

His strange look returns.

The driver has a strange look now, too, sending a startled glance to me in the back seat as I demand his other passenger kill me.

"Why the hostility?" Liam inquires, sounding as if he's actually interested. "After all, I'm the victim here."

A harsh laugh bursts from my chest. "*Victim*? You're as much of a victim as I am an orangutan."

He looks me up and down, his gaze razor sharp as it rakes over my body. His Irish brogue thick with sarcasm, he drawls, "Where could you be hiding your tail, I wonder?"

I stare at him in astonishment.

He's toying with me. He's laughing at me. He's going to kill me, but has decided to have some fun with me first.

The nerve!

I say through clenched teeth, "Orangutans don't have tails."

"I thought all monkeys had tails."

"They're not monkeys. They're apes." Since I'll be dead soon, I decide to add a little zinger for good measure. "Like you."

"An ape? I'll take it. I've been called much worse."

He doesn't look offended. On the contrary, he seems to be enjoying himself. He's smiling again, the psychopath.

We ride in silence for a while, staring at each other, until I can't stand it anymore. I demand, "At least tell me how you're going to do it."

His gaze drops to my mouth. He moistens his lips. "Do it?" he repeats, his tone gravelly. His gaze flashes back up to mine. Now his eyes are burning. "Do what?"

"Kill me."

The taxi driver swerves then overcorrects, throwing me against the door. Liam remains undisturbed in his seat, staring at me with the scorching intensity of a thousand suns.

He says, "I'm curious—"

"You'd like to have a sexual encounter with another man? Good for you. More men should admit they're heteroflexible. It's nothing to be ashamed of."

A muscle slides in his jaw. His gaze drops to my mouth again. His tone deadly soft, he says, "Oh, I'm crystal clear on my sexual preferences, little thief."

His dark lashes lift, and now he's incinerating me with his stare. "I'd give you a demonstration if I didn't already know how much you'd love it."

I refuse to break eye contact with this arrogant bastard, though I'm pretty sure I'm going to have PTSD if I somehow make it out of this cab alive.

Liam Black is the kind of violent jolt to the system that takes years of psychotherapy to unwind.

I say, "Don't flatter yourself."

"I'm not. And stop playing with that knife in your pocket. If you stab me, you'll only succeed in making me mad."

I stare at him for a long moment, debating whether or not to go ahead and pull the knife out and lunge at him like I'd been planning.

He presses his lips together. I suspect it's to stop from laughing out loud.

"As I was saying before I was so rudely interrupted, I'm curious: why donate what you stole from me?"

"I didn't steal it from you. I stole it from a warehouse."

"I own the warehouse."

"No, a shell corporation owns the warehouse."

"I own the shell corporation."

I say drily, "One of many."

"Aye. Too many to keep track. To be honest, I didn't even know about it before you pulled that stunt."

"Your minions set it up for you, huh? Just one more way to wash your dirty money?"

"Something like that."

"Well, in case you're wondering, you've got ninety-six of them."

"Diaper factories?"

"Shell corporations."

He pauses, examining my expression. His own reflects deepening interest and what I'd think was a glimmer of respect, if I didn't know better.

"Have you been studying up on me, little thief?"

"Something like that."

Ignoring how I threw his own words back at him, he says, "Why?"

"As a general rule, I do my homework before a job."

He studies me with the same ferocious focus I felt at the restaurant. His attention is like a physical force. A whisper of electricity zinging along my nerve endings. A finger reaching out to tap me on the shoulder.

A sledgehammer crashing into my chest.

He says, "What else did you discover about me in your studies?"

My temper—short even under the best of circumstances—snaps. "I'll tell you what I *didn't* discover."

"Which is?"

"That you're so annoyingly chatty. Are you gonna kill me or what? I've got better things to do with my time than talk to the likes of you."

Oh, god, that feels good. Watching the expression of astonishment cross his evil, chiseled features is sweet, sweet, sweet.

I bet he can't remember the last time someone disrespected him.

Especially a girl.

Score one for womankind.

My sense of satisfaction comes to an abrupt end when he grabs me by both arms and hauls me across the seat onto his lap.

I gasp as his arms close hard around me.

He's huge and impossibly strong, holding me easily even as I thrash and struggle. When I scream and kick out at the door, the cab driver squawks in panic.

"Hey! No rough stuff! I'll pull over and throw you both out!"

Liam says calmly, "Pull over and you'll get a bullet in your skull, mate. Keep driving."

When the sputtering driver turns the wheel and slows, headed to the side of the road, my captor adds, "I'm Liam Black."

Thirty seconds later, trapped and seething in his arms as the cab drives straight down the street at top speed, I say through gritted teeth, "Boy, that must really come in handy."

"It has its uses." He gazes down at me, helpless in the cage of his arms. "Answer my question."

"No."

"No?"

Judging by his tone, he can't decide if he's frustrated or amused by my flat refusal. He stares at my profile for a moment, then says suddenly, "You're not afraid of me."

He says it like he just discovered the lost city of Atlantis. With surprise and wonder and—weirdly—a touch of pride.

"Let's just say I have a healthy respect for your ability to make people dead. Now let me go."

"So you can break into another unsuspecting victim's business and steal infant care products?"

"So I can jab my thumbs into your eyeballs."

He clucks. "So violent."

"I'm not the one who just threatened the driver's life."

"Nobody's perfect."

"Especially not you, the guy who's about to sink my feet into cement blocks and throw me into the Charles River."

He bends his head to my ear. His voice drops to a husky whisper. "It would be the reservoir, not the river. But you already know I'm not going to hurt you. Now answer my goddamn question about why you donated what you took from me before I turn you over on my lap and give you something to really be snippy about. Which, let's be honest, both of us would enjoy."

Then he inhales deeply against my neck and makes a low sound of pleasure in the back of his throat.

I'm speechless.

My face is flaming, and my heart is pounding, and I can't get my mouth to form words.

Me, the girl who can talk straight through anything from a root canal to a funeral, cannot find the ability to speak, simply because a cold-blooded killer sniffed my throat.

There must be some kind of mind-altering agent in his cologne.

"I...I..."

He skims the tip of his nose against my earlobe, causing my

entire body to break out in gooseflesh.

"Hmm?"

My voice choked, I say, "Stop that."

"Stop what?"

He's all feigned innocence, the heartless SOB. "Let me go!"

"If you answer my question, I'll let you go."

That surprises me. He doesn't seem reasonable that way. "Really?"

His chuckle is low and full of self-satisfaction. "No."

At times like these, I really wish I had super powers. It would be so lovely to manifest a pair of poisonous barbed tentacles to wrap around his thick, smug neck.

"So in addition to being a general, all-around bad guy, you're a liar, too."

"Aye. Comes with the territory. But people in glass houses shouldn't throw stones, my mouthy little thief."

His lips move over the sensitive skin beneath my earlobe as he speaks, raising the hair on the back of my neck and sending my pulse haywire.

Then I realize he said "my" thief, and my heart stops altogether.

Because there are far, far worse things he could do to me than throw me into the Charles River. Catching the attention of a man like Liam Black doesn't have to end in blood.

If he decides he likes me, it could end in something worse than death.

"Easy," he says gruffly, pulling back to look at me. "What just happened?"

I can't look at him. My face is on fire, I'm as stiff as a board in his arms, and I can't risk looking into those dark, burning eyes, because I'm afraid of what I might see reflected back at me.

"Take a breath. Then unsheathe your fingernails from my arm. Then tell me why you're freaking out."

I blurt, "Because you're the most dangerous man in Boston—"

"In the world," he interrupts mildly.

"—and I'm about to die—"

"We've already been over this. I'm not going to hurt you."

"—and you admitted you're a liar—"

"Hmm. There is that."

"—and you're holding me in your lap and sniffing my neck and…and…"

"And?"

I swallow hard, still not able to look at him, my pulse flying at a breakneck speed.

Then his body tenses.

He deposits me back onto my side of the seat with an expression like he just smelled something rotten and barks at the cab driver, "Pull over."

The taxi screeches to a stop at the curb. Liam turns his head and pins me in his burning, unblinking gaze.

He growls something in a language I don't understand, then continues to glare at me.

I say, "Um…"

"Get out."

My mouth drops open. "You're letting me go?"

"No. I'm throwing you out."

Reaching around me, he opens the door and pushes on it, so it swings wide on its hinges. Then he retreats to his side of the car and stares straight ahead, his jaw hard and his energy that of barely controlled thermonuclear rage.

I have no idea what's happening.

But this isn't the time to wonder about a notorious gangster's unexpected mood swings.

This is the time to run the hell away.

I launch myself out of the cab and do just that, disappearing into the night as if it swallowed me.

5

JULES

"*I* don't get it."

"I don't either, Fin, but I'm telling you, that's what happened."

"He had you and then he just…let you go?"

"Yep."

Her brow crinkles. Seated next to Max on the baroque blue velvet love seat tucked into the corner of our favorite murder-mystery-themed dive bar, the Poison Pen, she's chewing her lip and frowning, white knuckling another bourbon as she watches me pace back and forth in front of the wooden coffee table separating us.

Max is watching me, too. But it's more of a "you're a bone-head" look than Fin's worried one.

She mutters, "You should've stabbed that fucker in the eye when you had the chance."

"I *didn't* have the chance, Max, that's what I'm saying!"

She's clearly dubious. "I dunno, Jules, it sounds like you two had quite the long talk. There must've been one second in between all that yammering when you could've shivved that son of a goat herder and made the world a whole lot better in the process."

She pauses to give me an accusing stare. "I mean...*Liam Black?*"

I turn and pace the other direction, wringing my hands distractedly. "We agreed it would be best if I kept the identity of the marks a secret. I pick the targets and research the job, you handle electronics and surveillance, Fin handles logistics and transportation. The details of each of our tasks we keep to ourselves in case one of us gets caught."

Max snorts. "Yeah, I know the rules. I just assumed our whole 'steal from the rich and give to the poor' girl gang ethos was about fat old billionaires who beat their kids and cheat on their taxes, not leaders of mafia syndicates."

Sipping her bourbon, Fin says absently, "Super-hot leaders of mafia syndicates."

"His hotness is irrelevant," says Max.

To which Fin replies, "It was relevant when you were ogling him at the bar and your panties were curling off you like burning paper."

"I didn't know who he was then. I'd never seen a picture of him."

"As if it would've mattered."

Max sniffs. "Excuse me, but I'd like to think I'm a little more discerning than that."

"Maybe *you* are, but your coochie has a mind of her own. Let's not forget that cute musician who couldn't find his way out of a paper bag."

"He was harmless!"

"He was clueless."

"An air-brained guitarist is *not* the same thing as the head of a multinational criminal empire!"

"My point is that when it comes to hot men, your vadge can't be trusted. If Satan had tats and a strong jaw, you'd fuck him."

Max says flatly, "This from the woman who falls in love with every leggy redhead who knows how to bat her lashes. No matter how conniving."

Bristling, Fin says, "Tess wasn't conniving. She was…clever!"

Max mutters, "Clever enough to make off with all the money in your bank account."

I have to stop this little spat before it can devolve into all-out war. "Girls! Please! Can we focus for a minute on the situation?"

Max huffs, Fin scowls, and I swing around and pace back the other direction. "Okay. First things first. How did he find us?"

"Don't look at me," Max says defensively. "The cameras at the warehouse and all around the drop zone were out. I did my job."

"What about around the field where we offloaded the truck?"

"Yes," she says with exaggerated patience, as if speaking to a child. "Those were out, too."

Fin says, "My side of the house is buttoned-up, too. I took all the usual precautions."

"There has to be a leak somewhere. A hole we didn't plug. Maybe someone saw us break into the warehouse and followed us from there?"

"Doubtful," says Fin. "There were no headlights behind us until we got on the highway, and that was ten miles from the warehouse. Besides, if someone saw us breaking in, they'd have called the police, not tailed us."

"Could the apartment be under surveillance?"

Max makes a face. "If the cops were watching us, they would've showed up at the restaurant, not *him*."

"Maybe they're on his payroll."

"Well, yeah, they probably are. My point is that we'd already be arrested. Instead we're sitting here, shitting our pants, wondering how soon it'll be before we get a bullet in our skulls."

I stop pacing to look at them. "That's the thing, though. He could've snapped my neck in the taxi if he wanted to. But he didn't. He let me go." I think for a moment. "Actually, that's not technically correct. He threw me out."

Fin sits up straighter. "Wait. What?"

I drop into the overstuffed leather chair across from the sofa and stare morosely at my feet. "Yeah. It was so strange. He was being weirdly pleasant and not killing me, then he went all Conan the Barbarian and threw me out of the cab."

Max and Fin gaze at me in loaded silence, until Max says, "What did you say to make him do that?"

My hackles go up at the way it sounds like an accusation. "Why does it have to be something I said?"

Fin says gently, "You do have a way of exasperating men, hun."

"What is *that* supposed to mean?"

With none of Fin's tact, Max says, "It means your mouth makes men crazy. And not in a good way."

Fin nods. "Like not in the wow-you-give-a-great-blowjob way."

I lift my chin and look down my nose at them. "I'll have you know I give an excellent blowjob."

Max snorts. "Really? When was the last time you gave someone a blowjob? And dreams don't count!"

I open my mouth to make a smart retort, but have to close it again when I realize I have no idea when the last time was that I performed that particular sexual act, in dreams or otherwise.

Best not to think about it. I've got more important things to be depressed about.

"Getting back to the subject at hand: Liam Black has our home address."

That hangs in the air ominously for a while, until Fin says, "I think the real subject at hand is what *specifically* you said to make him throw you out of the cab."

"I agree," says Max, nodding.

"How is that important?"

"If it was important enough to stop him from murdering you, it's important enough to consider." She motions to the waiter for another round of drinks, then turns her attention back to me. "So, what was it?"

I already know it's useless to try to divert Max from this line of conversation. She'll hound me until I answer. She's as stubborn as a Rottweiler. So I slouch lower in the chair, close my eyes, and think.

After several moments, it hits me. "Oh." I open my eyes and think some more, frowning. "No. That can't be right."

Fin and Max lean forward, all ears. They say in unison, "What?"

Still frowning, I look up into their eager faces. "I think...it's possible I might have insulted him."

After a beat, Fin turns to Max. "She thinks she insulted him."

Max turns to Fin. "The head of the Irish mafia."

"She insulted the head of the Irish mafia so badly, he forgot to kill her."

They turn back to me and stare at me in accusing silence.

"Jeez, you guys. Thanks for the support."

The waiter—a cute young guy with a man bun and a tattoo of Betty Boop on his forearm—returns with our drinks. He sets them on the coffee table, takes the empty glasses, and grins at Max. "You need anything else?"

One brow quirked, Max looks him up and down. When she opens her mouth, Fin elbows her in the ribcage.

Max sighs. "We're good, thanks."

He leaves with a wistful smile in her direction.

Fin watches him go with a curled lip. "Unbelievable. We're being hunted by the mob king as we speak, and you're flirting with hipsters."

"We're not being hunted by the mob king. He already found

us, and Devil Tongue here"—Max gestures to me—"scared him away."

"You're welcome," I say loudly, grabbing my second shot of vodka.

"Let's not get ahead of ourselves," says Fin, grabbing her own drink. "The reality is that Liam Black is probably plotting our deaths at this very moment. Our violent, hideous, painful deaths, which he'll take great pleasure in, considering we not only stole from him, but insulted him as well. *To his face*. For a man who can make grown men cry by the mere mention of his name, that's probably worse."

Aggravated, I shoot the vodka, wincing as it sears a path down my throat. "I said I *think* I might have insulted him, not that I was sure!"

Fin pushes a lock of hair behind her ear and sits forward. "Just tell us the words you spoke, and we'll go from there."

Sighing heavily, I shrug. "I just...he was sort of...sniffing my throat—"

"*Sniffing your throat?*" she interrupts, wide-eyed.

It sounds even worse out loud. "Um. Yes. I was on his lap and he was sniffing—"

"*On his lap?*" they say together.

I glance around in irritation. "Can you please keep your voices down?"

Max stares at me in open astonishment. "Your priorities right now are so out of whack, I don't even know where to start. Who cares what anybody in this bar thinks? *You were sitting on Liam Black's lap and he was sniffing your throat?* Shut the front door!"

"And god bless America," adds Fin, lifting her glass to me in a toast.

I really need to get better friends.

"It wasn't like it sounds," I start, only to get interrupted again.

"Oh, really?" Max laughs. "Because it sounds like a certain smoking hot evil gangster got sprung when he saw you at the bar, my friend."

"He couldn't have gotten 'sprung,' as you so charmingly put it, because he was staring at my back!"

Fin says, "Your back is hot," and guzzles her bourbon.

I drop my head into my hands and groan.

"Oh, stop your bellyaching. This is good news!"

I lift my head and glare at Max. "How, exactly, is this good news?"

"We're probably not going to die!" She pauses. "I mean, you're not." She pauses again. "I wonder if he'd forgive us all for a foursome?"

"I'm not having sex with you two bozos and a friggin' mobster!" I say with heat.

Meanwhile, Fin is looking at Max with pursed lips, like she's considering it.

"Fin. *No.*"

She blinks innocently at me. "I didn't say a word."

"Listen, can we *please* focus? He knows our address. He could have ten hitmen waiting for us at home right now!"

Max shakes her head. "He wouldn't have come to the restaurant himself if he were going to have his goons handle it. Besides, I'd get a notification on my phone if anyone broke into the apartment."

She sits back against the sofa, crosses her legs, and gazes at me.

"No, what I think happened here is that somehow Liam Black discovered who we were, got an eyeful of you, Natalie Portman, and decided he wanted to go in for a closer look."

I say flatly, "I don't even look like Natalie Portman's distant cousin."

Fin tilts her head, examining me. "There's a definite resemblance. Mostly that kind of bookish, nerdy, tomboy brunette thing. The hot Harvard grad vibe. I've always thought you were more of a Greta Garbo, myself. Very aloof and mysterious. Very 'I want to be alone.'"

"I do want to be alone." I look back and forth between them. "I have a very strong desire to be alone. Not here, having this ridiculous conversation, with two people who obviously took drugs at some earlier point in the evening."

We sit in silence for a moment, until Max says suddenly, "I know what we have to do."

"Really? What?"

"You have to call him and apologize."

I wait for the punchline. When I realize she's not joking, I scoff. "Oh, good plan, Einstein. I'll just call Gangster 4-1-1 and get his phone number, then say sorry we stole your stuff, please don't kill us."

"No, not that we're sorry for stealing his stuff. That *you're* sorry for insulting him."

I look over to Fin. "Help me out here."

But Fin isn't on my side, the traitor. "She has a point, Jules. I mean, from what you said, he told you straight out that he wasn't going to hurt you."

"He's a criminal! We can't believe a thing he says!"

"We can believe his actions. Exhibit A: you're still breathing."

"For now!"

"Exhibit B: we're criminals, too, and we're trustworthy."

She stares at me like what she just said makes complete sense. Groaning, I scrub my hands over my face. "Your logic makes my brain hurt."

"It's the whole honor among thieves thing, Jules," says Max. "The Code. He said he wouldn't hurt you, which is basically a promise." She pauses for effect, dropping her voice. "But he never said he wouldn't hurt me and Fin. So you have to call him and apologize."

I mutter, "This is insane."

Fin says, "I think it's worth a shot. Men like Liam Black are all about ego. Respect. Stealing from him is business, but insulting him?" She *tsk*s. "That's personal."

Max adds, "Especially insulting him while you were sitting in his lap." She gasps, her blue eyes going wide with panic. "Oh god."

I cry, "What now?"

"Please tell me you didn't make a crack about the size of his dick. Because then we *are* all dead, for sure."

I motion to the waiter for another round of drinks. He's been watching Max like she's his next meal, so he sees me right away and jumps into action.

"No, I didn't make a crack about the size of his dick."

Max exhales in relief.

"I think what happened is that he got that I'd rather have him kill me than…other stuff."

Fin understands right away. "Kidnapping," she says quietly, nodding her head.

Max stares at me in confusion. "You're saying you'd rather *die* than be kidnapped and held captive by that burning hunk of man?"

"Two minutes ago, you were arguing that I should've stabbed him in the eye."

"Well, yeah, if you thought he was going to kill you. But I said that before I knew you two were canoodling in the back of a taxi cab. There's a big difference between self-defense and canoodling."

"You also said the world would be a better place without him."

"*I* like to be supportive of my friends' choices in men." She sends Fin a pointed glance.

"Oh god. I give up."

When the waiter arrives with fresh drinks, I'm flattened in my chair, staring in defeat at the ceiling.

"Ladies," he says, grinning at Max. "This round's on the house."

"How sweet!" With a wink in my direction, a beaming Fin turns to Max and squeezes her thigh. "Honey, did you tell him we're newlyweds?"

I have to give him credit: the waiter doesn't fumble the drinks. His smile doesn't falter. But still, his disappointment permeates the air.

I feel sorry for him for all of half a second, until I see the light bulb go on over his head as he looks back and forth between my two pretty friends, his smile returning.

Men.

I think god actually created woman first, then created man after deciding we needed something to vex us so we didn't die of boredom in the Garden of Eden.

I say to Fin, "Hey, did you get that nasty rash cleared up? Max said you were on some pretty heavy antibiotics."

Fin nods, playing along. "Oh, girl, it was *so* bad. My gynie said she'd never seen such oozing sores. Unfortunately, by the time I got my meds, Max had it, too."

Watching the retreating back of our waiter as he hurries toward the bar, Max says dejectedly, "You guys suck."

"It's his own fault for assuming lesbians just need a good rogering to go straight."

"*I'm* not gay," says Max, "and I could really use a good rogering."

"Well, sorry for the cock block," says Fin, obviously not sorry at all. "But it's common knowledge that guys with man buns are bad lovers. They're too focused on their hair to focus on their partner. You deserve better than that."

"Thank you. I think."

We're all reaching for our drinks when the waiter returns.

Before I can tell him that we'll pay for that last round, he says, "Which one of you is Juliet Jameson?"

My stomach tightens. The three of us look at each other for a moment, until I say warily, "That's me. Why?"

He jerks his thumb over his shoulder. "You've got a phone call."

No one knows I'm here except Fin and Max. The tightness in my stomach turns to a knot.

"From who?"

The waiter shrugs. "Some Irish guy who says you owe him ninety thousand dollars."

6

JULES

*A*fter a few seconds of stunned silence, Max says, "Okay, that's freaky as hell. He's calling *you* after I just said you should call *him*? What are the odds of that?"

Fin glances around worriedly. "What's really freaky is how he knew we were here. Do you think he followed you after he kicked you out of the taxi?"

"He must've. I guess he likes playing games."

Like a cat with a mouse right before it delivers the killing bite that severs the spinal cord.

I grit my teeth, square my shoulders, and look around, expecting to see a bunch of big dudes wearing evil expressions and dark suits with suspicious bulges underneath. But I see no hitmen, only regular people talking and drinking, mingling near the bar.

I stand, my heart banging around inside my chest. "If I'm not back in five minutes, you guys know what to do."

Max nods. "Blow the place."

"What? No! Go to your safe spots and text the signal when you're all clear!"

Fin is frowning. "I thought 'if I'm not back in five minutes' was code for 'I'm going home with the hot piece of ass I just met, don't bother waiting up for me.'"

"Jesus," I say, glaring at them in disappointment. "We're the worst criminals who ever lived."

Fin replies, "At least Max and I know better than to insult the grand poohbah of the underworld, babe. Now go save our asses. We'll be right here getting drunk in case you fail."

Shaking my head, I leave them and head in the direction of the man bun, who's waiting for me at the end of the bar. He motions to a telephone booth near the back exit. It's one of those old-fashioned red ones from London that tourists love to take their pictures near.

Adrenaline courses through me like electricity. I enter the booth, pull the door shut, and take a deep breath. Then I lift the receiver off the top of the phone box and bring it to my ear.

The silence on the other end of the line crackles. Even through a phone wire, his presence is as palpable as a hand sliding over my skin.

Then: "I wasn't planning on that."

The voice is low, rough, and distinctive. Now that I've heard it, I'd recognize that rich Irish brogue anywhere.

I say, "On not killing me when you had the chance?"

"On losing my temper. I owe you an apology."

We breathe at each other until I recover my senses. "Are you joking?"

"No."

"Is this…some kind of game?"

"No."

I stare so hard at the buttons on the phone they start to blur. "Okay, I'm just gonna go ahead and admit I have no idea what's happening right now."

"What's happening is that I'm apologizing for throwing you out onto the street."

"After I stole ninety thousand dollars' worth of diapers from you?"

"Aye." A hint of warmth creeps into his solemn voice. "Though I'm told that technically they were stolen from a warehouse, not from me."

I long for a chair to collapse into, but sagging against the glass door of the narrow booth will have to do. Gripping the receiver in both hands, I demand loudly, "Are you going to kill us or what?"

He sighs. "Not this again."

"Is that a no?"

He says firmly, "Aye, lass, it's a no."

I ignore how I like being called "lass," and forge ahead. "Why? Because we're girls? If we were men, we'd already be dead, right?"

When he hesitates, I blurt, "Oh, god, you changed your mind."

"No. I'm just disappointed that my reputation includes harming women. I've never lifted a hand to a woman in my—"

He stops abruptly and curses under his breath.

When he doesn't continue, I say, "Um. You were saying?"

He exhales heavily. "I was about to tell you a lie. I did hit a woman once. I beat her, actually."

If my jaw drops open any lower, it will be resting on the tops of my shoes.

"It's one of my greatest regrets. I was under the impression she was trafficking girls—selling children—never mind. It's a long story. My point is that I don't want us to get off on the wrong foot, so I'm being honest."

When I'm silent too long, cross-eyed with shock and confusion, he says, "I killed the man who gave me that incorrect information. That Eva was a trafficker."

Swallowing around my dead lump of a tongue, I say, "Oh. Okay, then."

"I know it doesn't excuse what I did. I'm not saying it does.

I'm just giving the reason."

"Uh…"

"She's married now. Has twins. I watch them when her husband goes out of town for work. We've become good friends."

"So it all worked out in the end."

There. I managed to sound like a rational human being and not the mashed-potatoes-for-brains zombie I really am.

His tone turning firm, he commands, "Tell me why you donated what you stole from me to a charity. Why take the risk for no financial gain? What was in it for you?"

This guy is giving me whiplash. "What difference does it make?"

"Motivation speaks to character. Tell me."

God, he's bossy. I'm irritated until I think of Fin and Max, and what thin ice we're all skating on right now, and decide to relent. "All right. If you must know, to make amends."

A long, blistering silence follows. Then he says slowly, "Amends to whom?"

"Well…the world, I guess. To everyone."

There's another pause, this one longer. "And what kind of terrible sins have Robin Hood and her merry band of thieves committed that would require making amends to the entire world?"

"Not us," I say, my voice quiet.

"Then who?"

I don't know why I tell him.

Maybe because I've never said the words out loud before, or because I sense so much is riding on my answer, or because I've had a lot to drink. But the words are out before I can stop them. Along with them comes a strange sense of relief.

"Our fathers are all bad people. Very bad people. The kind who don't care who they have to hurt to get what they want. The people we steal from are all like that, too. What we do is kind of…it's our small way of giving back. Of trying to make up for being related to such gigantic assholes."

When he doesn't say anything for so long I start to get worried, I blurt, "I'm not lying."

"I believe you," he says, his voice surprisingly soft.

Then he doesn't say anything else, and panic kicks in. I start to babble.

"Um. So. That's it. That's the reason. We're actually pretty bad at what we do. One of us inevitably screws something up, and it's a miracle we're all not in jail already, and we do have day jobs, we're not total criminals, just sort of part-time you could say. Well, I don't mean to make it sound like we don't take it seriously, because obviously we do, it's dangerous stuff, but—"

"I want to see you."

His tone has lost all its softness. It's still low, but now it's tense, too, filled with a dark need that makes my panic skyrocket.

All the breath leaves my lungs. Swallowing around the lump in my throat, I whisper, "Why?"

His voice thick, he says, "You know why."

God help me, I do. And it's not because he wants to kill me.

I didn't even know my heart could do what it's doing, that throbbing, thrashing thing that's making my limbs weak and my entire body shake.

"I…I have a boyfriend."

He makes a soft sound of dissatisfaction. "We were doing so well with the truth telling, little thief. I know you don't have a boyfriend. I know you haven't been serious with anyone in years. I know your credit score and how much money you have in your checking account and that your name is probably fake, because I conducted a background check on you and found several interesting holes in your life history."

His voice drops. "I also know you like me, too, even though

you'd never admit it."

I can't speak. I doubt there are any words that could properly convey the depth of my shock, anyway.

Finally, I pull my head out of my ass and say the only thing that comes to mind, though it's not even in the top ten most relevant after those bombs he just dropped on me.

"How did you find me here?"

"I put a tracker on your jacket. Under the collar, left side."

My hand flies up to fumble around under the collar of my jacket, until my fingers close over a tiny, round piece of metal, smooth and cool against my skin.

I pull it off and stare at it in disbelief. Smaller than a dime, it's a little electronic *gotcha* winking at me under the phone booth's lights.

"I'd apologize, but I'm not sorry, and I want us to start off on the right foot, like I said. So no lying. *Either* of us," he adds sternly, as if he's being entirely reasonable.

As if he hasn't completely short-circuited my brain.

I say faintly, "What is *happening?*"

"Be in the alley behind the bar in sixty seconds, and I'll explain it to you."

The phone goes dead in my hand.

I stare at it, frozen, until someone knocks on the phone booth glass. I jump, looking up into Max's face.

She gives me a questioning thumbs-up.

Moving slowly, I hang up the phone and open the door.

She says impatiently, "Well? How'd it go?"

"I'm pretty sure he's not going to kill us."

She examines my expression for a moment. "Then why do you look like you're about to barf?"

"Because he's waiting for me outside."

She swings around to stare in shock at the exit I gestured to. "Here? Now? *Why?*"

"I...think we're going on a date."

She turns back to me, blinking so slowly it's comical. "A date."

"I think so. Either that, or he recently fired his therapist and needs to get some things off his chest."

"I have no idea what that means."

"It means that for a soulless, ruthless, cold-blooded gangster, he's surprisingly big on confessing his faults."

Max stares at me in silence.

"And honesty. He seems to be big on honesty, too. He kept insisting we weren't going to lie to each other." My laugh is small and semi-hysterical. "So we don't get off on the wrong foot."

She says, "Oh shit."

"Exactly."

We gaze at each other for a while, both of us knowing that my choices are limited.

I can try to run, putting my friends' lives in danger, in addition to my own if he finds me. Which I'm beginning to suspect he could easily do. He seems to have all kinds of tricks up his well-tailored sleeves.

And despite his promises to the contrary, there's no guarantee he won't kill us all if I don't comply with his wishes.

Or.

I can walk out the back door.

"Where's Fin?"

"She went to the restroom."

I take a deep breath, blow it out, and say a quick, silent prayer. "Don't go back to the apartment tonight. Go to your safe spots and stay there. And if you don't hear from me by dawn, contact my father."

Max blanches. "Your *father*? Why?"

I say grimly, "He's the only one who'll be able to protect you and Fin from Liam Black."

Then I give her a quick, hard hug, and head out.

7

JULES

$\mathcal{T}$he heavy back door of the bar closes behind me with an ominous *bang*. I step out into the alley.

I'm greeted by the unnerving sight of five black SUVs lined up in a row, windows blacked out, engines running. Exhaust from the tail pipes steams white in the night air.

The driver's door to the SUV in the middle opens. A big guy in a dark suit steps out, buttoning his jacket. He's got jet black hair, ice blue eyes, and a hard, handsome face.

Like his boss, he's disturbingly good-looking for a gangster.

Most of them have smashed noses or beady eyes or any number of scars and deformities from their time in the trenches. When my father and his associates get together, it looks like a gathering of trolls.

The driver opens the back door to the SUV and stands aside, waiting.

I hesitate, trying to muster my courage.

He says, "In you go, lass. Mr. Black doesn't like to be kept waiting."

Funny how a lilting Irish brogue can make everything sound lovely. Even a threat.

I walk forward, head held high, until I'm within a few feet of the car. Then I stop and skewer the driver with a look. "For future reference, *I* don't like being rushed."

He gazes at me like he's trying to restrain himself from rolling his eyes. He says drily, "I'll make a note of it, Your Highness. Now get your arse in the car."

"Declan."

The sharp reprimand comes from inside the SUV. It's Liam, leaning forward in his seat, gazing with steely-eyed disapproval at the driver.

"Sorry, boss." He inclines his head to me. "Apologies, lass."

Sincere apologies from not one but *two* killers in a single evening. I'm on a roll.

"No worries. I've recently been told I have a forked tongue, so I can hardly blame you." I shoot a glance at the car and mutter, "Plus, working for Prince Charmless must take its toll on your temper."

A ghost of a smile flits across his mouth, but he quickly suppresses it.

I climb into the car. The driver shuts the door behind me. In a moment, we pull away.

All heat and coiled tension, Liam simmers in the seat beside me.

After we've gone three blocks, he says, "How long are you going to make me wait until you look at me?"

"I'm working on regulating my breathing so I don't pass out. Maybe ten minutes?"

His chuckle is low and sensual, raising my blood pressure by at least two hundred points.

"You're tougher than that. I'll give you ten seconds."

When the seconds have ticked by, I turn my head and glance at him warily from the corner of my eye.

He stares at me with such blistering intensity that for a moment, I can't breathe.

His voice husky, he says, "Hullo again."

Holy crap, he's handsome. How can someone so evil be so hot?

My exhalation comes out in a burst. It's accompanied by a shudder. Then I clear my throat and pretend I'm a mentally functioning adult. "Hi."

He lets his gaze drift over me, head to toe, taking in every aspect of my clothing, posture, and expression.

"You still don't trust me."

I make a sound that's supposed to be a laugh, but it sounds more like a small animal being strangled. "Trust? I'm sorry, did you just say *trust*?"

"I did."

He's serious. I stare at him in astonishment. "Of course I don't trust you! You're…you!"

The driver pipes in from the front seat. "That's hardly fair, lass. You've only just met."

Through gritted teeth, Liam says, "*Declan*."

"Right. Sorry." Falling silent, he turns his attention back to the road.

Liam smiles reassuringly at me. "It's so hard to find good help these days."

I look back and forth between them, gobsmacked by the whole situation. I could be hallucinating. Maybe that hipster bartender put something into my drink.

I'm still pondering that when Liam leans over and settles his huge, hot hand around my throat.

I grip his thick wrist in both hands, gasping and shrinking back into the seat.

Looking into my eyes, he murmurs, "I'm not going to hurt you."

My voice comes out high and panicked. "This is a shitty way of proving that."

"I'm not trying to choke you, lass."

It's true, the pressure of his hand on my throat is gentle, but still. "Then what the hell are you doing?"

He slides his thumb back and forth over the throbbing vein in my neck. "Feeling your pulse."

Heart hammering, I stare at him. "Why?"

"Because I want to see how fast it gets when I kiss you."

I freeze. "Don't you dare."

He quirks one dark brow. "Why not?"

"I don't want you to."

He leans closer, his eyes burning into mine, his body heat and the warm scent of his skin surrounding me. He growls, "If you were telling the truth, little thief, I'd honor that request."

I blurt, "I'm not ready for that!"

Instantly, he stills. His dark gaze searches my face. Then, slowly, his full lips lift into a smile. "Then I suppose I'll have to wait until you are."

He stares hungrily at my mouth for a moment before releasing me.

I remain where he left me, frozen and wide-eyed, slumped against the door, staring at him and trying to convince myself of several important facts.

One, that I should be afraid. Because two, that there's at least a fifty-fifty chance he's going to snap my neck. And three, that I really *didn't* want him to kiss me.

Especially that I didn't want him to kiss me. Because what would it say about my sanity if I did?

Adjusting his tie and looking straight forward, he says, "Don't overthink it. But thank you for being honest. If this is going to work, we have to be honest with each other."

My laugh is weak and disbelieving. "This? There is no 'this!'"

He turns his head and sears me with his gaze. "Aye, lass," he says, his voice thick. "There is."

If my body hadn't just detonated with heat, I'd tell him to jump off a bridge, the arrogant prick.

Anger gives me the strength to sit upright. "I can't believe I have to say this, but I don't date gangsters. Gangster."

Looking at my mouth, he moistens his lips. "Who said anything about dating?"

Holy guacamole. He's not going to make this easy. My cheeks heating, I say primly, "I don't sleep with them either, okay?"

His eyes, good god, how darkly they burn. "I didn't say anything about sleeping, either, lass. Spend time with me, and you won't be getting any sleep at all."

It feels like my heart is up in my throat, which makes it hard to get the words out. "I don't want to spend time with you."

A muscle flexes in his jaw. He shakes his head, like he's disappointed in me.

"I don't!"

"You do. You're fascinated by me. You just can't wrap your head around why."

So aggravated I want to scream, I say, "I'd be crazy to be fascinated by you."

"Then you're crazy." He shrugs, as if he doesn't care. "But you're interesting, too."

More whiplash. He thinks I'm *interesting*? "I stole from you."

"I know. That's what makes you interesting." His tone goes from nonchalant to hungry. "That and that beautiful, smart fucking mouth."

We stare at each other. Adrenaline crackles through my veins, hot, dark, and dangerous.

Like him.

It occurs to me that perhaps this was inevitable. I was brought up around dangerous men. I was raised by one. Some

51

part of my brain must be wired to be attracted to Liam Black's particular brand of bad.

It doesn't help that he's so damn handsome. It's effortless to be revolted by a man whose face is as ugly as his soul, but when evil is dressed up in such a pretty package, it's not quite as easy to resist.

Before he got his ass kicked out of heaven, the devil was the most beautiful angel of all.

He demands, "What are you thinking?"

"That you're the devil."

"I went from an ape to the devil? That's quite a jump."

I know from my limited experience with him that we could go around and around like this forever, so I cut to the chase. "Where are you taking me?"

"Home."

That queasy feeling in my stomach tells me he isn't talking about my apartment. Horrified, I gaze at him.

His voice lowers. "Whatever comes out of your mouth next, please don't let it be a lie."

The "please" stops me short. He doesn't seem like a man who even knows the word, let alone allows himself to speak it.

"Okay. No lies. I'm on board with that. So here are some truths for you: I'm confused. I'm exhausted. I'm worried about my friends. I've had several drinks, and I don't think my brain is working the way it should be. I don't like you, but I can't honestly say you disgust me, either, which I very much wish you did. I'm disappointed in myself about that."

He's watching me with such blistering intensity I have to take a breath to steady myself before I go on.

"What else? Um. I'm relieved you haven't killed me yet—"

"I swear on my mother's grave, I will never harm you."

His voice is rough and urgent. His dark eyes shine like gems. There's something raw and open in his expression, something that seems to plead with me to accept that he's telling me the truth.

We gaze at each other in silence until I surprise myself by whispering, "Okay."

He seems surprised, too. "You believe me?"

"Yes."

After examining my face for a moment, he breathes, "Thank you."

I don't know why, but it's obvious what I've said means a great deal to him.

"What about my friends?"

"They're safe. You have my word."

He gazes at me like the sun is shining out of my head, and he's getting blinded by it. To be stared at with such unwavering intensity by a man so gorgeous, so powerful, and so completely masculine is disorienting.

It's also undeniably thrilling.

Except I'm supposed to hate him. I *do* hate him.

I think.

"About this you-taking-me-home thing."

"What about it?"

"If I tell you I don't want to go home with you, does it void anything you've promised me up to this point?"

"No."

"Good. Because I don't want to go home with you."

He gazes at me in silence for a moment. Then he smiles.

"Will you stop doing that?" I say, exasperated by his cockiness.

"I can't help it, lass. You've got a face a blind man could read."

"Please listen to me: I. Am not. Going home. With you."

"Actually, you are. We're driving there as we speak."

This man could make the pope go on a killing spree. "I don't want to engage in a semantics war, okay? What I'm saying is that it isn't a good idea."

"I think it's the best idea I've had in a decade."

"No! I need to be away from you! I need to process this insanity! I'm not going to your house!"

"It's not a house. It's a penthouse. In a skyscraper. The views are incredible. And you don't need to process anything, except the fact that this is happening. You'll go to my home, you'll take a look around, we'll have some wine, we'll talk a bit, you'll get more comfortable with me, and then we'll do what we've both wanted to do since the moment we laid eyes on each other."

I stare at him. He stares right back, daring me to contradict him.

At least I'm not the only one on the verge of a heart attack. For all his outward cool control, the pulse in his neck pounds as hard as my heart.

"This whole thing is very abnormal. You know that, right?"

"I've never lived a normal life. I have no intention of starting now. Here's the bottom line: I want you. You want me. End of story."

"I hope you won't throw me out of the car again, but I have to tell you that your idea of romance is profoundly lacking."

His voice drops. "It's not romance you need."

His expression tells me he's about to elaborate on that thought. I'm having none of it. "You can just leave that right there, thank you."

"You don't want me to leave it. You want me to tell you what I think you need. Then you want me to show you."

"Okay, that's just…wow. Your ego needs its own zip code."

He chuckles softly. "That's not the only part of me that needs its own zip code, lass."

I crinkle my nose. "You're crude."

"Don't believe me? I'll be happy to show you."

I say hotly, "If you try to unzip your pants right now, mister, I'll punch you in the throat."

His voice turns husky. "God, you're sexy when you're threatening me. I like it even more than when you're stealing things I own."

We're two feet apart and not touching, but we might as well be naked in bed with him on top of me and thrusting between my spread thighs for how intimate this feels, all this heat and friction and heavy breathing. I'm breaking out in a sweat.

This is a hundred different kinds of wrong. Jump out of the car, Jules. Just open the door and jump.

As it seems drawn to do, his gaze drops to my mouth. When I bite my lower lip, his eyes darken. He leans toward me, his own lips parting.

That's when the first hail of bullets explodes against the side of the car.

8

JULES

*W*hen I dive onto the floor behind the driver's seat, it's a reflex. No screaming, no panicking, just an action born of muscle memory in response to something I practiced repeatedly as a child.

I curl into a ball, cover my head with my arms, and close my eyes.

Meanwhile, the bullets keep flying.

The car swerves hard left, away from the direction of the gunfire. Liam shouts something to Declan in a foreign language —Gaelic, I assume—and the car lurches forward, accelerating, tires squealing against the asphalt.

Though we're under heavy fire, the windows don't shatter, and the bullets don't penetrate the car's steel skin.

Thank you, god, for armored vehicles.

Liam throws his body over mine and curves into a protective shield around me. "Just stay down, lass," he shouts. "Try to remain calm. We'll be to safety in a moment."

I shout back, "Unless this is only the opening act, and they're intentionally driving us toward something worse."

I feel his attention shift from the gunfire to me. "Have much experience with diversionary tactics, do you?"

Yes. And handling edged weapons, rappelling from tall buildings, and escaping from locked rooms. Grow up as a mob boss's only daughter and you're taught all kinds of useful survival skills for when you're inevitably kidnapped by daddy's enemies.

Men, for instance, like you.

Instead of saying any of that, I say, "I watch a lot of crime shows on TV."

"Oh, look, she's lying again. Seems to be a compulsion."

"You're not half as smart as you think you are, gangster."

"It occurs to me that you're unnaturally calm, considering the circumstances, yet you squawked about me killing you non-stop, despite my continued assurances to the contrary. Care to share?"

"No. Do you always talk like you ate a dictionary for breakfast?"

He puts his mouth close to my ear and lowers his voice. "No. Sometimes I talk like I fuck: dirty."

Without slowing, the car makes another hard turn around a corner. I tell myself that's what makes me red-faced and breathless.

Then, out of nowhere, another car slams into us from the passenger side.

The noise is deafening. The SUV spins in a half circle, then comes to a jolting stop when we hit another object on the driver's side of the car.

From there, it all happens so fast.

Liam is still on top of me, shouting at Declan in Gaelic. My door is yanked open from the outside. I lift my head and see a man dressed in black tactical gear and a ski mask. He gazes down at me with emotionless eyes. A semi-automatic rifle is gripped in his gloved hands.

He raises the rifle and points it at me, and my heart stops dead in my chest.

So here it is. Finally.

I've been waiting for this moment my whole life. I always knew it would come. Somewhere in the back of my mind, I knew I'd have to pay for being born into the family I was born into. For this tainted blood that flows through my veins.

No matter how much good I try to do, nothing can make up for the rot inside me. My father's sins have stained me to the bone.

The gunshot is painfully loud.

I flinch instinctively, but instead of a bullet ripping through my brain, the gunman's head explodes in a wet red burst from the back of his mask. He topples sideways, lands on the pavement, and doesn't move again.

Holding a smoking Glock in one hand, Liam jumps over me and out of the car, turns and grabs my arm, and hauls me out. He pushes me to a sitting position with my back against one of the SUV's big wheels.

Leaning down so his nose is inches from mine, he stares me straight in the eye.

"Stay down. Don't move from this position until I come for you. Understood?"

Though more gunshots ring out through the night and what sounds like several dozen men are shouting nearby, his tone and expression are calm.

He saved my life. The mob king just saved me.

When I don't respond, he raises his voice. "I've gotta go kill some people now. I promise no one is going to hurt you. Stay here until I come back. Nod if you understand."

I nod.

"Good." His tone gentles. "You're beautiful, by the way. I know you think I'm cocky and overbearing, but it's only because I'm relentless when it comes to getting what I want."

His dark eyes tell me in no uncertain terms that what he

wants right now—other than shooting some pesky dudes who're trying to kill him—is me.

He presses a soft kiss to my forehead, then straightens and disappears around the rear of the SUV.

Liam Black saved my life…and he wants me.

I broke into a warehouse owned by the head of the Irish mafia, stole a shitload of stuff from him, donated it to charity, then sassed him non-stop when he caught me.

And, for some bizarre reason, all that turned him on.

I'm not sure whether to laugh or cry.

"Get it together, Jules," I say faintly, dazed. "If you're still breathing after tonight, there'll be time for a breakdown later on."

The dead gunman lies sprawled on the pavement to my left, a dark pool of blood widening around his head. I lean over, grab his discarded rifle, and quickly huddle back against the wheel, cradling the weapon against my chest. It's bulky, its weight unwieldy, but holding it makes me feel safer.

I'm still carrying my knife in my coat pocket, but knives are useless in a gunfight.

I sit for what feels like a long time with a clenched jaw and a stiff spine, clutching the weapon like a life vest as gunfire and men's screams echo in my ears.

Then everything falls still.

He reappears like a vision from a dream or a nightmare, seeming to move in slow motion as he rounds the back of the car and strides smoothly toward me, a huge figure in a tailored black suit carrying a gun in each hand.

His intense gaze is trained on me. His dark hair is haloed in moonlight. Smoke swirls in misty gray eddies around his feet, and the devil wishes he were that beautiful.

Shoving the weapons under his belt buckle at the small of his back, he kneels down, removes the rifle from my grip, and tosses it aside. Then he wordlessly picks me up in his arms.

I stare at his handsome profile as he strides toward another SUV, one of the ones in his entourage. It's undamaged, idling with the driver's door open several yards away.

"Is it over?"

"Aye," he says, his voice low. "For now."

Off in the distance, sirens wail. I look over his shoulder to the street behind us. It's littered with bodies.

I close my eyes and swallow, banishing the image from my mind.

I've got too many similar ones stored in my memory banks already.

~

We drive.

Away from the massacre into the darkness, city streets flying by at warp speed. Liam is silent, but I sense his attention as he expertly navigates the roads, every so often glancing at me from the corner of his eye.

He's wondering why I'm so calm. Why I'm not screaming. Crying. Reacting with hysteria to having a gun pointed at my face and violence erupting all around me, like a normal person would.

If he asks, I'll tell him it's shock. The truth is too dark and far too dangerous.

He can never know who I really am.

We enter the downtown district. When we pull into the parking garage of a modern black glass building so tall it disappears into the clouds, I realize where we must be. My calm erodes around the edges.

Because he seems to notice everything, he notices that, too.

"You're in no danger from me," he murmurs.

"But you're taking me to your home."

"The two aren't mutually exclusive."

I moisten my dry lips, feeling my heart pound, wishing it wouldn't. "I can't…I don't want to have to—"

"I know, lass. I'll be on my best behavior."

What would that be, I wonder? For a man whose daily agenda includes murder, extortion, racketeering, and god only knows what else, what would good behavior look like?

Kicking his cat instead of skinning it?

He says, "What was that snort for?"

"You don't own a cat by any chance, do you?"

"No. Why do you ask?"

"Just wondering."

Liam pulls the car to a stop in front of a bank of elevators flanked by a group of hulking men in dark suits. He hops out of the car, leaving it running. I unbuckle my seatbelt, but before I can open my door, he's there, opening it for me. He pulls me out, his big hand curled possessively around my upper arm.

He keeps me right next to him as we walk to the elevators.

One of his men has already hit the call button, so the doors slide open as we approach.

Liam gives a sharp command in Gaelic. The men snap to attention, bristling like they're about to go to war.

Which, I suspect, they are.

The doors close behind us. The elevator hums as it lifts.

Then I find myself flattened against the back wall staring up into a pair of blistering dark eyes. His heat and bulk close in on me until our bodies are only inches apart. One big hand slides around my throat.

When I make a small sound of panic, he murmurs, "Easy."

"You keep saying that. I don't think you understand the definition of the word."

"Just breathe."

"I am."

"You're hyperventilating."

"It's a normal response to abnormal situations."

"You weren't hyperventilating on the street. Bullets flying all around, and there you were, Sarah Connor gripping an AR-15, calmly lying in wait to blow off the Terminator's head. The picture of composure. All you were missing was a cigarette dangling idly from your lips."

He waits for a response, gazing at me with unblinking eyes, his thumb moving gently back and forth over the throbbing pulse in my neck.

I almost—*almost*—say my unnatural calm during the gunfire was shock, as I'd planned, but something stops me.

I hope it isn't the fact that I promised him I wouldn't lie to him, because that would be downright pathetic.

Looking up at him, I say quietly, "Can I ask a favor?"

He replies without hesitation. "Anything."

"I'd like to have the option of not answering every question, if that's okay."

When he's silent too long, examining my expression, I add, "Since we're only supposed to be truth telling. And, um, I'm not really comfortable talking about myself."

The corners of his mouth lift in a wry smile. "I didn't ask a question."

"Don't be an ass. It was implied."

Back and forth that gentle thumb sweeps over my skin as he gazes at me thoughtfully, most likely fully aware that my nipples are hardening from his touch on my neck, and that I'm so angry about that, I'd like to smack myself in the face.

"Should we have a code word for when you'd rather duck my question than lie?"

His expression is neutral, but faint laughter underscores his words.

"Sure. How's this: up yours."

His lips twitch. "That's two words."

"Call it a code phrase, then."

His lips twitch again, and I realize it's because he's trying not to chuckle. He says, "Maybe something more respectful, considering you might have to say it in front of my men."

"Right. Can't tarnish that shiny alpha male glow. Aardvark?"

He wrinkles his nose in disapproval.

"Quadrangle? Collywobbles? Maltipoo?"

"And you accuse *me* of eating a dictionary for breakfast."

"I was only joking then. I'm sure what you really eat for breakfast are the souls of everyone who's displeased you."

He stares at me with a look I can't quite figure out, until he says gruffly, "Do you have any fucking idea how much I want to kiss you right now?"

After a moment, when I can catch my breath, I whisper, "Yes. Please don't."

Very slowly, he exhales. When he speaks again, his voice is thick. "I won't. At least not until you ask me to."

"That will never happen."

His gaze drills into mine. His thumb lazily strokes the pulse in my neck. "Aye, lass, it will. You'll hate yourself for it, but it *will* happen, because you want it as much as I do. Don't you."

The last part isn't a question, really. It's more of a dare. But he's got me trapped in the heat of his stare with his hand on my throat and all my nerve endings singing, and I don't think I could lie even if my life depended on it.

I turn my head and close my eyes. "Aardvark."

The elevator slows to a stop. A bell dings. The doors slide open.

Liam leans down and whispers hotly into my ear, "For the record, I'd burn down this whole goddamn city just to hear you admit it."

He's a criminal, a ruthless, heartless, overconfident SOB, but dear god this is the sexiest man I've ever met.

There is something very wrong with me.

He takes me by the hand and leads me into his house. Excuse me—his penthouse. We wander through the living room, vast and silent, and past an equally vast formal dining room, until we reach the kitchen. It's also huge. And, like everything else, decorated entirely in shades of gray and black.

He guides me to a counter stool at the big marble island and helps me into it, making sure I'm comfortable before rounding the island and opening a cabinet above the sink.

He removes a bottle of bourbon and two crystal glasses and pours a measure into both.

Then he shucks off his jacket, removes his cufflinks, rolls his shirtsleeves up his forearms, tugs on the knot in his tie, pulls the tie off over his head, and drops it onto the counter. For the final act, he loosens the top three buttons of the shirt, exposing a strong, tanned throat decorated on one side with a tattoo.

Of what, I can't tell. I'm too busy staring at his other tattoos, all along his muscular forearms.

Holy...how many more are there? And where? And do they all ripple like the ones on his arms?

"Penny for your thoughts."

I glance up from my awed inspection of his forearms to find him smirking at me.

I refuse to say "Aardvark" and give him the satisfaction, so instead I deflect to something still true, but much safer than what I was thinking. "I was wondering if your interior decorator got a good deal on all this black marble, or if she thought you were part bat."

His smirk turns to a genuine smile. "It is a bit monotone, isn't it?"

"Oh, no, it's fantastic," I say, looking around. "If you're blind. Or clinically depressed. Or undead."

Chuckling, he slides one of the bourbons over to me, then downs his own in one swallow. "I have to agree with you, there."

"Then why did you go with it?"

"It was like this when I moved in."

The answer is smooth, but he dropped his gaze to the empty

glass in his hand when he gave it. I don't think he's lying, not exactly, but there's a lot more to his words under the surface.

Mimicking his dry tone from the car when he was commenting on how calm I was despite the circumstances, I say, "Care to share?"

His gaze flashes up to mine. He holds me in it for a moment, a fly caught in amber, then murmurs, "Aardvark."

We gaze at each other across the island, both of us knowing we'll soon be wearing out that word.

I take a breath and ask the question that needs to be asked. "I'm not sleeping with you, Mr. Black. So why am I here?"

"I think we can dispense with the formalities of surnames, considering you watched me shoot a man in the face."

His logic passes the sniff test, so I start again. "Okay, Liam, why am I—"

"Killian."

The forcefulness with which he interrupts me is startling. "Excuse me?"

"Call me Killian."

I wait for him to provide an explanation, but he doesn't. "Why would I call you that, when it's not your name?"

His jaw works. He gazes at me in silence so long I almost start nervously laughing. Then he says, "It is my name."

I open my mouth, close it, then open it again. "So Liam is like a nickname or something?"

"No."

"Is it…your middle name?"

"No."

We stare at each other. Finally, I sigh. "You don't want to tell me."

"It's not that I don't want to. It's that I can't."

"Uh-huh." I narrow my eyes and peer suspiciously at him, but it feels as if he's telling me the truth. Since the situation is ludicrous anyway, I decide to roll with it. "Okay, fine. If we're going by other people's names, I want you to call me…Sophia. No, wait. Seraphina. That sounds kind of badass."

He says softly, "But you're already going by someone else's name, little thief."

I was picking up the bourbon to drink, but freeze with the glass halfway to my mouth.

"Aardvark?" he inquires, sounding amused.

I set the glass down carefully on the marble countertop. My heartbeat picks up, my hands turn clammy, and a knot forms in my stomach.

What the hell am I doing? This is dangerous. This is insane.

Looking at the glass instead of him, I say quietly, "I'd like to go home now."

After a tense moment, he says, "Look at me."

When I do, eyeing him warily, he shakes his head. "I don't care if you have secrets. I don't care if you call yourself Cinderella or Mary Poppins or anything else. What I care about is that you understand there's nothing more important to me than my honor."

"Meaning?"

His eyes burn straight through me. "Meaning I gave you my word I'd never harm you. That stands no matter what."

I don't understand him at all, and that frustrates me. My father could give his word you'd be safe with him, then five seconds later turn around and shoot you in the back.

I'm not exaggerating. I've seen it happen.

Because that's what gangsters do. That's what they are: liars.

"I believed you when you said you wouldn't hurt me, Li— Killian, but you can't promise the no matter what part."

"Aye, lass. I can."

Thunderclouds are gathering over his head, but I'm feeling reckless. "Even if I tried to kill you?"

His answer is swift and unequivocal. "Even if anything."

We stare at each other until he adds, "And the reason you're here is because there's nowhere safer for you."

I can't help but laugh at that. "A bunch of men in riot gear carrying military-grade weapons just tried to kill you. I don't think being near you is safe for me at all."

He pauses, his gaze dark and unreadable. Then he says softly, "I'm not so sure it was me they were after, Juliet."

9

KILLIAN

I watch her face pale. I watch her lips part. I watch her knuckles turn white around the glass.

I watch all that and know that this gutsy young thief with luminous brown eyes that convey emotion like a silent movie star's has skeletons in her closet that rival mine.

She might even have more, if that's possible.

Swallowing, she moistens her lips. She clears her throat. Then she says, "What makes you say that?"

Her voice is shaky. For the first time since we met, she looks vulnerable.

That causes such a strong surge of protectiveness to flood through me, I have to take a moment to steady myself before I speak. "One of them didn't recognize me."

"How could you tell?"

"He thought I was your bodyguard."

He sputtered it before he bled out from the bullet hole I'd put in his neck, cursing me for protecting "the girl."

The interesting part was that his curses were in Serbian. I don't have any Serbian enemies. I keep very careful lists.

Even more interesting is how still and pale Juliet has become, staring at me with wide, unblinking eyes.

Keeping my voice soft and low, I say, "If you tell me who you are, I can help you."

"I'm no one of importance," is her instant answer.

I've said those exact words to someone in the past, and it was a lie, too. "If you're so unimportant, why the need for a fake name?"

"Sorry—*Killian*—but Juliet *is* my real name."

Her eyes flash. Her tone is defiant. Every time she looks at me like that, with all that fire and fuck-you attitude, I want to push her down and pin her underneath me and kiss that smart mouth until she's begging me to kiss her everywhere else.

"And Jameson? Is that your real last name?"

She presses her lips together and incinerates me with her stare.

"That's what I thought."

She stands abruptly, abandoning the whiskey glass on the countertop and wiping her palms on the front of her jeans. She announces, "I'm leaving," and turns and heads toward the elevator doors, walking quickly with a stiff back and tense shoulders.

I let her go and pour myself another drink.

In a few minutes, she's back. Seething. "The elevator's locked."

"Aye."

"Open it."

"No."

Her voice rises. "I want you to let me go. Now."

I study her. There's an edge to her voice and a glint of panic in her eyes. It's almost as if she thinks I'm...

When it dawns on me, I feel like a complete idiot for not realizing it sooner.

She's afraid of being kidnapped.

Not raped, like I thought when she was freaking out in the taxi cab. Though that's likely part of it, too. But mainly her anxiety seems to revolve around being taken—and held—against her will.

Fear of becoming a hostage is a very specific kind of fear. One ingrained by a specific kind of upbringing. And possibly a specific kind of training.

Her words come back to me again.

"Our fathers are all bad people. Very bad people. The kind who don't care who they have to hurt to get what they want."

I thought she meant drug dealers, perhaps, or some other kind of commonplace felon. Maybe even a soulless billionaire CEO. But added together with the acid disdain in her voice every time she calls me a gangster, and the unnatural calm she displayed during the car chase and gunfight, and her paranoia about becoming a victim of kidnapping—and, frankly, everything else—I think my little thief is the offspring of someone a tad worse than I thought.

Watching my expression, she demands, "What?"

"Juliet," I say thoughtfully. "That's an Italian name if I've ever heard one."

"No. It's English."

"Not if it's given to a girl born into an Italian family."

As if she's been slapped, her face turns white.

Bingo.

Something on my face makes her take a step back, shaking her head, her eyes wide.

"I won't hurt you. There's no need to try to run away."

Her voice is strangled when she speaks. "Please let me go."

I say firmly, "Juliet, I don't care who your father is."

She freezes in place as if turned to stone. The pulse in the side of her neck is flying.

Keeping my tone low and unthreatening, I say, "I won't hold you against your will. I swear to you. But I need to find out who exactly was behind that attack and deal with him—or them—before you can go. For your own safety, as well as mine. All right?"

Her throat works. Her hands shake. I fight the urge to cross to her and take her into my arms and gesture to the corridor beyond the kitchen instead.

"There's a guest room at the end of the hall. You can stay there. I won't disturb you."

When she doesn't move, I add, "The door locks from the inside. The frame is reinforced with steel. No one can get in unless you let them in."

"Are there cameras?"

"No."

She licks her lips, shifting her weight from foot to foot, trying to decide whether or not to believe me.

"There's also a gun in the nightstand. It's loaded." I add mildly, "Judging by how you held that rifle, I'm guessing you're familiar with firearms."

She narrows her eyes at me. She's probably wishing she had a gun in hand right now.

Then she squares her shoulders and takes a deep breath. "How long do you think it will take you to find out what you need to know?"

"A few hours, at most."

She blinks. I hope it's because she's impressed.

"So I could...maybe just...relax for a while until you're done?"

I incline my head, watching her try to maintain her composure and fight against the urge to run screaming to the front door. Except there is no front door, which she's already well aware of.

I take a few steps toward her. When she backs up, startled, I stop and hold up a hand, feeling pained. "Please. Trust me."

Her laugh is small and dry. "Can you appreciate how crazy that request sounds, coming from you?"

"I did save your life."

"Oh. Yeah." She looks sheepish for a moment, then glances down at her feet. "Sorry. And, um…thank you."

Fuck, she's adorable. "You're welcome. Anytime."

She glances up from her feet, her mouth quirked. She studies me from under lowered brows for a moment, then sighs and throws her hands in the air.

"Oh, for fuck's sake. Fine. I'll stay here for a few hours. I don't want to believe you'll keep your word, but I do. Mostly. Against my better judgment."

Then she props her hands on her hips and sends me her signature glare. "So don't screw it up, okay?"

I say solemnly, "I'd rather die than disappoint you."

It was an attempt at dry humor, but I surprise myself by meaning it.

She rolls her eyes. "Let's hope that won't be necessary."

She turns on her heel and stalks off through the kitchen, toward the guest room down the hall. I hear a door slam and smile.

Then I take a plastic Ziploc bag from a drawer, put my hand inside it, pick up her whiskey glass with the same hand and pour the contents into the sink, and head whistling to my office to discover who my beautiful thief really is.

"You're pulling my leg."

"No."

"C'mon, Killian. Seriously. You're joking."

"I'm not, Declan. I'm telling you the truth."

"Really?"

"Aye. Fingerprints don't lie."

Silence crackles on the other end of the line for a moment,

then I hear a low, disbelieving laugh. "Well, fuck. What are the odds?"

"Approximately seven billion to one."

"Christ on a cracker. Antonio Moretti's daughter?" More laughter. "That's some serious shit right there."

I say drily, "You don't say?"

"So what's your next move?"

"Good question."

I gaze at the FBI report on my computer screen, my state of shock having only recently dulled to a more manageable amazement.

It isn't every day I discover that the most interesting and attractive woman I've ever met is none other than the only child of the head of an infamous New York Italian crime family.

A man so vicious his breath is probably toxic.

A man whom, inconveniently, has been trying to kill me for quite some time.

"You think he set her up on the job?"

The diaper theft, Declan means. "No. I can't find any evidence of contact between her and her father."

I don't tell him that her mother was killed in a car bomb explosion when Juliet was a child. I have a feeling that's not something she'd want me to share. I also don't share her years of homeschooling or her intensely sheltered lifestyle before she was sent away at thirteen to a boarding school in Vermont for the children of the ultra-rich. It seems her rebellious streak kicked in then, because as soon as she left her father's household, she got into near constant trouble.

Immediately after graduating at eighteen, she was arrested for shoplifting. The charges were dropped—daddy's influence, no doubt—but whoever was in charge of daddy's security team neglected to scrub her fingerprints from the police database.

A mistake I'd never make, but a lucky one for me.

After her arrest, the FBI file ends. They don't have her alias listed, or any current known address. Neither does Interpol or the NSA, and they know everyone. Which means she did an excellent job of covering her tracks.

Which means she's even more impressive than I thought she was.

"Huh. So why she'd target you for the diaper job, then?"

My lips lift into a smile. "Apparently, she and her two sidekicks only steal from bad guys. Somehow, I ended up on their list."

After a moment of silence, Declan says, "That explains it."

"What?"

"Why you like her."

"I don't follow."

"She's a do-gooder. That's your particular brand of Kryptonite."

"How the hell would you know? You haven't seen me with a woman since I took over for Liam."

"He told me."

I grit my teeth. This should be interesting. Annoying, but interesting. "What exactly did he say?"

"That the only time you've ever lowered your guard in your life was for a woman who was so in love with someone else, she died to save him."

"She *didn't* die," I say through a clenched jaw. "And *I* saved him."

I can't see it, but I know right now he's blowing smoke rings and waving a hand dismissively in the air. "Details. The point is, she was a do-gooder. Selfless. Generous. This one's the same."

"She's a *thief.*"

"A philanthropist thief," he corrects, sounding smug. "Who only steals from bad guys and donates the take to charity. I mean, if that's not the definition of a do-gooder, I don't know what is."

When I stay silent too long, Declan says, "I know you're

sitting there trying to figure out how to argue with me, which is a problem because you also know that I'm right."

"Actually, I was just picturing your slow and painful death by poisoning."

"Psh. Poison's a woman's weapon. You'd just shoot me point-blank in the face."

"A tempting thought. I'm hanging up now."

"Aren't you going to tell me you're glad I survived our little run-in with the Serbians?"

I deadpan, "I'm *thrilled,*" and jab my finger against the End button on my phone.

He calls me back five seconds later. "Got a call from my buddy at the department. Feds are at the scene now."

"Good. Have them give me everything they've got as soon as they've got it."

He mimics a pirate's accent. "Aye, aye, captain."

"Declan?"

"Hmm?"

"Don't *ever* say that again."

"You don't like it? It originated as a British Royal Navy nautical term meaning 'Yes, I will do as you command.' As opposed to the more generic 'I understand' in response to an order, which doesn't implicitly connote obedience. Because, you know, the military's real big on obedience."

"I do know. I was in the military."

His tone turns thoughtful. "That's right. I always forget. Probably because I can't picture you taking orders from anyone. I bet you got disciplined constantly, right?"

I mutter, "I should've shot you on sight," and hang up on him again.

I sit thinking for several long moments. When my stomach grumbles, I realize I haven't eaten anything for hours. I head to the kitchen to get something to eat, but stop in the living room, my ear cocked.

I hear the sound again. It's a low *thump*, like a blow against a wall.

It's coming from the corridor that leads to the guest room where Juliet is.

A few seconds later, I'm applying my knuckles firmly to the door of her room.

There's a pause before she opens up. A pause in which I find it surprisingly difficult not to start pounding my fist on the wood and shouting. Then the handle turns, the door swings wide, and there she is.

Red-faced, disheveled, and breathing hard.

Behind her, the room is a wreck.

I let my gaze wander around the overturned furniture, the artwork hanging askew on the walls, the bed stripped of sheets. A nightstand has been dragged underneath an air vent on the ceiling on one side of the room. The window coverings lie in a crumpled pile on the floor.

I fold my arms over my chest, lean my shoulder against the wall, and say mildly, "I see you've been redecorating."

"I was looking for cameras."

"And trying to find a way out."

"Yes."

"There isn't one."

"I discovered that. Thank you."

We stare at each other. She's so lovely with the color high in her cheeks and her eyes ablaze with anger. I want to reach out and stroke her face, but know I'd only get slapped for the effort.

"You said you believed I'd keep my word."

"I said I *mostly* believed you'd keep your word. And you can't blame me for having my doubts about your veracity." After a pause, she adds, "I'm sorry if that's insulting. I don't mean to insult you." She closes her eyes, sighs, and mutters, "I can't believe I'm apologizing."

"I appreciate the sentiment, though."

She opens her eyes and gazes at me with her brows drawn together, like I'm a frustrating puzzle she half wants to solve and half wants to set on fire and throw into the street.

"Are you hungry? I was just going to get something to eat."

Ignoring that, she demands, "Did you find out anything yet? Can I leave?"

Ouch.

I say softly, "I want you to trust me."

"And I want a unicorn pony. So here we are."

I have to bite my lower lip to keep from laughing, because I know it would only enrage her more. "I'll work on that. In the meantime, I'll feed you."

I turn around and walk away, feeling her gaze on my back as I go, trying to quell the dark, powerful surge of desire that moves through me when I hear her footstep on the marble and realize she's following.

JULES

Don't look at his ass, idiot. He's the devil, remember?
I follow Killian down the corridor to the kitchen, admiring his hard, perfect butt despite myself. He walks like a king. Head held high, broad shoulders squared, his effortless swagger conveying total confidence.

He's the shit, and he knows it.

I'd like to take off my shoe and chuck it at his conceited head to take him down a notch.

But I don't. I've already ruined the man's guest room. Demolishing décor will have to be enough for one evening.

My feet dragging with fatigue, I hop back onto the counter stool where I sat before, prop my chin in my hands, and watch as the head of the Irish mafia makes me a tuna fish sandwich.

I swear that hipster bartender put something into my drink.

When the sandwich is ready, Killian puts it on a plate and takes a knife from a drawer. From over his shoulder, he says, "Crusts or no crusts?"

Yeah, that's it. I'm definitely hallucinating. "Crusts are fine, thanks."

He slices the sandwich in half and turns and presents it to me. Then he folds his big arms over his big, stupid chest and gazes at me from under lowered lids with a smug half smile playing over his lips.

"Don't smirk," I say, picking up the sandwich. "It's unbecoming."

"It's not a smirk. That's just my face."

Holding his gaze, I bite into the sandwich, pretending it's the tender space between his forefinger and thumb.

I refuse to like him. He's a gangster, a killer, a bad guy to the bone. Just because he saved my life and made me a tuna fish sandwich doesn't change anything. Plus, the jury's still out on whether or not he's going to let me go like he said he would.

"I'm really not so bad, once you get to know me."

I chew for a moment, irritated that he can so easily read my face.

Then he completely flusters me by growling, "Fuck, you're beautiful."

"Flattery won't get you anywhere."

"It's not flattery. It's honesty."

I swallow and clear my throat, feeling blood pulse in my cheeks. "Well. Thank you."

"You're welcome."

He stares at me in unblinking intensity, studying every nuance of my face, radiating pure masculine sexuality, until I can't stand it anymore.

"Are you always like this?"

He cocks his head. "Like what?"

I wave my hand at him. "This. You know. *Alpha.*"

He shrugs, the picture of nonchalance. "Of course."

Jeez, what was I expecting? Humility?

He watches me chomp in aggravation for a few moments, then smiles. "I feel sorry for that sandwich."

I don't have a smart comeback, so I simply chew and swallow until the sandwich is gone.

His cell phone rings. He whips it from his shirt pocket and answers with a curt, "Aye."

He listens intently. I try to listen, too, but can't hear whatever the person on the other end is saying. Then he poses a series of rapid-fire questions, his jaw getting harder and harder between each one.

"Just the one? Conscious? Where? Who's with him? How long have we got?"

He listens, his expression growing darker, until finally he glances up at me.

His dark eyes have turned black.

"I'm on it," he says, and ends the call.

I push the plate away, a funny feeling in the pit of my stomach. "Let me guess. You have to go out for a while."

"Aye. I won't be long. Make yourself comfortable while I'm gone."

I smile sweetly at him. "Oh, sure, I'll just be here rifling through your drawers for evidence I can provide to the authorities."

If I thought that would make him think twice about leaving me alone—and possibly taking me with him, giving me a chance at escape—I was wrong.

"Have at it, lass. My office door's open. You won't be able to get into anything without a matching biometric fingerprint, so you'll be wasting your time, but you're certainly welcome to try."

He turns and strides toward the direction of the elevator banks, but stops and turns back around to look at me. His voice comes low and rough. His dark eyes glitter with secrets.

"And the authorities already know exactly what I am."

The man talks in riddles. There always seems to be layers under layers hidden beneath his words, a sly wink in his tone like he's the only one in on the joke. It's intriguing as much as it is irritating.

"I know who you are, too, gangster. Everyone in this town knows who you are."

"I didn't say who, lass. I said what."

I'm getting exasperated with his word games. "What's the difference?"

He murmurs, "Only everything that matters, little thief."

Eyes burning, he holds my gaze for a moment longer before turning and heading out.

When the elevator doors slide shut and he's gone, I shout after him, "What you are is annoying, devil man!"

It doesn't make me feel better.

Because I was raised to have good manners, I rinse my dish and put it in the dishwasher, then wipe up the crumbs from the counter. Then I go on the hunt for the devil man's office.

I find it at the opposite end of the corridor from the guest room I trashed. It's large and masculine, with a big black oak desk and all the requisite macho man décor, bulky leather sofas and the like.

I sit in his ridiculously large captain's chair and stare at his blank computer screen with pursed lips, thinking. My gaze drops to the keyboard, then to the surface of the desk.

I wish he were here to see my smile.

Shoving away from the desk, I trot out of the office and back down the corridor. When I find the master bedroom—decorated all in gray and black, what a surprise—I rummage through his bathroom drawers until I find what I was looking for.

I head back to his office with the talcum powder bottle in hand.

Seated in his captain's chair once again, I lightly sprinkle the talc over the edge of the desk near the keyboard. I blow gently, then lean down and take a closer look.

"Hello, there," I say to the outline of a fingerprint.

It's easy enough to find the Scotch tape because it's sitting right out on the blotter.

I press a piece of tape over the talc outline, then gingerly pull it up. Then I stick the tape onto a neon yellow Post-It note.

When that's complete, I look around, realizing I haven't seen a biometric fingerprint scanner anywhere. The door to Killian's office was standing wide open when I came in, and there's nothing on the desk to indicate secured access to the drawers or computer.

Wherever this blasted biometric thing is, it's hidden.

I mutter, "Well, hell."

I toggle the computer's mouse, but nothing happens. I try a drawer, but it won't open. I look underneath the desk and chair, but find nothing there.

Then I look at the keyboard.

I don't know which finger this print I pulled off the desk is from, so I start from left to right. First, I press the Post-It to the A key. Nothing happens. I move to the S key, but nothing happens there, either. I go down the line, trying each key where you set your hands to begin typing, but get no results at all.

Until I try the space bar.

The keyboard lights up. So does the computer screen. So does my face.

Grinning, I say loudly, "Ladies and gentlemen, we have liftoff!"

Then a box appears in the middle of the computer screen informing me that access is denied and all systems are shutting down due to a security breach. The screen and keyboard go dark.

Five seconds later, my cell phone rings.

I pull it from my coat pocket and look at the screen. The ID is blocked.

This is interesting, because the only two people in the world who have the number to this burner phone are Fin and Max. And their numbers are already programmed in.

I have a bad feeling I know who it is.

"Hello?"

"Hullo, lass. Having fun?"

I look up at the ceiling, wondering where the camera is. "Actually, I am. I'm planning on starting a small kitchen fire next."

"Watch out for the sprinklers. The fire suppression system dispenses about four hundred liters per minute, so I hope you can swim."

His rich brogue is tinged with laughter. He's not even a little bit worried, the jerk.

"How did you get this number?"

"I'm me."

He says it with such casual, supreme self-confidence, I want to throw the phone across the room. Instead, I demand, "No, seriously, how did you get it? I picked this phone up at a kiosk at the airport a week ago. I paid for it in cash. I've only used it twice."

"I know," he says, his tone indulgent. "And you'll get a new burner for the next job, and a new one for the job after that. I would've called you at your apartment, but you're not there at the moment."

Great. He has my unlisted home number, too. Stupid land line. I told Fin we shouldn't have signed up for that.

"While we're on the subject, how did you know it was us at the warehouse? Was there another security camera we didn't know about?"

"You forgot to disable the cameras at the factory across the street."

I close my eyes, cursing silently. What a stupid, obvious mistake. "And from there? How did you follow us? The cameras at the field where we unloaded the truck and at the drop zone were out. So were the street light cameras all around both places."

"I hacked an air force satellite."

I open my mouth, but no words come out. *He knows how to hack a government satellite? What kind of gangster am I dealing with?*

He knows I'm shocked. His chuckle is all kinds of pleased. "You still there, lass?"

"Man, I really can't stand it when you're smug."

"Oh, don't be sore. Admit it: you're impressed."

I am, but I will never, ever, not in a billion years admit it. "Was breaking into machines orbiting the earth something they taught you in mob school?"

"Ach, no. I learned to hack long before I was in the mafia."

I say flatly, "Really."

"It's not like it's difficult. There aren't any cybersecurity standards for satellites, so anyone with a basic understanding of computer systems and programming languages can get past the pathetic firewalls government defense departments sets up. I can show you, if you like."

My tone drips sarcasm. "That would be swell."

"Might come in handy for one of your future gigs."

I can tell he's trying not to laugh, the son of a—

"I'd love to keep chatting, but I'd rather get type-2 diabetes."

"Admit it, lass. You think I'm charming."

"You're as charming as a burning orphanage."

"You can't stop thinking about what it'll be like when I finally kiss you."

"Isn't there a bullet somewhere you should be jumping in front of?"

"If you really didn't like me, you would've stabbed me in the taxi when you had the chance. Or shot me with that gun you stole from my guest room nightstand that you stashed under your coat."

The way he notices every detail is truly unnerving. "I

should've done both. Your only purpose in life is as an organ donor."

When he breaks out into gales of laughter, I can't help but smile. But I keep my voice cool when I say, "Apply ice to that burn. Bye now."

I hang up, frustrated as hell. Then, because I assume he's watching through a hidden camera, I twirl around in his macho captain's chair like I don't have a care in the world.

Then I text Max that I'm still alive and that she and Fin shouldn't go home until she hears back from me. If the devil man is right and those guys were after me and not him, the apartment isn't safe.

In a few minutes, I get a thumbs-up text back from Max, though it doesn't do much to settle my nerves. The way my luck is going, she probably thinks "don't go home" is code for "we're out of toilet paper."

Then, with a dawning sense of horror, I realize that if Killian has this phone number, it's possible he's also monitoring my communications. Worse, he could be monitoring Max and Fin's phones, too…and using them to track our locations.

If the man knows how to hack a satellite to find us, manipulating a cell phone would be a piece of cake.

I send Max another text. *Update: all phones compromised. Destroy asap. Safehouse compromise possible. Dark mode until I message on VM with all-clear.*

It takes Max only moments to text back. *Please tell me you didn't insult him again.*

I text back *DARK MODE MEANS NO TALKING!* Then I remove the SIM card from the phone and smash it under my heel.

I put the pieces into my pocket. I don't want to chance leaving anything in his trash that he could somehow use. Knowing him, he'll probably make a surveillance device out of the crumbs of my tuna fish sandwich.

I spend about an hour wandering through the penthouse and snooping through his drawers, but find nothing personal, nothing of interest. If he has family, he doesn't own pictures of them. There's a huge collection of books in the library, but not a single knickknack on the shelves. There's not a house plant, not a magazine, not a crumpled receipt from a store. There's not even any dust. It's like he lives inside a museum.

Eventually, fatigue overwhelms me. I lie on my back on the sofa in the living room, hoping that he's one of those super anal neat freaks and will see me in one of his cameras and get annoyed that I didn't take off my shoes.

I don't mean to, but I promptly fall asleep.

I wake up in Killian's arms. He's carrying me toward the elevator.

"Relax, lass," he murmurs when I bleat in panic. "I'm taking you home."

I freeze, my eyes widening. "Home? Really?"

"Aye. Really."

We enter the elevator and the doors slide shut. We begin to descend.

Looking at his profile, I say, "Um. You could put me down now."

"I could. I just don't want to."

I ponder that for a moment, but decide I've got other, more important bones to pick. "Is it safe for me to go home?"

He turns his head and gazes at me through heated, half-lidded eyes. "Can't stand the thought of being away from me, hmm?"

I resist the urge to smack him on the shoulder. "Please tell me what's happening. Those men who attacked us—"

"Are all dead," he interrupts, his gaze going dark. "And I know now who sent them and why. And that person will soon be dead, too."

His intense gaze clings to mine, making me shiver. A million

86

questions fly through my mind, but I can only manage one. I whisper, "Who sent them?"

When he answers, his voice is chillingly soft. "An enemy of your father's."

He knows who I am. My heart stops dead in my chest.

I can't catch my breath or look away from the deep, dark power of Killian's gaze. We stare at each other in silence as the elevator descends smoothly, taking us down to who knows where.

I try to keep my voice steady when I speak. "Put me down."

"Not yet."

He's still staring at me with that strange intensity, his eyes locked onto mine. Panic begins to claw its way up my throat.

"You promised you'd never hurt me."

He inclines his head. I breathe a little easier, because for some insane reason, I believe him. Pretty much, anyway. But this still doesn't make any sense.

"But you...now you know who my father is?"

His tone is faintly dry. "Aye. And we're not exactly what you'd call besties."

Hello, understatement of the century. The only thing my father hates more than overcooked pasta is the Irish mob. They've been at war as long as I can remember, and from way before I was even born.

"But you're not going to use me to your advantage? Get money, concessions, terms?"

"You say that like it's an impossibility."

I scoff. "If my father had *your* daughter, you better believe he'd get something out of it. Something big."

The minute it leaves my mouth, I regret it. It sounded like a dare. But Killian simply gazes at me with that strange, dark intensity, his gaze never leaving mine.

He murmurs, "I am getting something out of it, lass."

My mouth goes dry. *Oh, shit. Here it comes. Soon I'll be missing my big toe.* I whisper, "What?"

"This."

He doesn't elaborate, and now I'm confused. "This...what?"

His big arms give me a gentle squeeze. "This moment. This memory. This time I've had with you."

I stare at him in disbelief with my mouth hanging open.

He's serious. He's actually *serious.*

I blurt, "What kind of gangster *are* you?"

He turns his head, breaking our gazes and leaving me feeling like I've been sprung from jail.

"Don't tell anyone," he says with a sigh. "Can't have word getting around that I'm a romantic. As soon as the sharks get a whiff of blood in the water, it all goes to hell."

The elevator doors slide open to reveal the building's parking garage. Six men in dark suits await in front of an idling SUV. Killian strides out of the elevator toward the car. One of his suited goons opens the back door for us.

But Killian doesn't get in with me.

He sets me gently on my feet next to the open door, straightens, then looks at me.

His tone and expression somber, he says, "It's been a pleasure, Miss Moretti."

I stare at him, feeling like I'm in an alternate universe and everything is backward. "I don't understand what's happening right now."

"What's happening is that Declan is going to take you home."

I look around in confusion. "But..."

"Here's my number. If you need anything, call me. No matter the time."

He holds out a small white card. I take it, blinking like an owl. The only thing on the card is a telephone number. No name, no address, no explanation as to why I'm feeling so deflated.

Seeing my expression, Killian's gaze turns smoldering. He moves closer and leans down to murmur into my ear.

"Whenever you're ready for that kiss, little thief, I'll be waiting."

He turns and strides away without a backward glance. The elevator doors slide shut behind him, and he's gone.

11

JULES

*W*hen Declan drops me off in front of my apartment, I wait for the SUV to drive out of sight before heading back down the street to flag a taxi. The sun is rising by the time I make it to the hotel. I check in, head to the room, and leave a voicemail for Fin and Max on a number designated for emergencies only.

Then, dead tired, I drop facedown onto the king-sized bed and go to sleep. I don't dream. I don't move. I fall off a cliff into grateful oblivion.

When I wake, the sun is setting in a spectacular golden light show over the Charles River. I take a shower, order a steak and a bottle of red wine from room service, and get dressed again in the same clothes I've been wearing from before I broke into the Irish mob king's diaper warehouse and my whole world was turned upside down.

When the hotel phone on the desk rings, I answer with the name I checked in under. "Katniss Everdeen speaking."

"It's me."

Sighing in relief, I sink into the desk chair and take a big swig of the wine. "Max. Thank god. Are you guys okay?"

"We're fine. How was the date?"

"Ha ha."

"I'm only asking because you sounded so hot and bothered in your message. We figured you and the crazy beautiful evil gangster got down to more than canoodling."

"Why don't you sound the least bit concerned that I could be dead right now?"

"You picked up the phone, dummy. Clearly, you're not dead."

"You know what I'm saying. He could've killed me!"

"Listen. When a man looks at a woman the way Liam Black looked at you, the only thing she's in danger of is a punctured lung from his raging boner."

Dear god. The inhumanity. I say drily, "Thanks for your prayers, Mother Teresa."

"Tell the truth. He likes you."

I chug the wine angrily.

Meanwhile, Max is laughing. "Yeah, that's what I thought. He doesn't want to hurt you, he wants to play footsie with you under the table with his giant feet. Which reminds me, did you get a look at the size of those puppies? I noticed them in the bar. The things are enormous. If all his body parts are that large, he probably *could* kill you with his boner."

"This isn't funny, Max. He could have done very bad things to me."

"But he didn't. You're safe. Not only did he keep his word he wouldn't harm you, he let you go...*again*." She pauses. "What do you think that means?"

"That he likes playing games."

"Maybe. Or maybe that he's got a soul under all that smoking hot badassery."

I snort. "A soul? Let's not get carried away. He is who he is, after all."

Except he told me to call him by a different name than the

one everyone else calls him, and he's done the opposite of everything I've expected him to do up to this point, so I really have no idea who he is at all. Or what he is, except a notorious gangster.

"I didn't say who, lass. I said what."

Whatever the hell he meant by that is just one more question to add to the growing pile.

Max says, "So when are you seeing him again?"

I reach into my pocket and run my finger along the edge of his little white card. "Hopefully, never. Change of subject: you ditched your burner phones, right?"

"Yes, we got rid of the burner phones."

"Good. And you're at your alternate safe spots? You weren't followed? No one knows where to find you?"

Max answers with exaggerated patience. "That is correct, Sister Neurosis of the Immaculate Order of High Anxiety."

"You act like I'm being unreasonable."

After a weighted pause, Max says, "Did it ever occur to you that all this stuff we do to try to make amends for being who we are is a total waste of time? That if we *really* wanted to make a difference in the world, all it would take would be for each of us to put a bullet in our fathers' brains?"

I blink in surprise. "Wow. The conversation has taken a dark turn."

Her voice grows hard. "We could save countless lives by doing that, Jules. We could end so much suffering. But instead, we're playing at being these underdog heroes who do the wrong thing for the right reasons. Or the right thing for the wrong reasons, I don't fucking know."

"Max—"

"My dad is one of the worst drug traffickers in the northern hemisphere. Fin's dad sells weapons to whichever global anarchist or authoritarian hungry for power who'll pay the most. Yours makes Michael Corleone look like a crybaby."

I listen to her breathe hard for a moment before saying, "What's your point?"

"When the three of us met at school when we were thirteen, that was fate. It was fate that we made a pact to help people instead of turning into what our genes and our childhoods had in store for us. It was fate that out of all the people in the entire world, you chose Liam Black to target for a job."

"Or maybe it was sheer stupidity."

She ignores me. "And it was fate that he let you go not once, but twice."

I crinkle my brow in confusion. "I'm not sure I follow."

"You influenced him."

She lets it sink in for a moment before continuing. "He didn't hurt you. He wasn't even angry about what you'd done. He followed you, and made smoldery bedroom eyes at you, and gave you his word you'd be safe with him, and kept his word by not using you in one of the million different ways a man like him could use a woman."

This time her pause is longer. "Imagine if our mothers could've had any influence over our fathers. Imagine how much different so many people's lives might have been."

"Question: what have you been smoking?"

"Nothing."

"Really? Because it sounds like you're suggesting I should attempt to have some kind of influence over Killian Black's evil empire."

"I am. Wait—who's Killian?"

I pinch the bridge of my nose between my fingers and close my eyes. "Smoldery isn't a word."

Max's voice drips sarcasm. "Oh, look, another random change of subject. Could it be because you don't want to explain to the smarter of your two best friends that you're hiding something about the hot criminal you keep pretending not to like?"

"I *don't* like him," I say between clenched teeth.

"Sure. And I'm Brad Pitt."

"Nice to meet you, Brad. You're so much more irritating in person."

"I'm going to say something now. You're not gonna like it."

"Keeping in line with the general theme of the conversation."

"If you can influence him to stop him from doing something bad, even one thing, you have an obligation to do it."

I open my eyes and stare at the wall. "You're right. I didn't like it."

We sit in tense silence for a while, unbroken only by the distant sounds of traffic drifting up from the street below. Then, trying to sound reasonable, Max says, "I'm not suggesting you should sleep with him."

"Good, because my vagina is all out of the magic pixie dust that makes bad men do good things."

"You don't give yourself enough credit."

"Oh, for god's sake. *Moving on.* Have you seen anything on the news about the gunfight? I've been passed out since this morning."

"Gunfight? What gunfight?"

"The one I was in after I left you guys at the Poison Pen."

Silence.

"The one where like ten dead bodies were littering Birchland Avenue?"

"I've read two papers front to back today, I've watched the news, and I've been on the internet. There's been nothing about a gunfight."

Is he that powerful that he can keep a massacre off the news? I don't think my father could even manage that.

"Hello? Anybody home?"

"Still here. Just thinking."

"I know. I can smell the struggle. So this gunfight you were in. Spill."

"Um. Some guys tried to kill us. Me. Well, I'm not exactly

sure which one of us they were after, but Ki—Liam said he thought it was me. He said they were enemies of my father, which I didn't think to clarify what exactly he meant by that because at the time he was carrying me. Which. You know. Is disorienting."

In Max's pause, I feel her astonishment. "Are you saying *he knows who you are*?"

"He does."

Her voice rises to a shout. "*And he still let you go?*"

I see her point. I was the golden egg dropped onto his lap, a prize opportunity for him to stick it to a rival mob king, and he didn't take it.

Why?

I chew my lip, unsure how to respond.

She takes pity on me and goes in another direction. "How did he find out who you are?"

"I don't know. He didn't say. But he's got an uncanny ability to do stuff like that. I think he might have friends in high places. Like government type high places. He said he ran a background check on me. He knew all kinds of weird stuff, like how I hadn't been serious with someone in years."

"That wouldn't show up on a regular background check."

"I know, that's what I'm saying. And guess how he found us after we left the warehouse."

"How?"

"He hacked an air force satellite."

After a moment of thinking, Max says, "If he knew someone high level in the government, he wouldn't have had to go to the trouble of hacking a satellite to find us. He could've just made a call and said, hey, buddy, here's the time and coordinates I need, can you get an image of these chicks stealing stuff from me so I can follow them home and discover their identities."

"Hmm. True."

"Which means—if he really did hack a satellite and that

wasn't just BS—he's got some mad skills for your garden-variety gangster."

"Maybe he was like a programmer for Google before he went bad."

"That is the stupidest thing I've ever heard."

I groan. "I know. I'm grasping at straws. I'm so confused about this entire situation that my eyes are crossed."

"You're making yourself confused. It's actually very simple."

I mutter, "I can't wait to hear this."

"He wants you. You want to help other people. Make him helping people a condition of getting you."

"You just said you weren't suggesting I sleep with him!"

"I was lying. You should definitely sleep with him. My god, Jules, *look* at the man. He's masculine beauty personified. I could climax just by seeing him naked."

I say flatly, "You're a terrible friend."

"Am not."

"Are too."

"Okay, fine. Make it a one-time thing, then. Tell him you'll have sex with him if…" She trails off, thinking. "If he donates a million dollars to the Red Cross."

"He's a billionaire, and you're pimping me out for only a million bucks? That's all I'm worth to you?"

I hear the shrug in her voice. "Hey, I'd do him for free."

"Have at it, then! I'll give you his phone number!"

"He doesn't want me, Jules. He wants you." She pauses. "You have his phone number?"

"He gave it to me." Her silence sounds accusing, so I add defensively, "In case I needed anything."

As soon as she starts to laugh, I realize that was the wrong thing to say.

"Oh ho! So you've got the Big Bad Wolf on speed dial in case you *need* something! The plot thickens!"

My sigh is weary. "You make me want to stab myself in the eye."

"You know what he's hoping you need is his big, fat—"

I say loudly, "I have to go now. The ledge outside my window is calling."

"Don't be such a prude. A roll in the sack with that man would make your entire life worth living."

"I really hope this is a dream and I wake up in a few minutes to a reality where my best friend isn't trying to barter my cooch to a notorious mobster in some kind of insane humanitarian mission gone horribly wrong."

Her tone turns thoughtful. "You know what? That's a good idea. Give me his number and I'll call him to set up your next date."

I pour myself another large glass of wine and start to drink. Meanwhile, Max is still talking.

"I could lay down the ground rules. Act like your manager."

"The word you're looking for is madam. And we're not making any deals to save the world with a man who once threw a waiter off the roof of the Capital Grille for spilling a drop of his wine."

"That's an urban legend. Probably."

"Look, just keep your head down until I can figure out what our next move is, okay?"

Max hoots. "Oh, you're gonna figure this out? The girl who's supposed to be a thief but can't even pick a lock or hotwire a vehicle?"

"Excuse me, but I'm not the one who forgot to disable the cameras at the warehouse across the street from the diaper factory."

Into her horrified pause, I say, "Yeah. Our friend, Mr. Black, mentioned that. So you're no Hans Gruber, either, babe."

"Hey, Hans Gruber was a bad guy!"

"Sorry. He was the only famous thief I could think of."

"Because you've seen *Die Hard* about a thousand times, no doubt."

"Oh, we're going there? Should we talk about how many times you've watched *The Fast and the Furious*?"

From there, the conversation devolves into an argument about our respective bad taste in cinema. We bicker like old men until a knock on my hotel room door distracts me.

"Hold on. Someone's at the door."

"Are you expecting anyone?"

Already standing, I stop short. Suddenly, the closed door looks very ominous. "No."

"Look through the peephole to see who it is."

"I have to put the phone down. The cord doesn't reach."

"I'll be here. Go for it."

I set the receiver on the desk then creep toward the door on tiptoe. I flatten myself against it and look through.

An older man in a concierge uniform stands at the door, holding a brown paper bag. He has white hair, a cheerful smile, and a gold name tag on his lapel that reads "Ernesto."

Ernesto doesn't look like he's here to kill me, but you never know. Squirrels are super cute, but they can carry the plague.

I call out, "Yes?"

"A delivery for Miss Everdeen." He holds up the bag, smiling wider.

"Will you please take it out and show me what it is?"

His smile falters, but he obliges. From the bag he pulls out something wrapped in purple tissue paper. It's oddly shaped, with a point one end.

"Um...can you unwrap it, please?"

Ernesto looks as if he's beginning to regret not leaving the package at the door and running away when he had the chance. He tears off the tissue paper from the pointy end of the object, exposing what looks like a horn.

A golden horn, covered in sparkly glitter.

I yank open the door, grab the object from the startled concierge, and rip off the remaining tissue paper.

Staring in astonishment at the stuffed animal in my hands, I breathe, "Son of a bitch."

"The gentleman who left the package also included a note." He jiggles the brown bag.

I take the bag from him and go back inside the room, too dazed to feel bad that I didn't give him a tip.

When I pick up the phone again, Max demands, "So? Who was it?"

"Not who. What."

"I don't get it."

Inside joke. "It was the concierge. He had a package for me."

"Like a welcome basket?"

"No. Like a gift someone left for me at his desk."

"A *gift*? That hotel is your safe spot! Who'd you tell you were there?"

"No one. I wasn't followed here, either. I'm sure of it."

"What's the gift?"

I stare in disbelief at the stuffed animal in my hands. At its golden glitter horn and its flowing rainbow mane and tail. At its four hooves encrusted with tiny rhinestone crystals.

"I want you to trust me."

"And I want a unicorn pony. So here we are."

Recalling my conversation with Killian, I start softly laughing. "It's a unicorn pony."

After a beat, Max says, "Is that code for dildo or something?"

I prop the receiver between my ear and shoulder and marvel at the unicorn, turning it over in my hands. "No, gutter brain. It's a stuffed animal."

"Who the hell is sending you stuffed animals? More importantly, why?"

"Wait, there's a note."

I pull a square white envelope from the brown bag, open it, and remove the card inside. I read aloud, "Two households, both alike in dignity, in fair Verona, where we lay our scene."

There's no signature, nothing else but the quote, but there doesn't have to be. A small, impressed voice deep inside me whispers *Wow, he's something, this guy* but I quickly squash it.

After a moment of silence, Max says, "That's Shakespeare."

"Yep. It's the first line of *Romeo and Juliet*."

She shouts, "Is that fucking unicorn pony from the Big Bad Wolf?"

"It is."

Her gasp is low and thrilled. "And he's sending you quotes from the most romantic love story ever written? Oh god. My heart."

"Don't sound so swoony, idiot! *Romeo and Juliet* isn't a romance, it's a tragedy! Six people die over the course of four days because of two stupid teenagers!"

Max isn't moved by my logic. "But you get the symbolism of that particular quote, right?"

I roll my eyes to the ceiling. "If I didn't, I'm sure you're about to enlighten me."

"You're Juliet—well, obviously—and he's Romeo. Two star-crossed lovers from feuding families, brought together by fate—"

I interrupt crossly, "Destined to die through a series of ridiculous miscommunications and bad timing."

"—bound by true love—"

"Puh-lease. Insta love is *not* true love. Romeo was pining over some other chick the night he first saw Juliet and decided she was his soul mate. Talk about fickle."

"—and ultimately ending the age-old vendetta between their families—"

"Because they died. They *died*! How are you not getting this?"

"This is a sign, Jules," she counters, sounding adamant. "Forget about the death part. He's sending you an olive branch."

"More like a warning."

"He's saying he knows who you are. He knows who he is. He knows what the stakes are. *And he still wants you!*"

"You have really gone off the deep end, my friend."

"When did you become so anti-love, anyway?"

After a moment, I say quietly, "When my mother was killed by the car bomb meant for the mobster she married."

Max's sigh is heavy. "Oh fuck. I'm sorry. Me and my big mouth."

"Don't worry about it. Ancient history." I throw the stuffed unicorn across the room. It bounces off the carpet, tumbling to a stop to gaze at me with hurt blue eyes.

"So…what are we going to do about this? He knows you're at that hotel. He might know Fin and my phone numbers, and possibly our safe spot locations, too, since he's got spooky good people finding skills. He knows our apartment address. He probably knows where we all work. And we can't hide forever."

I know what she's suggesting. I know she's right, too. But boy, I don't want to do it.

I want this thing—whatever it is—between me and the Big Bad Wolf to be over before it's begun.

Grudgingly, I pull the small white card from my pocket and stare at his number.

Stupid Romeo. I'd like to smash in your face. I tell Max, "Fine. I'll call him. Satisfied?"

"Don't forget to thank him for the gift."

I hang up before I throw anything else across the room and dial Killian's number.

JULES

$\mathcal{H}$e answers on the first ring, his rich brogue tinged with warmth. "Hullo, lass."

"Hi." I'm tongue-tied for a moment. He doesn't make it any easier on me by remaining silent. "Um. Thank you for the gift."

"You're welcome."

"This doesn't mean I trust you."

"I know."

"My friend was the one who suggested I call. I didn't want to."

"I understand."

I run out of things to say, so I sit in silence, chewing my lip, until he chuckles.

"Stop chewing your lip."

I suck in a startled breath and look around in panic. "Are you watching me?"

"No. It's just what you do when you can't decide if you want to break something over my head or kiss me."

The weight of his ego could cause entire solar systems to collapse. "We've been over this a hundred times. I don't want to kiss you."

"I know you can't see my face, but my expression is one of extreme displeasure. We agreed on no lying, remember?"

I'm going to rip that damn unicorn pony to shreds. With my teeth. And send this smug bastard the video. "If I ever did kiss you, it would only be to satisfy a morbid curiosity about what disappointment tastes like."

He roars with laughter.

It's so unexpected, I simply sit and listen to it for a moment, enjoying the quality of the sound, but also confused. "Why do you like it when I say things like that?"

He's still chuckling when he answers. "Because no one else would ever dare."

Like so much else about him, that he has a sense of humor is a surprise. And yes, his ego is enormous, but he can laugh at himself, too. I also have to admit that his manners are quite good.

He's obviously sophisticated, even more obviously intelligent, and—for a ruthless killer with a reputation for extreme violence—he's oddly self-controlled.

My father would never deny himself a woman he wanted.

If she resisted, he'd laugh and take her anyway. His appetites are legendary. So is his hair-trigger temper and his exquisite sensitivity to anything that could even slightly be interpreted as an insult: he slit his own tailor's throat for suggesting it might be necessary to let out the seams on his jacket.

But *this* man reacts to my insults with a laugh.

He reacts to my refusal to kiss him with acceptance.

He didn't lay a finger on me, though his desire to lay all ten of them on me was more than apparent.

He kept his word not to harm me and also to release me when he brought me to his home, though keeping me captive could have been extremely lucrative for him. I have no doubt my father would have paid dearly for my safe return, if only because the family honor demanded it.

If I didn't know better, I'd describe Killian Black as a gentleman.

A beautiful, dangerous, unconventional gentleman who can sear holes through a woman's body with the heat of his eyes.

He says, "Uh-oh. She's thinking. That never ends well."

His tone is soft and teasing. Gentle and warm. I'm hit with the impossible thought that Killian Black has a tender side.

I blurt, "I don't understand you."

His voice grows even softer. "But you want to."

"Yes." Horrified that slipped from my lips, I backpedal as fast as I can. "No!"

We're quiet for a moment, until I say, "I don't know." Aggravated, I close my eyes and draw a breath. "The truth is yes, but I don't want to admit that, because it would make me like myself less. It would make me feel like I was going against everything I stand for."

"Because…?"

"Because of who you are. What you are. What you do. All of it."

In the following pause, I sense his ambivalence. He's fighting himself about something, but I don't know what. Then his voice comes over the line in a husky rumble.

"What if I wasn't what you thought I was, lass?"

My answer is immediate. "But you are."

"But what if I wasn't?" he presses. His tone is gentle but intense.

"Okay. If we're taking a trip to fantasy land, I'll play along. If you weren't who and what you are, I'd…well, I'd…"

Want to have sex with you, number one. Lots and lots of steamy hot sex, because you are one helluva beautiful beast, and I'd like to ride you like a stallion I'm breaking in until we both collapse from exhaustion.

"Lass? You still there?"

My cheeks pulse with heat. I have to clear my throat before

I speak so I don't sound like a phone sex operator. "The reason I called is to find out what your intentions are regarding the information you have about me and my friends." I clear my throat again. "Also to find out how you knew I was at this hotel."

After a beat, he says in a throaty voice, "For the record, I'd like to do whatever it is you won't say, too."

I exhale a ragged breath, drop my head into my hand, and close my eyes.

He takes pity on me by not pursuing that any further. His tone turns businesslike. "The only thing I'm going to do with the information I have is help keep you safe."

"Safe? What do you mean?"

"You're in no immediate danger, but the Serbs will send more men for you—"

"I'm being hunted by Serbians?"

While my voice has gone up an octave, Killian's drops one. "They won't touch you. They'll never get near you. I promise you, Juliet, I will keep you safe."

His voice rings with conviction, but it doesn't help my nerves. My hands have turned clammy. I grip the phone, trying to keep my breathing under control. "Why are they after me?"

"Apparently, your father has escalated a skirmish over drug trade routes into a war. The Serbs are looking for collateral."

My mind struggles to make sense of this distressing new information. "But they shouldn't have been able to find me. I don't go by his last name. I haven't lived with him in more than a decade. I've covered my tracks."

He says gently, "Anyone can be found, lass. Everyone has a digital footprint, no matter how hard they try to erase it. Credit cards, internet use, cell phones, surveillance cameras, bank accounts, utility bills, airline manifests, satellite images, drones...I could go on. There are a million ways to find someone. Most of them are easier than you'd think."

He pauses. "You did a good job of covering your tracks, though. I erased what was in your FBI file, but it wasn't much."

I spend a while blinking rapidly to try to clear my vision. "I'm sorry, did you say I have an FBI file?"

"Had," he corrects. "It's gone now."

When I don't say anything, he continues.

"I'm also working on wiping any other digital remnants of your existence, but we should talk about what you want to do with your bank accounts and driver's license. A new name might be in order. You mentioned Seraphina, but personally I think that unless you're a circus performer, it's a little over-the-top."

"I...I..."

"I know. It's a lot. Think about it and let me know."

He could be making it all up. This could be some kind of elaborate mind fuck, a way for him to gain my trust. Some weird game he's playing.

Or maybe he's just really good with computers?

"Killian?"

"Aye, lass?"

"Did you follow me to this hotel?"

"No."

"Are there any other trackers on my clothing?"

"No."

"Then how did you know I was here?"

"The card I gave you with my telephone number on it has a microscopic geo-locator device embedded in the stock."

Of course it does. Because that's completely normal. There are also probably tiny robot cameras swimming around in my veins. "I see. That's very cool."

"It is. I agree." He pauses for a moment. "You're freaking out again."

"I think so, yes."

"Open the door."

Startled, I look at the closed hotel door. "Why? Is there another stuffed animal waiting for me?"

"Something like that."

His voice is warm and amused, as if he's enjoying a private joke. It makes me nervous.

"Did you get me a bunny rabbit or something? A potbellied pig? One of those fainting goats? Oh god, don't tell me it's an aardvark."

"Open the door and see."

He disconnects, leaving me hyperventilating.

I set the receiver back in the cradle and head to the door, feeling as if my arteries are about to explode from the extreme pressure they're under. I peek through the peephole…but no one is there.

I glance up and down the hallway. There is no evidence of a person, a potbellied pig, or anything else. All is still and silent.

I crack open the door and look through.

A big hand reaches out from beside the door and flattens over it. Then I'm pushed back into the room by the large and imposing presence of none other than Boston's mob king himself.

Before I can make even a peep of surprise, he kicks the door shut with his foot, grabs me by the upper arms, spins me around, and pins me against it.

"Ask me to kiss you, lass," he murmurs, rubbing his thumbs back and forth over my rigid biceps. My hands are flattened over the hard expanse of his chest. I'm pushing against it, to no avail. The man is built like a mountain.

I manage to eke out a *No.* Even he doesn't think it sounds too convincing, because his smile turns smug and his eyes start to smolder.

In an attempt to gather my wits, I drag in a deep breath through my nose. Unfortunately, along with it comes the heady smell of his skin, some intoxicating combination of musk and spice and virile male in his prime.

It's quite possible I have just become pregnant through osmosis.

Get it together! Kick him out! More firmly, I say, "No. Why are you here?"

"Because I want a kiss."

I pretend his look of intense longing directed at my mouth doesn't affect me one bit. "Don't you have an evil empire you should be out running?"

"Aye." He adds softly, "This is more important."

Oh no. He's decided to be charming. Where's a chastity belt when you need one? "I want you to leave."

He shakes his head and *tsks*. "One more lie, sweet little thief, and I'll take you over my knee."

He's threatening to spank me? Heat floods my face. My heart starts to bang around inside my chest. I stare at him in outrage. "You wouldn't."

"Try me."

He looks like there's nothing he wants more in the world.

Then he leans down and inhales deeply against my throat. As I stiffen, he says hotly, "Fuck. You smell like heaven."

He nuzzles his nose into my hair and inhales again. His hands tighten around my arms. His voice drops to a growl. "I bet you taste like heaven, too."

My mind, easily distracted under the best of circumstances, wipes blank. I forget all about hating him, asking him to leave, or anything else for that matter, and simply cling to his suit jacket and try to remain standing upright.

He presses the full length of his hard body against mine, fists one big hand into my hair at the nape of my neck, curls the other around my throat, and pulls away to stare into my eyes.

In his own is a raging inferno.

"Go ahead. Lie to me. Tell me you don't want me to bury my face between your legs. Because it's all I can think about."

He strokes his thumb slowly back and forth over the pulse in the side of my neck, no doubt feeling how wildly it's throbbing.

I whisper, "Aardvark."

His eyes flash. He moistens his lips, and holy fuck, that's the single sexiest thing I've ever seen.

Against my hip, his erection throbs.

Though I try to project strength and cool self-confidence, my voice comes out shaky when I speak. "I have something I want to ask you."

He stills, coiled to spring. His unblinking gaze focuses on mine. His breathing goes ragged.

"I want to ask that you take a step back. This is too over-whelming for me. *You're* too overwhelming. I can't think."

He examines my expression in silence. Heat bristles like an electrical current between us. His stare is so hot and intense I feel burned by it. Then, once again, his gaze drops to my mouth.

"Killian. Please."

His eyes drift shut. A muscle in his jaw jumps. He exhales slowly through his nose, then releases me.

When he steps back, my knees are so rubbery that I nearly slide to the floor.

Adjusting his tie, he clears his throat. "I'm sorry. You make me…I get a little…" He stops and draws a breath. His laugh is low and faintly bewildered. "I'm afraid you make me go slightly crazy."

"I'm familiar with the feeling."

Our gazes lock and hold. He's standing only about a foot or so away, and the air between our bodies feels supercharged. Magnetized. Like there's a powerful, invisible pull drawing us together, no matter how hard we're both trying to stay apart.

Our breathing falls in sync. My ears turn hot. Hanging by his sides, his hands flex and unflex, as if he's deliberately forcing himself not to reach for me.

I say, "This is very strange."

"Aye."

"Like, beyond strange. Like UFOs and haunted houses strange. Like supernatural."

"Just because you don't understand it doesn't mean it shouldn't happen."

"But it shouldn't happen. It *can't* happen. I'm me, and you're you."

"Aye, there's some baggage there. We don't have to unpack it all tonight."

His eyes are blistering with desire, but his voice is velvet soft, husky with emotion. The combination of animalistic lust and raw vulnerability is intoxicating. Especially coming from a man like him.

Still. I can't for the life of me figure this out.

"Not to be rude, but maybe you only like me because I'm always saying no. Maybe you're the kind of guy who loves a challenge. Maybe my appeal for you is only that I'm—"

"Your appeal is that you're *you*," he interrupts, his voice still that same velvet glove stroking over my skin. "You're brave, and smart, and tough, but also kind. And funny. And beautiful. God, you're just a pleasure to look at. And you don't even try.

"I like that you seem as if you have more important things to do than dress a certain way or act a certain way or pretend to be anything other than what you are to impress a man. You just go around being unapologetically you. Living by your own rules. Trusting your own instincts. You let yourself take up space. You refuse to shrink to fit in. So many women don't do that. You're just…free. It's refreshing. You make me feel…"

He searches for a word for a moment, before blinking slowly, as if coming to an unexpected—and not entirely welcome —understanding.

Then he shakes his head and looks away, swallowing.

He stands there like that, tense and silent, while I watch him struggle with everything he won't allow himself to say.

It's incredibly appealing, damn him.

"Hey. Gangster."

Without turning his head, he glances back at me. His eyes are guarded.

I find myself unexpectedly smiling up at him. "I like you like this. It gives me hope that somewhere deep down underneath all that hard black armor, you might actually have a heart."

"I'd say thank you, but I'm not sure that was a compliment."

We gaze at each other for a moment, neither of us moving, until I exhale a breath. "Is it safe for me and my friends to go back to our apartment?"

He doesn't hesitate when he answers. "Aye."

I examine his face, intuitively understanding what it is he left unsaid. "Because you'll be watching out for us."

"Aye."

"And you won't let anything bad happen."

"Aye."

"Because you...inexplicably...like me."

He reaches out and gently brushes his knuckles over my cheek. His gaze follows the path of his touch. He says softly, "It's not inexplicable. I like you the way Newton liked gravity."

"I don't know what you mean."

"Once he found it, everything else in the universe made sense."

I sit with that for a moment, allowing myself to feel all the things that sentence made me feel. Allowing myself space to take it in and sit with it.

Killian gives me time to work it over and simply waits.

He doesn't insist I respond. He doesn't push for any kind of reaction. He just stands quietly and watches me with no expectation.

I could laugh at him. I could rage at him. I could shower him with scorn. His gift to me is that he'd accept any of those things, and he'd still be glad he said it because it's his truth.

It dawns on me like the sunrise over mountains: he doesn't want to lie to me. He doesn't want to play games with me. He only wants to tell me his truths.

If my life were a movie, it would be co-directed by Alfred Hitchcock and Woody Allen.

I say gently, "Do you think it's possible you're having a midlife crisis?"

He throws his head back and laughs.

"I mean, we haven't even kissed."

Still chuckling, he says drily, "Not for lack of trying on my part."

"You have to admit, though, this pursuit of yours is over-the-top. It's practically fictional. Romeo himself would be impressed by your single-mindedness."

"If you think I'm over-the-top, you should meet my brother. He sat in the same section of a shitty diner for an entire year staring at his future wife and obsessing before ever speaking a word to her."

The moment he says it, he looks like mentioning his brother was a mistake.

I smile at him, strangely glad he did. "Don't worry, gangster. I won't tell anyone you're human. We'll just keep letting everyone think you got here when Pandora let you out of that box."

He sweeps his thumb thoughtfully over my cheekbone, then cups my chin in his hand. He gazes at me steadily for a moment, then says, "I'll give you a week to think about it."

"It?"

"The kiss. If you decide when a week's up that you really don't want to kiss me, I'll let it go. You'll never hear from me again." He pauses. "To clarify: I'll still be making sure you're safe. This isn't blackmail."

Incredibly, I believe him. But I can't admit that, so I go with sarcasm instead. "How gallant."

"Just because I'm the leader of an international criminal organization doesn't mean I can't be honorable, too."

"Funny, I was under the impression that's exactly what it means."

That sly, I've-got-a-secret twinkle returns to his eyes. "Where I'm concerned, lass, you should get used to being wrong."

He ducks his head, brushes his lips against my cheek, then takes me by the shoulders and moves me a few feet to one side. Then he leaves, letting the door slam shut behind him.

I stand unmoving where he left me for a long time, my hand to my face, feeling the ghost of his lips burn my skin, trying to convince myself that when Max said my collision with the elemental force that is Killian Black was fate, she was dead wrong.

Trying but not quite believing it.

JULES

I call Max back and tell her everything. Then I ask her what she thinks we should do.

"Aside from driving straight to the nearest adult store to stock up on lube and fishnet stockings? Book an appointment for a Brazilian wax. Then set up a video camera in the closet. I'm gonna want to watch the highlight reel over and over again."

"I'm not having sex with him. Also, you are a very disturbed person. I said what should *we* do? Stay in our safe spots for the time being, right?"

"He knows where your safe spot is, genius."

"I'll move to another one, obviously."

"Uh-huh. And what makes you think he couldn't find you there?"

She makes a good point. I touch my hair, wondering if he implanted another tracking device when he had his hand buried in it.

I decide the odds are good. I should take another shower.

"We can't go back to the apartment like nothing happened. That's reckless."

Max laughs. "Right. Because the three of us would never do anything reckless."

I sit on the edge of the bed and stare out at the view of the Charles River, where I accused him of planning to throw me while I sported a pair of cement shoes. I think of his face when he said he liked me the way Newton liked gravity.

I think of his eyes.

I say quietly, "Help me, Max. I'm lost."

She's silent for a long time. Then she says, "You're lost because you like him. And you hate yourself for liking him. Because he's everything he is. Because your worst nightmare is ending up like your mother: drunk in love, then dead as a result."

It's both a gift and a curse having another person know me this well. My chest constricts until it's painful.

I whisper, "I remember how she worshipped my father. How she hung on his every word. Even when I was little, I couldn't understand her devotion. I knew he was bad…why didn't she?"

Max says firmly, "You're not your mother. Or your father. You're you, not the sum of their parts. Let that shit go."

Letting go is what I've been trying to do my whole life. But a person's life history isn't a butterfly's cocoon or a snake's dead, outgrown skin. We can't walk away from it. We carry our history around in our hearts and our memories and deep within our bones. It's alive and well, circulating in our bloodstreams.

Our pasts know exactly who we are, even when we don't.

Or don't want to admit we do.

Perhaps that's my mistake: running away from the past instead of confronting it. Fleeing the dragon instead of slaying it.

Confusing hiding with moving on.

I look at the gun I stole from Killian's guest room resting on the nightstand. I remember the knife stashed in the pocket of my coat. I think of all the ways I've trained to save myself from danger, all the ways I've contorted myself to make up for the sins of a single man, and wonder if the point of all the training and striving hasn't been safety or penance, but preparation instead.

Every warrior has to go to battle. Everyone who trains with a sword must eventually use it to fight.

Max says, "Hello?"

"I'll go back to the apartment. For the time being, you and Fin stay out of sight."

"Jules—"

"I won't risk your safety."

She chuckles. "That's a sweet thought, babe, but it's not your decision. Wherever you go, we go, too. Without the other Musketeers, D'Artagnan was just a wannabe in a dumb cape."

A wave of emotion overwhelms me. I don't deserve this kind of loyalty, but damn, it sure is great. "I love you. You know that, right?"

She's silent for a moment. "Jesus. Don't make it sound so awful."

"What do you mean?"

"You saying 'I love you' sounds like anyone else saying, 'The dog's dead.'"

When I laugh, swiping at my watering eyes, Max says, "That's better. I'll see you at home."

She hangs up before I can make any more depressing statements.

Two hours later, Fin, Max, and I are standing together at the big bay window at the front of our apartment, looking down onto the street below.

Fin says, "What is he doing?"

We watch Killian stride back and forth between two parked SUVs. They're his, obviously, the big ones with blacked out windows, shiny rims, and general air of menace. He doesn't stop to speak to the men inside, he simply walks the half block distance between them then turns around and goes the other way.

Max says, "He's pacing."

"Why?"

"Maybe that's how he gets his exercise."

I know better.

I know that right now he's down there doing battle with himself. I recognize the signs. Hands flexing open and closed, thunderclouds gathered over his head, jaw muscles jumping.

He's trying to restrain himself from running up the steps, kicking down the front door, pulling me out of the house, throwing me over his shoulder, and taking me back to his bat cave. Even from a distance, he looks like a man obsessed.

I can't decide if I'm flattered or if I should call the police.

Without breaking his stride, he glances up at the window. Our gazes lock and hold. Heat flashes over me. I exhale a soft, mystified laugh, wondering how it's possible that merely looking at him could raise my temperature by several dozen degrees.

Fin elbows me in the side. "Don't be rude. Wave."

Max says, "Judging by the look on his face, a wave isn't what he wants from her. Dude is *intense*."

Fin makes a noise of agreement. "Maybe you should call him, hun."

"What would she say to him, Fin? 'Hi, I can see your boner from here. Looks majestic. Send it on up.'"

"I'm just saying that he might calm down a little if he heard her voice."

"Or he might explode into a million superheated mafia king pieces."

"We can't let him stomp back and forth across the sidewalk all night. You know Mrs. Lieberman downstairs is already on the phone with 9-1-1."

"I'm not calling him," I say quietly, watching him turn on his heel and go back in the opposite direction. "I'm not doing anything with him. He said he'd protect us from the Serbians, and if his way of handling it is to wear a groove into the cement, so be it. He won't get a reaction from me."

Fin's whistle is low and impressed. "Play on, player."

"No games. I just have to disengage, not escalate."

Max snorts. "I'd escalate it all the way to a hundred screaming orgasms, myself."

Fin says drily, "Gee, what a shocker."

I say, "To what end? It would be a disaster. A stupid, dangerous, and completely preventable disaster."

A man steps out of one of the SUVs. I recognize him. It's Declan, the handsome one who called me Your Highness and got a sharp rebuke from Killian over it.

Spotting him, Max says loudly, "Holy crap, what is this? The Evil Supermodel convention? The first annual Criminals Who Can Cut Steel with Their Cheekbones event?"

Declan approaches Killian. They share a few words, then Killian starts his pacing anew. Declan heads back into the car, shaking his head.

As for me, I turn away from the window and lie down in the middle of the living room floor. Staring up at the ceiling, I say, "Someone please bring me a Xanax. I have to get up for work in a few hours. At this rate, I'll have a heart attack before then."

Fin says, "Oh, shit, that's right. Tomorrow's Monday. It seems like lifetimes ago since we broke into that diaper warehouse." She turns, looks at me on the floor, and smiles. "Since *I* broke into that diaper warehouse."

I say without heat, "You suck. Also, you're wrong. I'm the one who used the bolt cutters to get through that chain, remember?"

"What I remember is you flailing around like a newborn giraffe until I *handed* you the bolt cutters. Which *I* brought."

I entreaty the ceiling, "Why must everything be a competition?"

Max chimes in, "Because you were Ms. Crabtree's favorite. She's never forgiven you for it."

I remember our glamorous ninth-grade teacher at boarding school, and say, "Oh god. Carolyn Crabtree. I wonder what she's doing now?"

Fin says, "Still slaying young men with her crystal blue eyes and masses of wavy red hair, no doubt." Her smile falters. She says more softly, "Young men and women."

Gazing at Fin fondly, Max says, "You always were a sucker for a ginger."

"And you always were a sucker for anything with a dick."

"They do have their charms."

"Name one. I'll wait."

Fin and Max grin at each other, while I lie on the floor, emitting plaintive moans. "Xanax!"

"You know we don't keep Xanax in the house, dummy." Max comes to sit cross-legged on the floor next to me. She takes my hand and pats it. "But I'll let you borrow my vibrator."

I close my eyes and heave a sigh. "So gross."

Fin sits down on my other side and takes my other hand. I say warily, "Are we about to start a séance here, or what?"

"More like group therapy," says Max, making me moan again.

"No. No therapy. I don't want to talk about this. About anything!"

No one says a word for a while. Fin starts to brush her fingers through my hair. The silence is heavy with anticipation.

I insist, "I'm not talking about him. I don't even want to say his name."

"Hmm," says Fin, exactly like a therapist would.

I open my eyes and glare at her. "He's a criminal! There's nothing to talk about!"

"Nothing except your deeply conflicted feelings about him and what he does to your libido."

I close my eyes again, wishing I were a hermit who lived alone on a tropical island and my only friends were a parrot and a tree snail.

A mute parrot and a tree snail.

When the silence grows so pregnant it's about to give birth, I relent. "Fine. Who's going first?"

"I am," says Fin briskly, already in interrogation mode. "Max filled me in on the unicorn pony situation, but I want to backtrack to before any of this started. To the very beginning. How did you pick him for the job in the first place?"

"I saw him on the news a year ago. He was being arrested. Led in handcuffs up the steps of the courthouse by a bunch of federal agents. Except it looked like *he* was leading *them*. Ugh. You've never seen such confidence. Such conceit. Even his hair looked smug. It really, really pissed me off." Thinking about it, I'm getting pissed off again.

"I remember that," muses Fin. "He was let go pretty quickly, right?"

"Literally the same day. No charges filed. The government nabs the guy after months of intense investigation, and not one of the charges they slapped on him stuck for even twenty-four hours."

Max nods. "You were indignant."

"Righteously indignant," adds Fin, her tone soothing.

"Hell, yes, I was! Here was this man—"

"This incredibly gorgeous hunk of man. This extreme example of uber-manliness. This scorching hot, barn burner of a man, who can produce spontaneous orgasms in whole swaths of the female population with merely a smile."

I direct my glare to Max. "May I continue?"

She has the decency to look bashful. "Sorry. It's just that he's freaking *beautiful*, Jules."

"No one is denying the man is attractive. Panthers have

lovely, strokeable, furry torsos, but nobody is dumb enough to stick their hand close enough to cop a feel."

"Point taken. Proceed."

"Thank you. As I was saying…what was I saying?"

Fin says, "You were indignant."

"Yes! Thank you. I was indignant. Here was this man, this infamous criminal, oozing self-confidence and superiority like sap from a tree. I hated him on sight. It's like he *knew* he'd get off scot-free. I could see it on his face. That…that…"

Sounding impressed, Fin says, "Boldness."

Sounding dreamy, Max says, "Élan."

"Give me a break here, girls. I'm running out of glares."

They apologize, and I continue. "Arrogance is the word I was looking for. Arrogance was coming off him like fumes. And not only that—entitlement. He knew he'd get off because he is who he is. Because he thought *he deserved to*. Because for a man like him, nothing in the world is impossible or out of reach. The heartless bastard."

I seethe for a moment, until Fin observes, "I'm sensing some Daddy issues."

My tone drips sarcasm. "You think?"

Max says, "To be fair, if Daddy issues were plutonium, the three of us would have enough nuclear power to run the entire galaxy."

"True," says Fin, nodding. "We were all emotionally abandoned as children."

"We're emotional driftwood."

We sit in gloomy silence until I say, "This sure has been a great talk. Very uplifting. I feel so much better now."

While I'm busy marinating in my discontent, Max is looking at me funny. She says, "Wait. If my math is right, we've pulled off four jobs in the last year."

"Yeah? So?"

"So you said you saw Liam Black on the news one year ago."

"And?"

She eyeballs me. "And you've been stewing about him ever since."

I issue an automatic denial, to which Max says, "No? Then why wasn't his job the first job we planned after you saw that news story?"

"I was doing research."

"Research. Uh-huh. An entire year's worth of research."

Her tone makes me feel defensive. "Exactly."

She's not buying it. "It takes you a few months to research and plan all the rest of our jobs...why did it take a *year* with him?"

"Maybe I was being extra careful!"

"Or maybe you knew, deep down, that this one wouldn't be just another job."

I sit up, drag my hands through my hair, and huff out a weary breath. "Please don't start with the fate stuff again."

"Fate is a real thing, Jules."

"Sure. So is the Tooth Fairy."

"No, that's a BS story parents tell their kids. Fate is as real as...well, as love. Just because you can't see it, doesn't mean it doesn't exist. All the most important things in life are invisible."

Fin and I look at each other, then back at Max. She shrugs.

Fin says, "What other invisible stuff is important? The mental break with reality you're having?"

Good. She doesn't believe in fate, either. I knew Max was wrong when she claimed to be the smarter of the two.

But Max is undeterred. She lifts her nose in the air just far enough to look down it at us. "Things like loyalty. Things like faith. Things like *friendship*, dumbasses."

"One could only wish friendship were invisible," says Fin with a sweet smile.

Max scowls at her. "I'm gonna make that condescending smile invisible in a minute. When I slap it off your face."

I stand and head into my bedroom, calling over my shoulder, "Wake me up if I need to help one of you bury the other one's body. Otherwise, I'll see you two nightmares in the morning."

I head to my room and lock the door, knowing they won't be the only faces I'll see in the morning.

Knowing without knowing how that tomorrow, Killian Black will be right where I left him, pacing in agitation outside the window.

My dark, deadly Romeo waiting for his Juliet.

Thank god I don't have a balcony.

1 4

KILLIAN

*B*y the time Liam answers the phone, I'm ready to smash something.

"Brother," he says, his voice thick with sleep. "Tell me this is an emergency. Tell me you're not calling me at three o'clock in the morning for a family chat."

I growl, "It's two here. And aye, it's a fucking emergency." I spin on my heel and turn back to pace the other direction, ignoring Declan inside the SUV. He's watching me, shaking his head like I'm a lost cause.

Hearing my tone, Liam's sharpens. "What is it? Are you all right?"

"No, I'm not all right. I'm the opposite of all right, whatever that is."

"What's going on?"

I glance up at Juliet's apartment window. It's dark. The whole street is dark, except for the streetlights and the nuclear glow of my agitation. I demand, "How did you make Tru fall in love with you?"

After a short silence, Liam says warily, "Come again?"

"You heard what I said. Answer the question."

"I don't understand."

"There's nothing to understand. It's a simple question."

"Not coming from you, it isn't."

I stop short, drop my head back, and stare up into the starry night sky. Closing my eyes, I exhale heavily. I encapsulate the direness of the situation into three words.

"There's a woman."

Silence. Then, flatly: "You're joking."

"No."

More silence. Somewhere off in the distance, a dog howls at the moon. I know exactly how the poor creature feels.

Liam says, "Thank you for waiting while I picked my jaw up off the floor. How bad is it?"

My laugh is low and disbelieving. "Bad. Fucking...*bad*."

After another heavy pause, Liam says, "Does she know?"

"Aye."

"Does she feel the same way?"

I picture Juliet's face. The way she looks at me with those big brown eyes filled with anger, disgust, curiosity, and desire. I know it's only hope on my part that I think the desire has a good chance of winning out.

"She's not as clear about her feelings as I am about mine."

Liam's tone turns dismissive. "Then she's daft."

"She's not daft. She's perfect. She can hardly stand the sight of me, and she doesn't trust me for shit, and she mocks me every bloody chance she gets..." My sigh is heavy and hopeless. "And she's perfect."

"Good god," says Liam, alarmed. "Who the hell am I talking to? You sound like an actual human being!"

"I know. It's awful. Help."

After a stunned silence, Liam says, "Did the word 'help' just come out of your mouth? Because if it did, I'll know this phone call is a dream brought on by the red wine I had with dinner. To the *real* Killian Black, 'help' is almost as foul a four-letter word as 'love' is."

A disgruntled growl rumbles through my chest.

Liam laughs in delight, the fucker. "I think you should get off the phone with me and call an ambulance, brother. You don't seem to be doing so well. A massive cardiac arrest could be in your immediate future."

"I'm glad you're enjoying this," I snap. "Now fucking tell me how you got Tru to fucking fall in love with you."

"All right, calm down. If you must know, I kidnapped her."

It's my turn to be stunned into silence.

Sounding defensive, he says, "It's not ideal, I know."

"You're serious."

"I am."

"And it *worked*?"

"She's sleeping beside me. Wearing my ring. Carrying my child. I'd say it worked."

His voice has grown warm and soft, and I know that he's looking at the sleeping form of his wife snuggled against him in bed. I feel a disturbing pang of what can only be described as envy.

No. It has to be hunger. I've never been envious of anyone in my entire life.

Then I realize there was one man I was envious of once. A man who had something that looked beautiful from the outside, the same way that what my brother has with Tru looks beautiful from the outside.

I'll never have that. That beautiful thing will never be mine. I made a life for myself built on revenge and dead bodies, and beautiful things such as that are not meant for men such as me.

The anguish I feel is so crushing I have to force myself to breathe through it so I don't smash the phone to pieces in my hand.

"Killian?"

"I'm here."

"Don't hate me for saying this, but whatever is meant to be will be. Fate will take care of it."

I scoff. "Belief in fate is for children and fools. I'm neither."

"You don't have to believe in something for it to be true. Just because you have an opinion doesn't mean it's right."

"Of course it does. I'm always right."

I hear the smile in Liam's voice when he speaks. "There he is. I was beginning to think you'd been possessed." He stifles a chuckle. "By the ghost of Romeo Montague."

"Speaking of which, you'll enjoy this: her name is Juliet."

He laughs. "Now *that's* funny."

"It's not a joke. Guess what else?"

"She thinks the Republic of Ireland is in the UK."

"Worse. She's Antonio Moretti's daughter."

My brother doesn't gasp. It's simply not a thing he does. But from across the phone line comes the distinctive sound of a hard breath being dragged in from shock.

Then he starts coughing. Hacking, like a big piece of meat is lodged in his throat.

"Aye," I say drily. "Now you know how I feel."

"Antonio—Moretti's—daughter?"

The words are garbled, choked out between strangled coughs. In the background, Tru's voice is a worried murmur.

Shit. I've woken her up. "I'm sorry for calling so late. I'll let you get back to your wife."

"No! Hold on!" An elephantine trumpeting nearly deafens me. He's clearing his throat. Then he comes back on the line and thunders, "*What the hell do you mean she's Antonio Moretti's daughter?*"

"I mean exactly that. Her name is Juliet Moretti. Daddy Dearest is our good friend, Antonio. Welcome to my life."

He wheezes. I imagine him, bug-eyed, sitting up in bed with the phone clenched so hard in his hand his knuckles are white, his pretty young wife hovering over him in hand-wringing worry as he tries not to topple over from the stroke he's having.

The image is strangely satisfying.

"No more pithy platitudes about fate for me, brother? No sage advice about how not to fall hard for our mortal enemy's only child?"

He barks, "Does she know who you are?"

"Aye."

"No wonder she can't stand you! They're the Capulets and we're the Montagues! It's the family business to hate us!"

"She and her father are estranged. They haven't had contact in years."

"Oh."

"She's also a thief who steals from bad guys like her father and donates everything to charity. It's how we met."

"At a charity event?"

"No, when she broke into one of my warehouses and stole two thousand diapers from me."

After a moment, Liam says, "That can't be true."

"Hand to god, brother."

"Huh. No wonder you're in such a state."

I groan in frustration. "This is what I've been trying to tell you."

After a slight pause, he says, "When was the last time you were serious about a woman?"

"Thirty years ago."

"I'm not fucking around."

"Neither am I. The last time I felt like this, I was ten years old. Her name was Katie Dunham. She lived down the street from us. Black hair. Green eyes. Big gap between her front teeth."

He thinks for a moment. "The one who was always eating handfuls of dirt?"

"That was her sister, Lizzie."

"So all these years—as an adult—you've never been in—"

"No," I say curtly before he can continue. I couldn't bear it if he said it out loud. "I came close once. But she belonged to someone else. This one..."

I drag a hand through my hair, struggling for the words to describe it. "This one is different. I feel like I've been electrocuted. Like I've been set on fire. Like I've got cancer and only have a few weeks left to live. I'm terminal. I'm fucking desperate. It's the worst."

"It sounds like the worst," says Liam, chuckling.

"And I haven't even kissed her yet."

In a conversation made up of many different types of pauses and silences, this one is the longest. It's long and loud and echoes with incredulity. Then Liam says, "Have you recently had a fall? Hit your head on a sharp object?"

"No," I say through gritted teeth. I turn around and pace in the other direction, savagely kicking a rock out of my path as I go.

"Because I'm concerned about your brain. It doesn't seem to be working right."

"It isn't! Haven't you heard a word I've said?"

"This isn't like you."

"Jesus Christ on a crutch, *I know*!"

"You're this worked up over a woman who stole from you, who doesn't like you, and whom you've never even kissed?"

I say flatly, "This from the man who stalked his wife for a *year* before he mustered the courage to speak to her. And then *kidnapped* her, because that's high on every woman's list of most romantic gestures."

"At least her father hasn't tried to kill me six times."

"He's only tried to kill me twice."

"I was talking about me. I ran things before you got there, remember?"

"Oh. Right. Sorry."

"So between the two of us, Antonio Moretti has racked up *eight* assassination attempts." Liam pauses. "Guess you won't be inviting him to the wedding."

He's laughing at me. I can hear it in his voice. "Remind me to punch you in the nose the next time we see each other."

"Oh, don't sound so depressed. This is good for you!"

"How is it good for me?"

He stifles a laugh. "Pain builds character."

I growl, "Piss off, wanker."

"Don't hang up on me yet, I have something helpful to tell you."

Finally. "I'm listening."

"If there's one thing I've learned about women since meeting Tru, it's that they hate—and I mean *hate*—to feel controlled."

I furrow my brow in confusion. "How is that helpful?"

He muses, "How do I put this delicately?" After a beat: "You're the most controlling arsehole who's ever lived."

"I'm commanding, not controlling. Like the captain of a ship."

"I hate to break it to you, but women aren't sailors. They don't enjoy having orders barked at them while they're swabbing the deck."

I think of how many times since meeting Juliet that I've demanded this or that from her, and feel a faint flush of dismay.

"They also hate it when you're overly dominating. Strong and confident is one thing, but caveman-like domination is another. Except in bed. Dominance is allowed in bed. Outside the bedroom, it's a no-no. Oh, and don't be condescending. That will make a woman want to set fire to your face and put it out with a hammer. Let's see, what else?"

"It doesn't matter what else. I'm already doomed."

He ignores me and continues. "Don't explain something to her unless she specifically asks for an explanation."

"Like what, for instance?"

"Like anything. Economics. Parallel parking. How to correctly load the dishwasher."

"Why is an explanation bad?"

"Who knows? It just is. They even have a word for it: mansplaining. It drives them crazy."

I mutter, "This is why blowup dolls were invented."

"I'm only getting started. We could be on the phone all night." He pauses. "Maybe I should just email you a list."

"What I'm hearing you say is, in a nutshell, don't be me."

"Exactly. Be anyone else but you. Be...Ryan Reynolds. Women seem to like him. He's funny, charming, and self-deprecating." Snicker. "I know those words are unfamiliar to you, but you can Google them to see what they mean."

I stop pacing long enough to drag a hand over my face and sigh. "I'm so glad I called."

"Me, too. I thought I'd never see the day when my hardass brother exposed his soft underbelly."

I say flatly, "I don't have a soft fucking underbelly. Good night."

As I'm disconnecting, he's saying loudly, "Remember—Ryan Reynolds!"

It must be so nice to be an only child.

15

JULES

I wake when it's still dark out. My first instinct is to go to the window, but I take a shower and eat breakfast instead.

Then I sit at the kitchen table and do something I rarely allow myself to do.

I think about my father.

My mother was twenty-five when she married him. The same age I am now. He was already notorious, the youngest of four sons and by far the most ambitious. And the most violent. According to the stories, when my grandfather wanted to send a message to a rival family that wouldn't be ignored, it was Antonio he'd send to do the job.

My grandfather was a mafioso, too. *Capo dei capi*, boss of all bosses. Just like my father.

This shit runs in my veins.

When the bomb meant for my father took my mother instead, I was twelve years old. I had just gotten my first period. I had no friends outside of the family, no female I could talk to who wasn't a cousin or aunt. My grandmother was still alive—my father's mother—but she was a dour old woman, frighteningly religious, always dressed in black even in the deadening heat of summer. The only two pleasures in her life were cooking and god.

Intensely introverted, I lived my life inside the safety of books. The trifecta of homeschooling, security training, and the closed circle of my family made me extraordinarily distrustful of strangers and awkward to the extreme. I had no idea how to operate in the "real" world.

Then my mother was killed, and the real world came knocking on my door. I was sent away to a boarding school in another state.

At the time, my father explained that it was for my own safety. Now, I think that with my mother gone, he simply didn't know what to do with me. His only child. A pre-teen girl.

So off I went to a private school for rich kids in Vermont.

It was the best thing that ever happened to me. I met Fin and Max and had friends for the first time in my life.

My mother didn't have any friends. She wasn't allowed to have them. Originally from California, she met my father during a vacation to Manhattan. After knowing him only a week, she gave up her entire life to go live in New York with him. That's how in love she was.

Or how lonely.

If she didn't know what he was before she moved there, she certainly found out fast.

He was a king. Wealthy. Proud. Charismatic. Both feared and respected, and known by all for his commitment to his honor but especially for his thirst for violence.

Exactly like Liam Black.

"Killian," I say aloud, correcting myself.

Killian. Not a nickname, not a middle name, not a name he's called by anyone else. It makes no sense that he would demand I call him that. It irks me.

What irks me more is that I haven't told Fin and Max about

it. I've always been good at keeping secrets, but not from them. This name thing, though…I'm still working it out. There's something important there. A clue. But to what, I don't know.

The last time I spoke to my father was seven years ago. I'd been arrested for shoplifting. It was the only time I'd seen the inside of a police station, before or since. The bail was only five hundred dollars, but I had no money of my own. I didn't have a job. My father paid for everything. It was the day after graduation, and I was scheduled to return to New York within the week.

But that phone call with my father changed everything.

In the mafia, a thief is the lowest form of garbage aside from a snitch. Made men will happily profit from the spoils of stolen goods, but they would never themselves stoop to the actual procuring of it. Their "honor" won't allow it. They have associates who do that sort of thing instead—people not allowed in the mafia ranks. Non-Italians, those of poor reputation, etcetera. So when I had to call my father to wire bail money, and he discovered that I'd dishonored the family name by stealing, he flew into a rage. He screamed at me. He called me names.

He said I was stupid, my mother's daughter to the core.

And something inside me snapped.

I was done. Done with all of it. Especially done with him.

I hung up the phone in the middle of his tirade.

I told the arresting officer I'd stay in jail until the arraignment. He looked at me strangely, then said he'd talk to the judge. I seemed like a nice girl, he said. And it was my first offense. He had a daughter about my age, and it didn't make much sense to have me in jail with the sex offenders and drug dealers for stealing a ten-dollar lipstick from a department store.

The judge decided to be lenient. I was released after twelve hours sitting alone in a cell, thinking. It was the first time I'd truly been alone in my life.

I loved it. There were bars on the door and window, but I'd never felt as free.

I knew my father would come for me, even though he was furious. I belonged to the family. I was chattel. I had value as a bride for a favored ally or payment for a debt: it was unthinkable to simply let me go.

I disappeared instead.

I moved to Boston with Fin and Max. Fin knew someone who knew someone who got me a fake ID. I got a job working in the mailroom of a local paper.

I was terrible at it, but I learned.

From the mailroom, I was quickly promoted to the advertising department, and from there to an assistant position for one of the staff writers in the features department. Hank had aspirations to grandeur: he wanted to win a Pulitzer for reporting. He was dogged in his pursuit of "real news" and taught me how to do data mining on the internet for research, how to piece together seemingly unrelated tidbits of information, and, most importantly, how to verify facts.

I became adept at all those things. In my spare time, I used those skills to find our marks.

Criminals—the "good" ones, at least—are also skilled, especially at hiding their criminal activities. When I saw the news report about Liam Black's arrest and almost immediate release, I decided to find out more about him.

But for a man with such a huge reputation, there was curiously little to find. No verifiable address, no history of arrest before the recent one, no social media presence, no photographs. It was as if he existed by word of mouth alone. As if he were a ghost, a Bogeyman parents used to frighten their misbehaving kids.

My interest grew.

I kept digging until I found something: in the Massachusetts Secretary of State's corporate licensing database, there was a listing for Black Irish Enterprises, Inc. The name jumped out at me. The corporate headquarters address was a post office box. All the officer positions were listed under the name Mail Kcalb.

A name that made absolutely no sense, until you spelled it backward.

After more digging, I discovered that Mr. Kcalb was the owner of ninety-five other companies, most of them in foreign countries and operating under DBAs. The majority of them were shell corporations. Meaning they had no employees, no active business operations, and no significant assets.

Suggesting they were formed only for the purposes of money laundering and tax evasion.

I played the clip of Liam Black being led into the federal building by FBI agents over and over again, memorizing his face, making note of the tattoos on the knuckles of his left hand. He left an indelible impression on me. I'd never seen a criminal as beautiful as that one, or half as smug.

The combination was infuriating.

By that time, I'd lived in Boston for over a decade. It was long enough to have heard the stories about the Irish mafia and its ruthless leader. Remembering how my father had screamed that I was stupid, I decided there was another arrogant mobster who needed to be shown he wasn't actually king of the universe. That there was someone out there who wasn't afraid of him.

That being a girl—younger, smaller, powerless—didn't mean I couldn't beat him at his own game.

Max was right, though. I did stew about it for months. Months and months and still more months, until almost a year had gone by before I finally pulled the trigger on the job.

In all that time, I never once asked myself why I was stalling.

Now, sitting here at my kitchen table, grappling with the past, I have to admit Max was right about something else. I knew from the moment I laid eyes on him that the formidable Mr. Black was lightning, and I was a lightning rod.

Made to attract his strike.

I say darkly to the empty kitchen, "Okay, gangster. You want to play this game? Let's play."

But I'm in it to win.

The coffee steams in the cool morning air, sending up perfect white whorls like in a commercial. Approaching the SUV with a mug in each hand, I'm careful not to spill any on the front of my pretty white dress.

When I'm twenty steps away, Killian bursts from the passenger seat as if the car spat him out.

He stands stock still as I approach. Staring at me. Eating me up with his eyes.

I stop in front of him and look up into his burning gaze. Holding out one of the mugs, I say pleasantly, "Good morning."

He accepts the mug without looking away from my face. "Good morning."

"You look like shit."

"I haven't slept."

"The front seat of your macho truck isn't good for that sort of thing, hmm?"

He licks his lips. Drinks his coffee. Licks his lips again.

I say, "Have you considered that you hanging out here on the street with your goombahs will bring a certain amount of attention? Considering you're trying to keep me safe, it might not be the best strategy." I look him up and down. "You're not exactly incognito."

"I'm not trying to be incognito. That's the point."

We stare at each other. We drink our coffee. A slight breeze rustles the leaves on the trees.

He says, "In Irish, a goombah is called a *comhlach*."

"Sounds like you're trying to clear your throat."

His lips lift into a wry smile. "Aye. Much of Irish sounds like that."

I tilt my head and consider him. "It's not called Gaelic?"

"It is, but at home we call it Irish. As opposed to Scottish Gaelic, which is a completely different thing."

I'm hyper aware that the cool morning air has caused my nipples to harden, and also that Killian has noticed it, too. We both pretend we haven't.

"Say the same word in Irish and in Scottish Gaelic."

He thinks for a moment. "Áilleacht. Brèagha."

"Those are the same words?"

"Aye."

"What do they mean?"

His voice turns husky. His gaze turns intense. "Beauty."

I drink more coffee, willing my cheeks not to turn red.

He says, "Brèagha was what my father always called my mother. She was Scottish. He wanted to say it in her language, so I grew up thinking it was an Irish word. It wasn't until long after they were both dead that I learned it wasn't."

This personal family anecdote is unexpected. He isn't the kind of man I imagine as ever being a boy or having parents. He seems like he arrived on this planet a fully formed adult, kicking ass and incinerating panties.

"So you're half and half."

"Aye."

"In the Italian mafia, you can't be a made man unless you're full-blooded Italian."

"I guess it's a good thing I'm not aspiring to the Italian mafia, then."

"I'm half and half, too. My mother's family was British."

He nods. "From Leeds, in the north." When I simply stare at him in shock, he adds, "Beautiful part of the country."

I take a moment to gather my wits, then say, "That background check was pretty extensive, huh?"

His gaze softens, and so does his voice. "It didn't tell me everything."

"No? Well, ask away. I'll be happy to fill you in. What would you like to know? My shoe size? Favorite color? How I like my eggs?"

"Eight-and-a-half. Violet blue. Scrambled, with a side of bacon."

Oh, I thought I was so smart. I thought I'd have it all under control, didn't I? And here he is, throwing me for loops within two minutes of the start of the conversation.

He smiles at the expression on my face, then says gently, "There are some things I don't know about you."

I say tartly, "Like what? Which utensil I'd most like to gouge out your eyes with?"

He stares straight into my eyes. "Like how you sound when you come."

In a wave, heat rushes up my neck to flood my face.

"Or how you laugh when you're truly happy instead of bitter. Or sarcastic. Or angry."

I open my mouth but shut it again, not knowing what to say.

His voice drops an octave. "Or how long you're going to punish me for reminding you of your father."

My cheeks flame hotter. My heart jumps into my throat. I hate it that he can push my buttons like this. That he knows things about me, all kinds of painful, personal things he shouldn't.

I hate it, and I hate him.

"Forever," I say hotly. "And you don't only remind me of him. You *are* him. Just in a different body."

"I'm not, lass. I'm really not."

A faint trace of melancholy colors his tone. Melancholy, longing, and regret. We gaze at each other in crackling loud silence for so long it becomes unbearable. I look away, struggling for breath.

He says softly, "You wore that dress to punish me, too, didn't you? That dress with no bra underneath so I can see exactly what I can't have. What you know I want but you're unwilling to give me."

I close my eyes. My hands are beginning to shake. "Stop it."

He continues, his voice still that gentle caress. "I know you did. And I'll take it. Whatever punishment you need to dispense, I'll take all of it, lass. Because I know that once we get past the anger and you give me all of you, it will have been worth every pint of blood you needed to extract."

I open my eyes and look at him, fury lighting up every nerve ending and flooding through my veins. "You conceited, insufferable, stuck-up *ass*."

"Guilty. But right."

I'm so angry, I want to spit. I want to hit something. I can feel the rage coming off me in superheated waves. I step closer to him, my hand curled so hard around the coffee mug I'm surprised it doesn't shatter.

My voice shaking, I say, "You will never have me. *Never*. I'd rather die than give myself to you. I'd rather be thrown naked from a cliff into a pool of starving piranha. I'd rather have all my skin peeled off and be rolled in salt, then tarred and feathered. I'd rather—"

He drops his mug, knocks mine from my hand, grabs my face, and kisses me.

16

KILLIAN

Fuck Ryan Reynolds.

I'm not funny. I'm not charming. I'm *definitely* not self-deprecating.

I'm Killian fucking Black.

JULES

*O*nce upon a time, I was a lonely little girl who played with dolls and had an invisible friend and daydreamed about the day my Prince Charming would arrive to sweep me off my feet and take me away from my cloistered, claustrophobic life to live with him in his beautiful castle.

My prince was kind. He was noble. He was strong and brave, but most of all, he was good.

He was so damn good that a dragon would throw itself at his feet and stretch out its neck willingly for the honor of being slain by a man of such goodness.

My prince did not kill other men.

My prince also did not lie, cheat, steal, extort protection money from merchants, or run prostitution rings, drug cartels, or illegal gambling operations.

He wasn't arrogant. Nor was he irritating, nor bossy, nor vain.

He was not the subject of government criminal investigations.

He owned clothing other than black Armani suits.

He was, in short, the most perfect specimen of manhood that an innocent child could imagine.

But I never, in all my wildest dreams, imagined that my good prince could kiss like *this*.

Killian's mouth is hot and demanding, fused to mine with ferocious need. He kisses me like he's starving. Like he's dying. Like he's been waiting for this exact moment his entire life and now that it's here, he's going to wring every drop of pleasure from it or kill himself trying.

He spins me around, pushes me up against the car, flattens his body against mine, and thrusts his tongue deeper into my mouth. When I arch against him, digging my fingers into the muscles of his back, he makes a sound of pleasure low in his throat that is utterly masculine and sexual.

It's a growl. A rumble. A lion's guttural grunt of dominance as he mounts his lioness.

When he realizes I'm not fighting him or trying to push him away, he moans into my mouth, moving one hand to encircle my throat and burying the other in my hair.

He pulls my head back and kisses me deeper.

The kiss goes on until I'm delirious. My breasts feel heavy and begin to ache. Heat pulses between my legs. My heart is a trapped bird beating frantically against the cage of my chest, and my mind is empty except for a drunken, repeated chant of *yes yes holy mother of god YES.*

He rocks his hips into mine so I feel the whole hard length of his cock, throbbing insistently, as demanding as his mouth is.

Even when I sag against him, weak and mewling, he refuses to let me go.

Just as I'm sure I'm going to pass out, he breaks the kiss abruptly and puts his mouth next to my ear. Breathing hard, he says roughly, "Fuck yes, baby. Feel it. Feel it with me."

He fits his mouth against mine again, covering my moan.

This time the kiss is softer. Slower. More luxurious. Like melting into a steaming hot bath, all my muscles liquid heat. I forget about hating him and wind my arms up around his broad shoulders. I press my breasts against the hard expanse of his chest.

A high, sweet thrill sings through me when he groans.

He slides the hand encircling my neck down to my breast, cupping it through my dress, rubbing his thumb back and forth over the rigid peak of my nipple.

I know if he put his demanding hot mouth there and sucked, I'd come.

He breaks the kiss again, this time to nuzzle my neck and whisper hotly into my ear. His lips move over my skin. His beard tickles me. I don't understand the words he's saying: they're not in English. It's Irish he's speaking, and somehow that makes it even more of a turn-on. My whole body feels as if it's on fire.

I drop my head back, gasping for breath.

When my head hits the car window, it's with a flat, unsexy *thud* that acts like a wake-up alarm to my woozy brain.

Wait. What the hell am I doing?

I freeze.

Feeling the change in me, Killian stills, too. He straightens, frames my face in his big hands, and gazes down at me. Entire planets are burning in his eyes.

"Don't run away yet," he says gruffly. "Sit with it for a moment longer."

We stare at each other, nose to nose, breathing raggedly. My lips feel bruised. My heart feels bruised. My knees are shaking, my panties are soaked, and I think I have just gone out of my mind.

I whisper in horror, "You kissed me."

"Aye. What's really gonna make you tear your hair out later on is remembering how lustily you kissed me back."

I flatten my hands over his chest and shove, pushing him

away far enough to jerk out of his arms. I stand several feet away, my hand cupped over my mouth, unable to look at him.

He says, "For the record, I fucking loved it, too."

I spin around and slap his face.

His head snaps to the side. He stands still for seconds that feel like lifetimes, then he slowly turns his head around and locks his burning gaze onto mine.

He licks his lips. I know it's taking every ounce of his willpower not to lunge for me.

I turn around and head back to the apartment, breaking into a run halfway across the street.

Moving in a daze, I take off the dress, leaving it in a pile in the middle of my bedroom floor. I change into jeans, a T-shirt, a light jacket and boots, then use the back stairs of the building to enter the parking garage.

Then I get into my car and head to work.

It's still early. Traffic is light. I'm at my desk within fifteen minutes, staring blankly at a dark computer screen, my hands still trembling, my mouth still feeling bruised.

I'm sitting in the exact same spot an hour later when my boss comes in.

"Hey, kiddo. How was your weekend?"

Hank says it in passing, rapping his knuckles on the top of my cubicle as he goes. I mumble an answer. I couldn't say what.

He stops, backtracks, and looks at me with concern in his dark blue eyes. At fifty, he's ruggedly handsome, tan and fit with a full head of sandy blond hair. I've always thought he looks like an advertisement for the benefits of healthy living.

"Did someone die?"

"No. Why?"

"You're as white as a sheet." He glances at my hands. "And your hands are shaking."

I slide my hands under my desk, wringing them together guiltily. "I'm fine. Didn't sleep very well last night."

His gaze is steady. His expression is unconvinced. I should know by now that the man has such acute observation skills, he could find a mouse hiding in the dark.

"You want to talk about it?"

My laugh is faint and semi-hysterical. "I wouldn't know where to begin."

He jerks his head to one side. "Come in my office. I'll get us some coffee."

Coffee, ha ha. Maybe that's not such a good idea. The last time I had coffee with a man, I went insane and turned into a giant, pulsing clitoris.

I rise, walk unsteadily into his office, and sink into the nearest chair. Hank returns in a few minutes with two Styrofoam cups and hands me one. Then he sits behind his big mahogany desk and looks at me.

"So. Give it to me. Who, what, when, where, and why?"

I laugh despite myself. He's such a reporter. Taking a sip of bitter coffee to buy a moment, I look at all the framed awards hanging on the wall behind his desk. The office is small but comfortable, decorated all in beiges and creams. Conspicuously absent are any photos of family.

I say, "Do you ever regret not having children?"

His brows shoot up. "The question assumes I've ever met a woman I wanted to have children with."

Embarrassed, I look down at the ugly white cup in my hands. "I'm sorry. That was rude. It's none of my business."

After a moment of silence, Hank says, "I'll answer it in a sec, but first I want to point out that this is a momentous occasion."

I glance up at him from under my brows.

He smiles, dimples flashing in both cheeks. "In the five years since you became my assistant, today's the first time you've ever asked me a personal question."

"It's not because I don't care."

"I know." His voice gentles. "It's because you don't want any personal questions asked in return."

Oh god. I'm that obvious?

His tone turns brisk. "Anyway. To answer your question, no. I don't regret not having children. They absolutely terrify me."

That makes me laugh. "Kids scare you?"

"Their sole purpose is to grow up and replace us. We're breeding our replacements. Have you ever thought of that?"

"You've been watching too many alien movies."

"My sister has six of the little monsters. *Six.*" He shudders. "Visiting her house is like descending into Dante's seventh circle of hell. Half a dozen violent, miniature tyrants going around smashing things and screaming like a bunch of Vikings on crack. It's total chaos. She's forty-two but she looks a hundred and two. If I hadn't gotten a vasectomy in my twenties, watching her raise those future criminals would've definitely sent me running to the doctor."

I feel a cold pang of panic. "Do you think people can be born bad? Like they come out that way, pre-programmed, and no matter how they try to be good, they'll always be rotten?"

He cocks his head, frowning at me. "No. I'm being hyperbolic. My sister is a very good mother. Her kids will turn out fine. What are you really asking?"

I look down at the cup in my hands, horrified to discover it's blurry. My eyes are watering. I clear my throat and blow out a hard breath. *What the hell. Just say it. You've got nothing to lose.*

"I'm asking for advice." When Hank doesn't say anything, I glance up at him. "I need a man's opinion. An older man. Someone smart. Worldly. Like you."

"Okay. That's flattering, thank you. But couldn't you ask your father?"

"We're not close. Actually, we haven't spoken in years."

He digests that information for a moment. "I'm sorry to hear that."

"Don't be. He's a bad guy. The kind of bad that's malignant, like cancer."

I can tell by his expression that he's dying to sit forward in his chair and interrogate me, because that's his instinct. His reporter's instinct kicking in, the way a dog's instinct to chase kicks in when it spots a squirrel. But he restrains himself and simply nods, indicating he's listening.

"I met a man." I stop and take another breath.

"Go on."

I look down again. This is way too hard. "Um. He's..." *Beautiful. Complicated. Aggravating. Interesting. A king among criminals. Sexy beyond compare.* "I can't decide if I like him or I hate him. I mean, I *should* hate him. He's everything I shouldn't want. But he's also...unexpected. Intelligent. Fascinating."

I close my eyes and think of Killian's face. "He's by far the most interesting man I've ever met. And—aside from my father —also the most dangerous."

"Dangerous?"

I open my eyes to find Hank staring at me with lifted brows, his expression incredulous. "Like how dangerous? On a scale of driving while intoxicated to Darth Vader."

I answer without hesitation. "Darth Vader is a mama's boy compared to him. He's more like the love child of Lex Luther and Maleficent. Times ten thousand."

We stare at each other in silence, until Hank says carefully, "If this man is harming you, Juliet, we need to go to the police and report it."

All my held breath bursts out of me in a loud, wild laugh. "God, no. The only danger he poses to me is the ruination of my entire collection of panties."

Hank blinks.

I pull my lips between my teeth and stare at him in horror. "Sorry."

He makes a face and drags a hand through his hair, then chuckles nervously. "It's no problem, I just wasn't expecting that. Well." It's his turn to clear his throat. "This, ah, this dangerous man of yours. How did you meet him?"

"I stole something from him. A lot of things, actually. I mean it was all the same type of thing, just a bunch of them."

Hank is beginning to look like he regrets embarking on this particular chat. He spends a moment choosing his words, then says, "You committed a theft."

"Oh, yeah. A big one. Then this dangerous man discovered it was me who did it—I won't bore you with the details of how he found out it was me, but they're pretty interesting—and he followed me. And he kept following me, because he liked me, even when he discovered that my father is, like, his worst enemy."

Hank peers at me. He's starting to look confused. "Uh-huh."

Warming up to the subject, I sit up straighter in my chair. "And that's the main problem, really. Not that the two of them are enemies, but that he's in the same line of work as my father. He basically has the same type of lifestyle."

"The malignant type."

"Yes."

"May I ask a personal question?"

"Sure."

"Have you considered professional therapy?"

I stare at him, strangely hurt. "Jeez, Hank."

He says gently, "That's not a rebuke. I say it out of genuine concern. Because what I'm hearing is that you have an intense sexual attraction to a man you know you should stay away from, but can't." He pauses. "Also, the theft thing is a problem."

"It's more like a hobby."

His voice rises. "You've stolen something more than once?"

I'm feeling reckless, so I admit it. Might as well keep the scandalous admissions train going full steam ahead. "Oh, god, yeah. Lots of times."

He gapes at me. "You could end up in prison!"

"Yeah." I shrug. "I've been in jail before. It's surprisingly relaxing. You get a lot of good thinking done."

Hank sits back into his chair slowly, his brow furrowed, his expression one of dismay.

"I know," I say softly, watching his face. "I seem like such a nice girl."

"You *are* a nice girl. Honestly, this is shocking."

"What if I told you that I only steal from bad guys and that all the stuff I take goes to help the less fortunate?"

"I'd say that story's as old as the hills."

"So's the story of Moses. Doesn't mean it isn't true."

He props his elbows on his desk, drops his head into his hands, and groans. "Please stop talking."

This is why you don't confide in people. The truth makes them twitchy. "Oh, relax, Hank. I'm only kidding. Not about the guy I shouldn't like, but about everything else."

When he looks up at me, I send him my most winsome smile. He narrows his eyes, clearly dubious. "So you didn't steal anything from him?"

I wave my hand in the air dismissively. "Of course not. Don't be silly."

"And he's not dangerous?"

"He's an accountant."

"Why shouldn't you like him, then?"

"Because my father's an accountant, too. I swore I'd never marry one. All that bean counting could drive a girl nuts."

We stare at each other. Me with a straight face, Hank with a face like he's painfully constipated.

Finally, he sighs. "Okay. Here's my advice. Take it for what it's worth. You ready?"

"Yes."

"Life is short. You don't get a do-over. Kiss who you need to kiss, love who you need to love, tell anyone who disrespects you to go fuck themselves. Let your heart lead you where it wants to. Don't ever make a decision based on fear. In fact, if it scares you, that's the thing you should run fastest toward, because that's where real life is. In the scary parts. In the messy parts. In the parts that aren't so pretty. Dive in and take a swim in all the pain and beauty that life has to offer, so that at the end of it, you don't have any regrets.

"We only come this way once. Our obligation for receiving the miraculous gift of life is to truly, fully live it."

He pauses, blinking. "Wow. I wish I'd recorded that. It was brilliant."

My voice choked, I say, "I'll transcribe it for you. I'm pretty sure it's etched into my soul."

"Oh god. You're crying."

"I am not," I say through a sob. Swiping at my watering eyes, I add, "I'm just on my period."

Shaking his head, Hank chuckles. "So glad we're finally doing the sharing thing at eight o'clock on a Monday morning. I should've called in sick."

I stand, round his desk, and throw my arms around his neck. Still in his chair, he pats my back in a fatherly way.

After a moment, he clears his throat. "Okay. This is the limit of my paternal instincts, kiddo. If you need more help, I'm gonna send you to Ruth in Human Resources because I literally have no idea how to handle emotional young women."

I straighten and smile down at him. "You're a good egg, Hank Hauser."

He waves me off. "Quit trying to butter me up. You're not due for a wage increase for another five months."

A knock on Hank's office door makes us turn.

A young man stands in the doorway. He's Latino, good-looking, maybe late twenties, dressed in an expensive black suit and a white dress shirt open at the collar. He's carrying a big bouquet of dark red roses and a flat black velvet box, about twelve inches square, tied with black ribbon.

"Juliet," he says sternly, gazing at me like I'm being accused of a terrible wrongdoing.

Oh god. What's this? "She's out sick today."

He quirks his mouth and shakes his head. "Nice try. You want these here?" He jerks his chin toward Hank's desk.

Bemused at this new development, Hank makes a sweeping gesture with his arm. "By all means, mister…"

"Diego. Just Diego."

Diego is obviously not your average delivery boy. Aside from the suit, he's also got that cocky swagger that I know all too well.

Made men all walk like they've got a million dollars in cash stuck up their butts.

He sets the bouquet of roses down, puts the black box next to it, then turns and heads back toward the door. Before he walks out, he stops abruptly and looks at me.

"He's not what you think he is."

We gaze at each other steadily. I feel Hank looking back and forth between us in concern, unsure if he should intervene or let this odd little drama play out.

I want it to play out. I've had enough of this "not who but what" BS.

"Tell me what he is, then."

Diego glances at Hank. He looks back at me. His voice low, he says, "He bought my mother a house. Paid it off. Gave her the deed. Nobody in my family's ever owned property."

"That's a touching story, Diego. My father once bought someone property, too. Gave him the deed, moved him and his whole family in. The house burned to the ground within a week, with everyone still in it. Guess who lit the match that started the fire?"

Hank's mouth drops open.

Diego's eyes flash. He says, "That's fucked up."

"It is. Bad people can sometimes act like they're doing good things, but it's only a game. It's make-believe. If I were you, I'd tell your mother to find another place to live before your employer shows his true colors and lights a match."

Hank stands, hands spread wide like he's conducting an intervention. "Okay, this is getting weird. Diego, I think it's time for you to—"

"What did they do?" says Diego, aggressively cutting him off. "The family who got burned in the fire—what did they do to deserve it?"

I say softly, "Oh. You still think it's about honor, huh? This little club you've joined, you think it's a brotherhood based on principles, when really it's just an excuse for cruel men to grind people under their heels."

We stare at each other. Hank looks on in dismay.

Then Diego says, "I come from bad people, too. My employer isn't one of them. I thought he was at the beginning. But my ignorance doesn't equal his guilt."

At the end of my patience, I demand, "What does it equal, then?"

He gazes at me, dark eyes glittering. "I hope you figure it out. Because he's worth it. And what he's doing is important work."

My mouth drops open. *Being a gangster is important work?*

Diego turns around and strides out.

After a moment, Hank says my name. He looks up from the black velvet box he's holding. He's undone the ribbon, and the lid stands open in his hands. He turns the box around so I can see what's inside.

It's a necklace. Diamonds glitter against black velvet, three fat rows of them nestled together around a large center stone, big as a robin's egg and black as ink.

My gut tells me that's a diamond, too.

Hank says drily, "So, this accountant of yours. Not only does he have loyal underlings and extraordinary taste in jewelry, he's quite the romantic, too."

He doesn't bother to wait for me to respond, he simply holds up the small white card that came with the gift and reads aloud from it. "Thus with a kiss I die."

More Shakespeare. It's Romeo's final line from the play, after he drinks the poison to join his love in the afterlife. A chill of foreboding runs through me.

Looking at me steadily, Hank says, "Must've been some kiss, Juliet."

My laugh is utterly without mirth. "Yeah. It was a real killer."

JULES

*D*eciding I won't be of any use to him in my current state, Hank tells me to take the day off. He suggests I take a drive out to the country to clear my head.

He also tells me to call a therapist as soon as I can, but I know it's not more talking I need. I need to *do* something.

Only I have no idea what that something is.

The first place I stop after I leave work is my bank. I rent a safety deposit box and leave the necklace in it. I'll get an estimate of its value later on, after I can think straight again. I know nothing about diamonds, only that the bigger and brighter they are, the more they cost, so Killian's present will probably bring a hefty chunk of change when I sell it.

I haven't decided yet if I'll give the money to charity or light it all on fire and watch it burn.

I make another stop at a convenience store to buy bottled water and fill up on gas, then hit the highway and start driving. I don't have a destination in mind, but it feels good to go fast, look in the rearview mirror, and not see any big black SUVs following behind me.

It feels good for all of one minute, until I see a plane flying overhead and realize that's not the only way Killian could follow me.

The man seems to have eyes everywhere, including the sky.

"Stupid satellites," I mutter, pulling into the parking garage of a mall.

I park in the middle of a crowded row of cars, head inside, and hunt for a payphone. I find one near the restrooms and call a taxi for a ride. When the cab arrives, I slouch down in the back seat and tell the driver to take me somewhere pretty.

"Manchester-by-the-Sea," he says instantly. "Pretty beach. Pretty marina. Pretty everything. Only a forty-minute drive."

"Let's go."

On the way, I force myself to do everything but think about Killian.

I count the number of red cars I see. I count the number of churches we pass. I try to remember all the lyrics to "Let It Be," by the Beatles, my mother's favorite song. I engage the driver in Twenty Questions, grilling him about where he's from, how he likes Boston, and what he thinks of the President.

Then I sit back and listen to him rant with only enough attention to insert a polite "Mmm" and "uh-huh" here and there.

By the time we arrive at our destination, I need a drink. Not thinking about someone is a surprisingly hard amount of work.

It's too early to hit a bar, so I spend a few hours wandering around the marina and its charming little shops until it's time for lunch. Starving, I shovel food into my mouth like a farm animal. I drink two pints of cold beer. Afterward, I feel much better. More clear-headed. It's probably only the sea air, but I'll take it.

I decide I like the place so much, I want to stay longer.

I call Hank from a payphone near the restaurant's restrooms.

"How much vacation time do I have accrued?"

"You've worked for me for five years. You get two weeks of paid vacation a year. You've never taken one. You do the math. Why do you ask?"

"The therapist I went to this morning said it would be good for me to take some time off work."

Hank pauses, then sighs. "That's a lie, isn't it?"

"Yes."

"Juliet, I'm worried about you."

"I'll be fine. I just need a few days off."

"How many days?"

"Like…a hundred and eighty-seven?"

"You've got through the end of the week," he says firmly. "Get your head on straight and come back fresh next Monday. Deal?"

"Deal," I say, relieved.

"And kiddo?"

"Yes?"

His voice drops. "You're a smart girl. You already know what to do with your accountant. Trust your gut."

I can hear the air quotes around the word "accountant."

"I would, but my gut is currently waging a bloody war between my head and my loins. Things are ugly. The casualties are piling up."

He chuckles. "Ah, to be young with an overabundance of hormones. I'm so glad I'm old. Things are far less confusing."

"You're not old!"

"I've been alive twice as long as you have. That's half a century."

"Half a century isn't old. My grandmother was ninety-two and still going strong the last time I saw her."

"And I'll bet she looked as fresh as a daisy, didn't she?"

When I don't say anything, he laughs. "Yeah, that's what I thought. Fifty isn't old in mind or spirit, but trust me, kiddo, you get to my age and you start avoiding mirrors. Your skin becomes forested with weird moles. Sleeping the whole night through without having to get up to pee is a thing of the distant past. Anything that can possibly sag, wrinkle, or dangle, does."

"Please excuse me while I go throw up."

"Hey, don't blame me for gravity."

"I like you the way Newton liked gravity. Once he found it, everything else made sense."

I close my eyes and rest my forehead against the cool metal housing of the pay phone, praying for some miracle that will block Killian's words—and his beautiful face—from my mind.

"You still there?"

"Yes. Just wondering if there's a way to bleach my brain of the hideous images you've branded onto it. I'm traumatized. I'll never be able to look you in the eye again."

"You'll live. See you Monday." He hangs up without waiting for a response.

The next call I make is to the voicemail Fin, Max, and I use for emergencies. I leave a message saying I'll be out of town for a few days, but I'll check in so they know I'm OK. Out of an overabundance of caution, I don't say more. Especially not where I'm staying. I know they'll understand.

I rent a room for the rest of the week at a motel right on the water's edge. It has a view of the boats bobbing peacefully in the marina, a fully stocked minibar, and a whirlpool bathtub big enough for three people. If I thought heaven was anything like this, I might start trying to be a better person.

Then I call back the voicemail and tell Fin where I left my car in the mall so it doesn't get towed. There's a spare key in the kitchen drawer, but knowing her, she'll hotwire it just to rub it in.

There's a small gift shop in the motel lobby where I buy toothpaste and a few toiletries. A boutique down the street catering to tourists sells T-shirts and shorts, flip-flops and breezy, floral dresses. I splurge on several things, wondering when was the last time I bought myself clothes.

Unlike Fin, the fashion plate, or Max, who always looks like she's auditioning for a role in the next installment of *Tomb Raider*, I'm usually dressed down in jeans.

I spend the afternoon wandering around on foot, no destination in mind. When the sun is sinking below the horizon and my empty stomach is protesting, I look for a place to eat dinner. I settle on an oyster bar with a crowded outdoor patio and a live band playing classic rock covers in one corner of the dining room.

I take a seat at the bar inside and order a chardonnay from the leather-skinned, wild-haired bartender, who is approximately two hundred years old. He tells me his name is Harley after the motorcycle, that he's lived in this town since the day he was born, and also that he's in love with me.

"I love you, too, Harley," I tell him, smiling. "Let's run away to Mexico together."

He cackles, then sends a glance down the bar to my right. He lowers his voice. "I'd take you up on that, sweetheart, but I think you might have bigger fish to fry tonight."

Following his head tilt, I turn in that direction.

Seated backward on a stool with both elbows propped up on the bar top, a man faces the crowd. Clad in denim, one long leg is stuck out into the aisle, the other is casually kicked up on the footrest under the stool. He's wearing sunglasses, Western boots, a cowboy hat, a tight white T-shirt that showcases every ripple of his washboard abs, and the collective lust of every woman in the place.

Tattoos cover his muscular arms from his bulging biceps all the way down to his thick wrists.

He runs a hand over the short black beard on his square jaw, giving me a perfect view of his other tattoos.

The ones on his knuckles.

I can't describe this feeling. It's shock, fury, disbelief, pleasure, horror, awe, and an almost overpowering urge to commit bloody homicide with a cocktail pick in a room full of people, all rolled into one.

Killian turns his head and looks at me. I can't see his eyes behind the mirrored glasses, but I feel them, fiery red Superman laser beams slicing me in two.

I turn my attention back to Harley. "You know what? This wine isn't gonna do it for me. I need a shot of tequila."

"Atta girl!" He produces a shot glass from under the bar, sloppily pours tequila into it, hands it to me, and says, "Just remember, sweetheart: no glove, no love."

And this is my life.

Harley wanders away to tend to his other customers. I wait, heart pounding, as Killian takes the stool beside mine.

He pretends to peruse the menu written in chalk hanging on the wall behind the bar. Then, sounding exactly like he walked off a cattle ranch in Texas, he drawls, "Hey, there, darlin'. How ya'll doin' tonight?"

I resist the urge to slam my forehead onto the bar and shoot my tequila instead.

Then, *with no accent whatsoever*, he says, "Not feeling the cowboy vibe, huh? I knew I should've gone with a British accent. Women love a British accent."

"Actually, what we love is plunging a pitchfork through the chest of an annoying man who's tied to a chair, then lighting him on fire."

"Hmm. I don't know if there's an accent for that."

I hear the smothered laughter in his voice and wave at Harley for another tequila. "What are you doing here?"

"Same as you, darlin'. Sightseein'. Havin' a drink. Lookin' at all the pretty people."

The Texas accent is back. I wish I could say it sounds incredibly stupid, but it doesn't. Instead, it sounds incredibly hot, which is incredibly aggravating. "So you followed me. Again."

"Did you forget about the part where I said I'd keep you safe?"

"I didn't think it meant you'd always be within shouting

distance. And I'm perfectly able to take care of myself, thank you."

"One doesn't cancel out the other."

"God, I hate it when you talk like that."

"Like what?"

"Like I'm being irrational."

"I don't think you're irrational. The people who are looking for you aren't irrational, either, just better armed."

The oblique mention of the Serbians sends a chill along my spine. I moisten my lips, feeling like he's a socket I just stuck my finger into and wondering how bad the shock is going to be.

"How did you find me?"

The Texas drawl returns full force, but this time, it's teasing. "Now, now, darlin'. You know I can't tell you all my secrets." He chuckles. "There wouldn't be any mystery left for you to obsess over."

It's official: I'm going to kill him.

Unsmiling, I turn his way. I stare at my reflection in his aviators, barely recognizing the woman staring back at me. She's angry, yes, but she also looks like she really needs to be kissed.

She looks…like a wild animal that's been caged for years and is about to be unleashed.

Killian slowly removes the glasses. He sets them on the bar without breaking eye contact with me.

He's not laughing anymore. In fact, he seems like a ravenous wolf about to devour me whole. Energy arcs between us. It's an attraction so powerful, I wouldn't be surprised if it can be seen.

"You already know what to do. Trust your gut."

Recalling Hank's words, something rises up inside me. A pressure builds. Some dark, nameless emotion expands inside my chest, crushing my lungs and flattening my heart until it's barely able to beat.

It's my gut, screaming at me to let it take the lead.

Oh no. I'm about to do something really dumb. I take a deep breath, blow it out, and jump.

"Chris Hemsworth."

Killian cocks one dark brow. "Excuse me?"

"Can you sound like Chris Hemsworth, the actor?"

He knows what I'm asking. His eyes flare. Dark and dangerous, desire glints in their depths. He says softly, "Course I can. I can do anything, Juliet. You oughta know that by now."

His Australian accent is perfect.

I bite my lip so hard I taste blood.

Killian says my name again. This time it's barely audible. Our gazes are locked together. We're not touching, but every inch of my skin feels him. Every cell in my body feels burned by his heat.

My pulse roaring in my ears, I say quietly, "Once. One time. One night. That's it, then it's over."

Killian doesn't wait for me to draw my next breath before he jolts to his feet, throws cash onto the bar, picks me up, and strides out of the restaurant, carrying me in his arms.

19

JULES

$\mathcal{M}$y hotel is only a few minutes from the restaurant, but the drive there seems like it takes forever.

I feel every tiny bump in the road. Every frantic beat of my heart. Every loud rev of the engine as Killian stomps his foot against the gas pedal when a traffic light turns from red to green.

Before we took off, he buckled me into the passenger seat and kissed me, hard, one hand around my throat and the other fisted in my hair. When he broke away, it seemed as if it took everything he had to leave me sitting there instead of tearing off my safety belt, pushing me face down onto the seat, ripping off my panties, and shoving inside me, right there in the parking lot.

I know exactly how he feels.

Every nerve ending in my body screams for him. For what I know he'll give me.

For release.

The only thing I remember from the trip from the parking spot in front of the motel to my room are the ravenous kisses in the elevator. His mouth so hot. His body so hard. His hands shaking as they roved all over me. By the time we're standing in front of my door, my hands are shaking, too, so badly I drop the key twice before he rips it out of my hands and unlocks the door himself.

He pushes me inside, kicks the door shut behind him, grabs me, and throws me down onto the bed.

I bounce once before he's on me.

I feel dwarfed underneath him. He's so big and deliciously heavy. His weight makes me sink into the mattress. Makes me feel weirdly safe, like his bulk alone could protect me from anything.

His mouth. Oh, god, his mouth. I could drown in these kisses.

When I moan, he breaks away, breathing raggedly.

"Am I hurting you?"

Dazed, I blink, looking up into his face. His eyes are wild. His nostrils are flared. His lips are wet from my kisses. He's so beautiful, it's physically painful. Looking at him is like having an arrow shot straight through my heart.

I whisper, "No. But if you do, I don't want it to stop you. If I'm bruised tomorrow, so be it."

I sink my hands into his hair and pull his head down. His mouth meets mine as he's exhaling a groan.

We kiss until I'm squirming underneath him, dizzy and mewling, rocking my hips into his. Long and hard, his erection is trapped between us.

The dress I'm wearing is one I bought at the tourist boutique. It's a gauzy, flowing thing, patterned with tropical flowers. When he rears up onto his knees and grabs the neckline, it rips apart like gossamer in his hands. He shoves up my bra impatiently.

Then I get his beautiful hot mouth on my breasts, devouring them.

I arch, moaning. My head tips back. My eyes slide shut. The feel of him sucking my hard nipples—one after the other, back and forth—is so insanely pleasurable I know if he kept it up, I'd climax from that alone.

I dig my fingers deeper into his hair, pulling on it. Rocking my hips. Gasping for air.

He pinches the nipple he's not sucking on. I jerk, whimpering.

What am I doing? What the hell am I DOING?

Don't think. Just feel. You can hate yourself tomorrow.

Suddenly, his mouth disappears. He rears back to sit on his heels and stare down at me. His chest heaving, he licks his lips. Then he shoves the skirt of my dress up to my hips, puts his face between my legs, and inhales deeply against my panties.

It's so carnal and raw. So animal.

At any other time and with any other person, I would die of embarrassment. But with him, I simply spread my legs wider. I watch, heart pounding, as he pulls my panties aside and exposes me.

He whispers, "Fuck, baby. Look at you." He leans down and presses the gentlest of kisses right on my clit. When I inhale sharply, he glances up at me. Then he lowers his mouth to my flesh and starts to suck.

It feels incredible. The noise I make doesn't even sound human.

He continues to suck, holding eye contact with me. The prude part of me is shocked at this intimacy, but it's no match for the other part of me—the bigger, stronger part—that has gone full porn star. I moan, let my head fall back against the mattress, and rock my hips against his face.

He growls against my flesh and reaches up to squeeze my breasts as he eats me.

He pinches my nipples, then does it again, harder, when I react with a low, broken moan of pleasure. I writhe against his mouth, starting to sweat. I'm dying to feel him inside me.

"Please, Killian. I need you. I need—"

"You need to come in my mouth, baby," he growls. "I'll tell you what else you need after that."

Oh god. The Australian accent. Chris Hemsworth is between my legs. I'm going to die.

He goes back to sucking my clit, sliding a thick finger inside me. He's relentless, holding me down with one big hand splayed over my belly as I start to buck helplessly against his face.

When my orgasm hits, it steals my breath.

I stiffen and cry out. The hard contractions pound through my body like waves. It feels like all of me is splitting wide open. I'm falling apart at the seams.

Between my legs, Killian makes animal grunts of approval.

When the wild contractions have faded to the occasional twitch, I lie panting on the mattress, limp and sated, and watch as Killian rises to his knees and pulls his T-shirt off over his head. He drops it to the floor.

I get my first look at his chest and abs, and my eyes widen. I exhale a breath that feels like fire.

I say faintly, "Holy shit, gangster."

Gazing down at me with hot, dark eyes, he smiles. "I wish I had a camera, lass. That look is priceless."

He had to have been carved from stone by a master sculptor. He's beautifully proportioned, from the breadth of his strong shoulders down to his tapered waist. His stomach is flat, except for where it ripples with muscles. His pecs are glorious. His biceps...there are no words.

And everywhere—blinding me—are tattoos.

Along with small round scars that I recognize instantly as made by bullets.

When I glance up at his face, he isn't smiling anymore.

My heart beating fast, I whisper, "How many times have you been shot?"

"Shot at or shot?"

"Shot."

"Twelve."

Twelve. I think that's astonishing, until he adds, "Shot at, probably in the thousands."

"That can't be true."

"I don't lie to you." He rips open the fly of his jeans. His voice drops an octave. "You and only one other person alive."

Before I can process that, he yanks my panties down my legs and tosses them over his shoulder. He rips the rest of my flimsy dress open down to the hem, then rolls me this way and that, tearing it off me. He discards my bra, opening it with a professional flick of his fingers, then pushes me facedown onto my belly and grasps the back of my neck, holding me down.

I lie still, staring at the wall, clutching the bedspread with my heart in my throat, as he stands silently and looks me over.

After a moment, he exhales. His voice barely audible, he whispers, "Lass. You're so goddamn beautiful."

He bends, pressing a gentle kiss to the small of my back. His other hand squeezes the back of my thigh, then slides higher. He puts a knee between my thighs, pushing them farther apart.

"Killian—"

"Hush. I won't do anything you don't like. Tell me to stop, and I will."

I moisten my lips, but it doesn't help. My mouth is so dry. My hands are trembling. It's not fear I'm feeling, just pure adrenaline.

He slides his lips to my tailbone, his touch feather light. His hand creeps higher, squeezing my flesh. He cups my bottom, then nips it, his teeth sinking into my tender skin.

"So goddamn beautiful," he whispers again, to himself it seems.

His fingers find the center of me, still wet from his mouth. He strokes my clit. He tugs on it. He pinches it, crooning when I gasp. When he slides his finger inside me and I arch back to meet its press with a moan and a shudder, he mutters, "Bloody fucking hell."

I don't know why he's going so slow, but I'm over it.

I need him inside me, and I need it *now*.

I say crossly, "Do you need a minute to take your heart medication, old man? Because I'm about to set this bed on fire."

My answer is a chuckle, dark and low. "Ah, lass. That smart mouth will be the death of me."

He flips me over, drags me to the edge of the mattress, and throws my heels up onto his shoulders. From the back pocket of his jeans, he produces a condom and tears the foil wrapper open with his teeth. He unsheathes his enormous erection from his briefs, rolls the condom on, and shoves his hard cock deep inside me.

I grab onto his steel biceps. My eyes roll back into my head. My gasp is so loud they can probably hear it down in the lobby.

He growls, "Are we done with the sassing?"

I shudder, unable to speak. I'm impaled on his cock, stretched open by the size of him. I love it so much it's quite possible I could burst into tears from sheer pleasure.

"That's what I thought," he says between gritted teeth, and starts thrusting.

This time when he kisses me, it's savage. He bends over me, pressing my thighs down until my knees are over his shoulders, and takes my mouth with a hard, rough kiss, his teeth clashing against mine.

Propped up on his elbows as he fucks me, he tangles his hands into my hair.

I dig my fingers into the hard muscles of his back.

From somewhere deep in his chest, a groan rises.

The motion of our hips falls into sync. Soon I'm cresting that wave again, riding it high into the sky until I think I'll be blinded by all the heat and light we're producing.

I grab the hard globes of his ass and come, jerking.

His voice hoarse at my ear, he says, "Ah, fuck. You're coming. God, yes, give it to me, baby. Give it to me."

He slows his thrusts until he's unmoving, buried deep inside me, groaning in pleasure as I convulse around him. I sob, grinding my pelvis against his and digging my fingernails into his ass.

He kisses my neck and starts to whisper to me in Irish as I arch against him, crying out, delirious. I hear that word that he said meant "beauty," and know he's praising me. I know from the passionate but tender tone of his voice that this one-night stand of ours is as intense for him as it is for me.

I also know one night isn't going to be enough. It could never be enough, not with a man like him.

He commands, "Open your eyes."

My eyelids drift open. My gaze meets his. Another hard contraction deep inside me makes me shudder.

Our gazes locked together, he starts to thrust again, slowly, driving into me through every contraction, wringing them out of me with the steady motion of his hips. He watches every nuance of emotion in my eyes with rapt fascination, like he's gazing into a crystal ball to discover his future.

When it gets too intense and I try to turn my head, he forces me to keep looking at him with a hand clasped around my jaw.

"No running away," he says in a husky whisper. "If one night is all I get, I'm damn sure gonna get every piece of you that you have to give."

"I—I can't—it's too much—"

"You can. Be brave, baby. Come on. *Give me everything.*"

My heart is flying. I feel as if I'm floating or falling, like gravity has ceased to exist. Like the world has ceased to exist. In the entire universe, there's only this bed and this room and the two of us, doing what lovers have done since the beginning of time but somehow it seems like we invented it.

Something in the middle of my chest feels as if it's cracking open wide.

That sensation is immediately followed by a cold jolt of terror. *Not with him. Oh god, no. I can't feel this with him.*

Moisture wells in my eyes, slips down my temple. Killian whispers my name.

I drag in a hitching breath and slide my hands up his bare back. With a soft groan, he kisses me deeply, releasing me from the cage of his eyes when he closes them.

He hides his face in my neck and thrusts harder, his breath coming fast. I know he's close when a shudder rocks his whole body and he slows the motion of his hips, moaning.

"Kiss me," I whisper into his ear. "I want you to kiss me when you come."

He lifts his head and gazes at me, his eyes hazy and half-lidded. In a throaty voice, he says, "You're not in charge here, lass."

I flex my hips, pulling another moan from him. Braced on either side of my head, his arms have started to shake.

Smiling up into his face, I say, "Sorry, gangster, but I am."

I pull his head down and kiss him, rocking my hips, urging him on with my body. He allows it for a few moments, then pulls out of me abruptly and flips me onto my stomach. He hikes my ass in the air, spreads my legs apart, grips my hips in his big hands, and drives inside me from behind.

When I groan in mindless pleasure, he chuckles. He leans over me, planting a hand on the mattress next to my face, and reaches around my waist to fondle my throbbing clit. I groan again, louder.

He teases, "Tell me again how you're in charge?"

"Arrogant bastard."

"Aye, lass. And you wouldn't have it any other way."

My breasts swing as he fucks me. My face is buried in the blankets. He's grunting and I'm moaning and it's dirty and sexy and hot, especially because he was too impatient to take off his boots and jeans.

He starts to speak in Irish again, the words rasped between panted breaths.

When I'm sweating and whimpering, almost over the edge a third time, he slows. He slides his hands around my waist, up my spine, and to my shoulders. He fists one hand into my hair and pulls my head back, then he rubs the fingers he just had between my legs against my mouth.

He orders gruffly, "Suck."

I open my mouth and take his fingers between my lips, greedily sucking my taste and wetness from them, feeling like I'm starring in a porno and loving every second of it.

He seems to love it, too: the growl that rumbles through his chest sounds thrillingly dangerous. His thrusts pick up speed again until he's pistoning into me, grunting and starting to lose control.

"Juliet. My beautiful thief. You drive me fucking crazy."

His moan is low and broken. He drops his forehead between my shoulder blades and takes his fingers from my mouth. He slides his hand between my legs, to the place where we're joined.

Then he tugs firmly on my clit, and I lose myself completely.

My orgasm slams through me, violent and intense. Crying out, I buck underneath him.

Killian says something in hoarse, garbled Irish, his entire body jerking. He stiffens. Then he comes, moaning against my back.

He throbs and pulses inside me, straining to get farther into me, to get as far as he can go. He gasps my name. Then he grabs my jaw, turns my head, and kisses me.

He's bent over and I'm bent back, both of us contorting to get that extra contact we need. That extra hot, delicious bond of our bodies.

That terrifyingly intimate bond of something far beyond merely that.

I wanted this to be only physical. I told myself that's all it would be: a release.

But I was wrong.

Whatever I thought this was between me and my beautiful criminal, this ravenous, emotional kiss as we climax together lets me know in no uncertain terms that my father was right about me.

I *am* my mother's daughter. We both have the same weakness for bad men.

But unlike her, I'm nobody's fool.

I won't surrender my heart, even if it kills me.

20

JULES

*W*hen I wake, it's to the distant, melancholy call of a fog horn. The room is dark, but brightening around the edges. It's close to morning, and the world outside the windows is quiet and still.

I'm alone.

That hurts for a sharp, cold second, until I push my ego aside and sit up in bed.

The first thing I notice is the white-and-green Starbucks coffee cup on the dresser. Beneath it is a folded piece of paper. My heartbeat ticking up, I swing my legs over the edge of the mattress and cross the room.

When I pick up the coffee and remove the lid, it's steaming hot. He must've only been gone for minutes.

I unfold the note and read.

You make me want to live a different kind of life. You make me want to be a different kind of man. Juliet. Juliet. You are why every love song was ever written.

The paper trembling in my hand, I stand there rereading it over and over again until the coffee has grown cold.

I spend the day pacing the motel room, my mind a snarl of tangled thoughts. I don't eat anything or go anywhere. I don't trust myself to venture outside. I doubt I have the presence of mind not to stumble into oncoming traffic.

When the sun is setting, I decide to go back to the same restaurant I went to last night.

It's an unconscious decision. My feet take me in that direction of their own will. I look up from my day-long daze to find myself standing in front of the restaurant's door with no recollection of how I got there.

I go inside. Take a seat at the bar. Order a white wine from Harley.

He takes one look at my face and whistles, shaking his head.

"Sweetheart, I think you need something stronger." He pushes a shot of tequila in front of me and leaves me alone.

I close my eyes and shoot the tequila, savoring the burn as it works its way down my windpipe because it distracts from the burn a few inches lower inside my chest.

To my right, a low voice says, "I only left because you said 'once.' If I'd stayed until you woke in my arms, I wouldn't have been able to honor that."

My heart. Oh, my poor heart. It's never had to deal with anything like this. It doesn't know whether to explode or stop beating altogether.

I turn and look at Killian, seated on the stool beside me.

He's dressed in jeans and a white T-shirt again, but this time he's missing the Western boots and cowboy hat. All the masculine beauty and scorching sexuality are still there though, in spades. The woman on the stool on his other side stares at him with an unfurled tongue and heaving bosom.

I say, "I got your note." That's all I can get out before my throat closes.

174

Eyes burning, he watches me swallow. Watches as I struggle to pull myself together, turning away to blow out a hard breath.

My heart pounds so hard it could be fatal. Having him this close to me after everything that happened last night is causing nerves I didn't even know I owned to bolt upright and start screaming.

He reaches out, slides his big hand under my hair, and gently squeezes the back of my neck. Then he leans over and presses a soft kiss against my temple. Into my ear, he murmurs, "I know, lass. Me too."

How can he see me so clearly? How does he always know what I'm feeling without me speaking a word?

I whisper, "This can't happen."

"It already has."

Anger forms a hot, sour ball in my stomach, but only because I know he's right.

"Look at me."

It takes me a moment to gather the courage to do as he commanded. When I do, I find him staring back at me with searing intensity.

His voice low, he says, "But what happens next is up to you. I won't pressure you. I'll disappear if that's what you really want. I only ask that you're honest with me. Let's not play any games."

His expression is dead serious. His eyes search mine. His thumb gently strokes the nape of my neck, raising goosebumps all along my spine.

Fighting the emotion clawing its way up my throat, I say, "I forgot to thank you for the necklace."

"You're welcome. Tell me when I can kiss you. I need your mouth."

I break eye contact, trying not to hyperventilate but failing. Looking at the chalkboard menu on the wall behind the bar, I stammer, "And—and the roses. Thank you for those, too."

"I can't stop thinking about how you taste. How you sound. How you claw my back when you come. I want more of all of it. I want more of you."

Closing my eyes, I whisper, "Killian. Please."

He drags me off my barstool, onto his lap, and into his arms.

Squeezing me tight, he inhales deeply against my throat. His voice comes out husky. "Let me in. Let me take care of you. Give me your trust, and I'll give you the world. I'll give you anything you ask for."

"This is insane."

"Aye. Who cares? It's real, and that's what matters."

The sweetness of his words, the gentleness of his voice, the tender way he's holding me…the man is breaking my heart.

My face hidden in his neck, I whisper, "Can you understand how hard this is for me? How this seems like it could be the stupidest thing I've ever done?"

"I'm not your father, Juliet."

When I groan and try to pull away, he takes my jaw in his hand and forces me to look at him.

"*I'm not your fucking father.*"

His tone is rough. His eyes blaze with anger. He's upset, and insulted, and some small, pathetic part of me clasps her hands to her chest and sighs.

I choke that dumb bitch unconscious.

"I know you're not him," I say, staring him in the eye as my heart throbs wildly. "But what I don't know is who—or what— you really are. Because from where I'm standing, the view is quite confusing."

"How so?"

"You hack satellites. You run background checks. Your business cards have advanced geo-location technology. You quote Shakespeare and give lavish gifts and live in a skyscraper all alone, with only miles of black marble for company. Everyone in the world knows you by one name, yet you ask me to call you by another. You have a reputation as a brutal killer, yet with me, you're a complete gentleman." My cheeks color. "Except in bed."

He growls, "You don't need a gentleman in bed, woman."

"No, I don't! That you know that is exactly my point! What am I supposed to do with all this contradictory information? You keep your word and make thoughtful gestures and write beautiful love notes and *literally* sweep me off my feet, but you also kill men in a shootout in the middle of the street!

"How can you seem like the perfect guy—except you're a *gangster*? What the hell does it all *mean*?"

After a moment, he says, "Well, nobody's perfect."

I groan in exasperation, trying to pull out of his arms again. And again, he doesn't allow it, pulling me closer instead.

"It means things aren't always what they appear on the surface," he says, his voice urgent now. As urgent as the look in his eyes. "It means you should trust yourself, and you should trust me. If you do—if you can—I swear, I'll tell you everything. But you have to go first, lass. You have to let go of all that shit in your head and your past and trust your heart."

I say flatly, "My mother trusted her heart. She ended up blown to pieces."

He stares at me with a look of such intensity it steals my breath. His voice dropping an octave, he says slowly, "Do you really believe I would ever let anything like that happen to you?"

I open my mouth, but close it again, because the automatic "yes" I was about to blurt isn't the truth.

The truth—no matter how ridiculous, impossible, or crazy— is that I believe he'd sacrifice his own life without hesitation if it would save mine.

My voice comes out in a faint, shocked whisper. "No. I think you'd always keep me safe."

"I would," he insists, his eyes shining with emotion. "I *will*. I swear it."

We stare at each other until the woman at the bar stool on his other side says, "If she's not interested, hot stuff, I sure am."

We ignore her.

"But I can't…this lifestyle of yours…it's…it's *wrong.*"

He looks frustrated, like there are things he's dying to tell me, but can't.

Or won't.

Because hello, big secrets. The things on which solid relationships are definitely *not* built.

This is when my little detour into fantasy land ends with an abrupt screech, like locked tires against asphalt.

I exhale, popping the shiny bubble I'd formed over my head with the visions of me and Killian sharing a happy future together.

God, I'm an idiot. A pretty face and pretty promises and my legs split open like a hot dog bun.

"Oh no," he says softly, examining my expression. "There you go again."

With as much dignity as I can muster, I extricate myself from his arms. I stand, smooth a hand over my hair, straighten my shoulders. Then I look at him and say, "I'm here for the rest of the week. I assume you already know that."

A muscle in his jaw jumping, he nods curtly. Thunderclouds are gathering over his head. He doesn't like the turn in the conversation.

Too bad. He's not in charge.

"Okay. So here's what I propose. This thing we've got going —it's unsustainable. It's not real life. But for the next five days, it can be…" I search for the right word, but can't find one. "It can be whatever the hell it is. Here, only. In this town. When I go back home on Sunday, it's over. For good."

I stand and wait for his response, pretending I didn't tell him just last night that it would only be the one time. My mother always said a woman reserves the right to change her mind.

He says through gritted teeth, "So that's your offer. Five days. Then we go our separate ways forever."

"Yes."

Standing to tower over me, he grinds his molars together. Getting a full look at his body and height for the first time, the woman next to him at the bar gasps softly. I wouldn't be surprised if she toppled unconscious off her stool.

He leans down until we're eye to eye. He growls, "No deal."

Then he brushes past me and strides out of the bar, leaving a trail of swooning females in his wake.

I throw my hands into the air and shout, "For heaven's sake, pull yourselves together!"

Then I storm out in the opposite direction Killian left.

Back in my motel room, I order room service and try to watch TV. After ten minutes, I turn it off impatiently. I try pacing again, but it doesn't help. I'd tear out my hair, but that seems unnecessarily dramatic and painful. So I wait, sitting on the edge of my bed, until the food arrives.

I shovel it down without tasting a bite. I take a bath in scalding water. I don't feel the heat until I get out and look at myself in the mirror. Steam rises from my skin. My entire body is red. I look like a freshly cooked lobster.

I leave a message for Fin and Max, then start to pace again. When I check the clock on the wall, I groan out loud when I realize that only an hour has passed since I left the bar.

At this rate, I'll be in a straightjacket by morning.

I start pacing again, wringing my hands, but some intuition makes me stop in the middle of the room and look at the windows. The gauzy white curtains are drawn. Beyond them, evening has taken the marina.

There's no reason for me to notice the windows, but I feel a pull I can't describe. I drift toward them almost unwillingly, my heart in my throat.

I stand to one side and draw back a corner of the curtain, peeking out to the street below.

And there, pacing back and forth like a man possessed, is Killian.

I drop the curtain and flatten myself against the wall.

"Don't look again, Juliet. Don't you dare open those curtains and look at him again. Get drunk. Go to sleep. Knit a fucking scarf if you have to. Whatever it is, *don't look at him.*"

Closing my eyes, I stand there against the wall, holding my breath and listening to my pulse roar in my ears. Then I exhale in a giant gust and open the curtains again, this time sliding them apart.

Back and forth he goes, from one streetlight to another, flexing his hands open and closed, until he spots me in the window. Then he stops dead in his tracks and stares up at me.

All the longing, frustration, anger, and desire is right there on his face. All of it.

And I'm even more of a fool than I thought I was, because before I know what I'm doing, my fingers are finding the way of the buttons on the front of my dress.

Even from across the street, I see his eyes flare. I feel his attention sharpen. Sense his focus shift the way a predator's shifts, catching a whiff of his prey on the wind.

He stands perfectly still and watches me as the bodice of the dress parts under my swiftly working fingers, exposing me to my waist. I'm wearing a bra, the outline of which I trace slowly with my fingertips.

He mutters something. An oath, no doubt. His eyes are two burning coals, frighteningly intense and piercing.

I know it's a dangerous game I'm playing, but there's a thrill in my blood and the sound of crashing waves in my ears. I'm not sure if I could stop, even if I wanted to.

I slide the dress off my shoulders so it pools around my waist. I reach behind my back and unhook the bra. I slide it down my arms, drop it, then stand with my hands cupped over my bare breasts, gazing down at him.

Then, trembling, I back away from the windows and sit on the edge of the bed.

He doesn't make me wait long.

In less than sixty seconds, he crashes through the door.

JULES

$\mathcal{H}$e pushes me to my back on the mattress, straddles me, and pins my arms over my head.

"Okay, thief," he growls, his eyes blazing with anger. "We'll do this your way. Five days it is. But just remember when it's over that I would've given you anything you'd asked for if you'd only given me your heart."

He crushes his mouth to mine.

And oh, god, the sweet thrill that runs through my body. He's furious with me, I know he's going to be rough, yet I'm so turned on I'm almost vibrating.

He breaks the kiss, rolls me onto my belly, shoves my dress up to my waist, and yanks my panties down. I hear him tear open the fly of his jeans. Then he pins my wrists over my head again, using only one of his hands.

He thrusts inside me with no preliminaries, without seeing if I'm ready, without uttering another word.

I cry out, arching.

"Aye," he rasps. "That's what you want, isn't it? That's all you want from me. And you're gonna get it, thief." His voice drops dangerously low. "You're gonna get it all."

He grabs my hip, holds me down, and starts to fuck me. As he does, he speaks to me in Irish through gritted teeth.

These don't sound like love words. It's a torrent of harsh fricatives, grunts, and growls, like an animal's language. Like one long, complicated curse. He thrusts into me, over and over, his hand gripped tight around my wrists, his breath coming in rough pants.

I come so hard I start sobbing.

He instantly freezes. Releasing my wrists, he leans down over me, planting his elbows on either side of my head.

Sounding anguished, he whispers, "Oh god. Oh fuck. I'm so sorry. I've hurt you."

"N-no. You didn't. Please don't stop."

He brushes my hair off my face and tenderly kisses my cheek. His breathing is hard and irregular. "Promise me I didn't hurt you. I couldn't stand it if I did."

"I promise. I swear."

"You would tell me?"

"Yes."

"This isn't—you're not afraid right now? You're not just trying to placate me?"

I roll my hips, softly moaning. "Killian. I adore it. You feel amazing."

He whispers, "Then why are you crying, love?"

Love. Oh, how that hurts. It hurts like a sword shoved straight through my heart.

I squeeze my eyes shut and turn my face to the sheets. My voice strangled, I say, "You know why."

He's still except for his ragged breathing. Buried deep inside me, his cock throbs, but he ignores it. He kisses my cheek again, nuzzles his nose into my hair.

Then he slides out of me, rolls me over to my back, and pushes into me again, framing my face in his hands. His eyes blazing with emotion, he whispers, "No. Tell me."

That look in his eyes is overwhelming. That need. That desperate longing. I turn my head, sucking in a hitching breath.

He kisses my neck, my jaw, my temple. He tangles his fingers into my hair. He presses deeper into me, watching my face like his life depends on it.

I wrap my legs around his waist and my arms around his back and close my eyes.

"Tell me," he says next to my ear.

I roll my hips and stay silent. I know if I opened my mouth, all that would come out are more sobs.

"Tell me it's because you know you won't be able to go back to who you were before we met," he whispers. "Like I won't."

"Killian—"

"Tell me it's because you want me the same way I want you, even though it doesn't make sense. Even though it's impossible."

I can't catch my breath. He's inside me, all over me, his weight and his heat and his intensity, and I'm exposed in every way underneath him. I'm nothing but a beating heart and a naked bundle of raw nerves.

He says gently, "Tell me it's because you know nothing else could ever be as good as this."

I beg, "Please don't be sweet. I don't have any defenses against you when you're sweet."

He bends his head to my breasts and nuzzles them, licking my hard nipples, gently testing them with his teeth.

Delirious with pleasure, I moan and arch into his mouth.

He starts a slow, steady motion of his hips, thrusting deep but gently. Greedy for him, I slide my hands underneath his T-shirt and up his back, loving the feel of his muscles as they work. Loving the smoothness and warmth of his skin.

He goes back and forth between my breasts, sucking and licking, cupping them in his huge hands as he flexes his hips. I'm panting. Sweating. Trying desperately not to crumble.

When I'm writhing and shaking, on the edge of another

orgasm, he puts his hand around my throat and presses his thumb against my jugular vein.

Then he fucks me harder.

I gasp his name.

He lifts his head from my breasts and puts his mouth next to my ear. His voice is a dark, irresistible command.

"Come."

I do, instantly.

He groans as I convulse around him, my head tipped back, crying out. My nails dig into the muscles of his back. My thighs clench around his hips. Still hot and wet from his mouth, my nipples throb and ache in the cool air.

He discards the smooth, rolling motion of his hips and pumps into me faster and more frantically. The headboard starts to slam over and over again into the wall. He's moaning and shaking, pulling my hair.

Then he falls still with a sound like he's in extreme pain.

My eyes fly open, and I see he's wearing an expression of extreme pain, too. I say breathlessly, "What is it? What's wrong?"

He answers through a clenched jaw. "Didn't wear a condom."

"God, you scared me." I relax against the mattress, letting the tension drain from my limbs. "Roll over."

His gaze hazy, he blinks at me in confusion. "Why?"

"Do you want to come in my mouth or not?"

He stops breathing. Then, in a flash, he's on his back and I'm straddling him, smiling down into his fierce, wild-eyed face.

I whisper, "That's what I thought, gangster."

I roll my hips, and he groans. He reaches up to fondle my bare breasts. His eyes drift shut. I flatten hands over his broad chest and roll my hips again, grinding my clit against his pelvis.

"You're drenched," he says faintly. "Your pussy is so wet. So hot. So fucking—"

He breaks off with another groan when I start to grind faster, finding a rhythm that sends shockwaves of pleasure surging through me and makes my breasts bounce in his hands.

He grabs my hips and thrusts up into me, his body jerking, all the tendons standing out in his neck.

"You're so hard for me." I gasp. "Oh god. I'm going to come again. Killian. Killian—"

He pinches both my nipples at the same time. I climax, shuddering and moaning on top of him, my head thrown back.

"Baby—ah fuck, I can't—I can't—"

A deep, broken moan breaks from his chest. He falls completely still, every muscle in his body straining. I barely have enough time to scramble off him and take his throbbing cock into my mouth before he's spilling onto my tongue. I wrap my hand around his shaft and suck.

His fingers twisted in my hair, he thrusts up into my mouth, shouting.

It's a strange sort of elation I feel, watching him fall apart. Watching as he completely loses himself to the pleasure I'm giving him with my mouth and my hands, with every stroke and slide of my tongue. He's so huge, so strong and powerful, but he's helpless, jerking into my mouth uncontrolled, calling out my name like a prayer.

I close my eyes and swallow every drop of what he gives me.

Along with it goes my final shreds of denial that this thing between us is going to be anything but a total catastrophe.

I knew it, but it wasn't until just now that I accepted it.

We're going to burn each other to the ground.

I awake sometime later on my side, nestled against him, my head resting on his chest and my leg caught between his. The room is dark except for the small blue light glowing on the cable box on the dresser across the room. Beneath my ear, Killian's heart is a slow and steady thump.

He murmurs, "You said my name in your sleep."

I hope he's making that up because otherwise, I'm going to die of humiliation. "Do you ever sleep?"

"Not around you."

Toying with my hair, he presses a kiss to the top of my head. He's so big and warm and comfortable. Dangerously comfortable. I could stay right here in this bed for the rest of my life.

"I have a question for you."

"Hmm."

"How do you always know where to find me?"

His voice achingly gentle, he says, "The same way a compass knows how to find true north."

Oh shit. He's being sweet again. I shut my eyes and draw a slow, steadying breath.

He gives me a squeeze, chuckling. "Such a big softie," he whispers.

"Look who's talking. And compasses don't point true north. They point to magnetic north, which isn't the same thing."

"I know. But it wouldn't have had the same romantic ring to it. True north being a euphemism for—"

"Don't say it," I beg. "God. Please. Are you *trying* to kill me, or what?"

"No, lass. Just trying to scale the fortress walls."

"Well, stop it."

"No."

I exhale in a ragged gust. I swear, I'm going to need some kind of cardiac surgery after this. A quadruple bypass, at the very least.

We lie in silence for a moment, long enough for my pulse to

return to near normal levels. My fingers decide to take a lingering stroll over the architecture of his abdomen. His skin is satin. His abs are steel. When I lightly trace the outline of his belly button with my forefinger, a delicate shudder runs through his chest.

I whisper, "Killian?"

"Aye, lass?"

"If I asked you to give a million dollars to the Red Cross, would you do it?"

"Of course." Thoughtful pause. "Are you asking?"

"I think so. Yes."

"Done."

"Okay. Thank you." It's my turn to pause. "How will I know?"

His voice turns warm. "I'll think of something. Any other charitable donations you'd like me to make, while we're on the topic?"

Thinking, I run my finger around and around that fascinating little indentation in the middle of his hard belly. I resist the urge to lean down and stroke it with my tongue. "Um. Probably? But…"

I feel his attention sharpen. "But what?"

"Never mind. It'll sound weird."

"If you think I'll let this go now, you don't know me at all."

Sighing, I say, "Fine. What I'd like you to do instead of another charitable donation is, um…not something bad."

"What is it?"

"No, that's it. I want you to not do something bad."

He considers that in silence for a while, running his fingers through my hair. "Like what kind of something, for instance?"

"Pick one. You're a mob boss. I'm sure there are a dozen bad things you do in your daily schedule that you could name right off the top of your head."

He pretends to think. "So, like…don't run over a grandmother with my car? Because I've got that scheduled for Tuesdays."

"Ha ha."

"Wednesdays I usually shoot up a barrel full of puppies. Thursdays are for helping blind people cross the street but leaving them in the middle of the crosswalk when the light changes, and Fridays I like to commit a little light fraud. Identity theft, telemarketing scams, that sort of thing."

"You're a jerk."

"Oh—you'll like this—on the weekends I usually buy a few dozen powdered donuts and take them down to the local home-less shelter."

He waits until I relent, rolling my eyes. "Okay, I'll play your silly game. Why is that bad?"

He stifles a laugh. "Because the powdered donuts are actu-ally plain ones that I rolled in glue and baby powder."

I sigh.

He pushes me onto my back, throws one heavy leg over both of mine, props himself up on his elbow, and smiles down at me. "Wait til I tell you what I've got scheduled for Mondays, lass."

I say tartly, "Let me guess. Bombing a hospital? Poisoning a municipal water supply? Killing off an entire comedy club audi-ence with your awful stand-up routine?"

His smile turns to a grin, stunning in its beauty. Even in the shadows, lit with only a dim blue glow, the man is breathtaking.

"Better. Deflowering virgins."

I snort. "And making the poor things fall in love with you, no doubt."

His smile fades. He presses a gentle kiss to my lips. "Hopefully."

I turn my head, hiding my face in his neck. He runs his hand up my arm and over my shoulder, then cradles my head. He whispers, "'And where two raging fires meet together, they do consume the thing that feeds their fury.'"

My voice comes out choked. "If you quote *Romeo and Juliet* to me one more time, I won't be responsible for what happens."

"That wasn't from *Romeo and Juliet*, lass. That was *The Taming of the Shrew*."

"Oh. So I'm a shrew now?"

"Considering my naked testicles are within easy reach of your angry fists, I decline to answer."

I wrinkle my nose. "Don't say testicles."

"Why not?"

"It's a gross word. Almost as gross as 'moist.'"

He chuckles. "I'll make a note of it. Any other forbidden words I should be aware of?"

I scowl into his neck. "If it's in the dictionary, it's forbidden."

"Ah. So what I'm hearing you say is shut up."

"Yes. Now. Or my angry fists will get to work."

Gathering me closer in his arms, his chest shakes with silent laughter. When I push against his stomach, irritated, he peppers soft, tender kisses all along my neck.

I mutter, "You're killing me, devil man."

"Right back atcha, little thief." He palms my ass, squeezing it, flexing his hips into mine so I feel his erection. His voice turns husky. "I need to be inside you now."

"If it'll get you to stop talking, I'm on board."

"Are you *sure* you want me to be quiet? Because from what I remember, you liked it an awful lot when I talked like this."

The Australian accent has made a reappearance. He's Chris Hemsworth again, the evil bastard.

But I'm not stupid. I spread my legs and draw him inside me, closing my eyes to pretend it's the actor I'd rather have make love to me, rather than my dangerous gangster with the heart of a poet and a thousand unspoken secrets swimming in the darkness behind his eyes.

22

JULES

*W*hen I wake the next morning, he's gone again. It hurts even more this time than it did the last.

I spend the day wandering aimlessly through town. I think it will become my new routine. When the sun is setting over the ocean, I head back to the same restaurant I've visited for the past two nights, knowing I'll find him there.

Or he'll find me. Magnets have a funny way of attracting each other like that.

This time when he arrives, he's in a gorgeous navy blue pinstripe suit with a white silk pocket square and black leather loafers polished to a mirror shine.

His hair is perfect. His beard is trimmed. He's not wearing a tie, so the strong column of his throat is exposed, tattoo and all. The combination of sleek sophistication with raw masculinity is devastating.

As is the British accent.

Instead of Chris Hemsworth, tonight he's James Bond.

Leaning an elbow on the bar, he says to Harley, "Vodka martini. Shaken, not stirred."

Harley stares at him, nonplussed. "You've gotta be fuckin' kidding me."

I lift my wine glass to him in a mock salute. "Amen."

Killian smiles blandly at the bartender. "And don't shake too vigorously. The ice will bruise the vodka." He turns to me, sending me a hot, half-lidded look. "Hello there."

"Hello yourself, Mr. Craig."

He lifts his brows. "Who's Mr. Craig?"

I look him up and down. "Daniel Craig. As in, the actor? As in, James Bond?"

Killian laughs a husky, sexy-as-hell, ovulation inducing laugh. "No. Sean Connery is the best and only Bond. All those other blokes are just window dressing."

"I'll give you the macho, devil-may-care thing. You've got that one pinned down. But Sean Connery had a super thick Scottish accent."

Killian leans closer to me, smirking. "A super thick Scottish accent like this?"

Yes, exactly like that. I could strangle him with my bare hands.

"Were you an actor before you turned to a life of crime?"

He switches back to the posh British Bond accent. "No. I was a farm boy. Acting didn't come until after I turned to a life of crime."

He holds my gaze. His own is unflinching. He's just told me the truth, strange as it is.

"A farm boy," I muse, warming to the idea. "In Ireland?"

He nods.

"Did your parents make you do chores?"

He nods again.

Fascinated, I try to picture it. Killian as a young boy, on the farm, completing his daily chores. Mucking out horse stalls. Feeding the chickens. Milking the cows.

Impossible.

"Do you have siblings?"

His pause is infinitesimal. "One."

I search his face, knowing he left something unsaid. "One...?"

"Left," he says, his voice lower. "I have one sibling left now."

"That's right. Your brother. You told me." After a beat, I say, "Wait. *Left?*"

Hesitating, he moistens his lips. "There were eight of us. Only two are still alive."

Surprised, I stare at him. Accidents? Illnesses? Something worse? What would take six siblings in the same family before middle age? I'm dying to ask, but I don't want to pry.

Idiotic, considering I've swallowed the man's ejaculate.

Reading my expression, Killian says softly, "There was a fire."

My heart stops. My hand flies up to cover my mouth. "Oh god. I'm so sorry."

He reaches out to stroke a lock of my hair, gazing at it intently as he runs it slowly through two fingers. "Thank you."

"And...and your parents? Are they still alive?"

His eyes very far away, he murmurs, "Gone. Everyone. Everything. Anything that mattered. All that was left for me was revenge."

He's somewhere distant for a moment before he snaps back to himself. His hazy gaze sharpens. His eyes gather the light, glinting dangerously like the edge of a blade. He drops his hand to his side and straightens, facing the bar.

Harley sets a martini in front of him with a dramatic flourish. "If your vodka's bruised, King Arthur, feel free to lodge a complaint with management."

He dodders off, cackling.

Cheeks ruddy, jaw tight, Killian grabs the martini and downs it in a single swallow.

193

Meanwhile, I stare at his profile with one word that he said echoing over and over inside my mind.

Revenge.

The fire that took his family wasn't an accident.

I feel as if a forbidden, locked door has cracked open, revealing a sliver of light.

He was a boy, his family was killed in a fire, and all that was left for him was to avenge their deaths.

I say quietly, "You knew who did it."

He sets the empty martini glass carefully on the bar. His throat works. He doesn't look at me.

"You killed him. Or them."

He's stiff and unresponsive, his silence giving an answer without words.

"And that's how it all started," I whisper, knowing as I say it that I'm right. "The farm boy got a taste for vengeance, and he never looked back."

He turns to me abruptly, bristling, his eyes ablaze. He says gruffly, "I look back every fucking day. Remembering where I came from and why I do what I do is the only thing that keeps me going."

His normal voice is back. That rich, lilting Irish brogue, thick with emotion now. He's himself again, all hard edges and sharp angles, a whirlwind of chaotic feelings contained by an iron will underneath a pretty, polished shell.

But I've peeked behind the curtain now. I've gotten a look at the backstage of his Broadway show.

Killian Black is a criminal not because he was born bad or because he's good at it or because there's nothing else he'd rather be.

He's a criminal because the world broke his heart, and the only way he knew how to deal with the magnitude of his pain was through violence.

Through vengeance.

Through the spilling of blood.

Holding his gaze, I say, "I was wrong about something."

He snaps, "What?"

"You're not like my father. He loves hurting people. He gets off on it."

Killian stares at me, his chest rising and falling rapidly, his jaw and his hands clenched. His eyes are dark, so dark they're unfathomable.

I whisper, "I don't think you like what you do at all."

He falls so still he doesn't appear to be breathing. His lips part, but he remains silent, his expression stunned.

We stay like that, locked in a breathless, intense bubble, until Killian exhales and the bubble bursts.

He grabs my arm and strides toward the back of the restaurant, steering me through the crowd.

"Where are we going?"

He doesn't answer. He simply keeps walking, holding my arm firmly in his grasp.

We pass table after table until I realize we're headed toward the kitchen. Killian throws open the swinging kitchen doors and guides me through aisles crowded with sous chefs cooking or plating food, all of whom give us only a cursory glance before turning back to their work.

He turns me left past a huge walk-in fridge, then right past a row of metal baker's racks stacked with serving trays and water carafes, then yanks open an unmarked door.

He pulls me inside, shuts the door, and kisses me with so much raw passion it takes my breath away.

The kiss goes on and on. It's greedy and possessive, like he's staking a claim. When he finally breaks away, my knees are shaking and my heart is beating like mad.

We're in a small supply closet. Shelves stretch from floor to ceiling on all sides. They're stacked with dish towels, cleaning supplies, and miscellaneous other items I glimpse only quickly because Killian has pushed me up against the shelf of towels and is kissing me again.

Groaning, he reaches between my legs and squeezes.

I know what he needs. It's the same thing I need. That release only the other can give, the whip-crack burn that arrives with the speed of lightning and hits with the force of a bomb.

I tear at his belt. He yanks at his zipper. His hard cock springs out into my hands. We keep kissing frantically as he shoves my skirt up my thighs. He can't wait long enough to remove my panties, so he simply pulls them aside.

With fumbling hands, I guide him to my entrance. I lift a knee and brace my foot against a shelf, gasping in pleasure when he pushes inside me.

Grabbing my ass with both hands, he thrusts deep, grunting. I cling to his shoulders as he fucks me, fast and hard, his fingers digging into my bottom and his face turned to my neck.

A stack of towels falls from a top shelf. Spray cans of industrial window cleaner clatter to the floor. A big sack of flour topples over, splitting a seam when it hits the tile and sending a white pouf into the air. It settles over our shoes like a dusting of snow.

He leans down and bites my hard nipple right through my dress.

I come hard but silently. My mouth is open but no sound comes out. The pleasure is too intense.

As I jerk and convulse around him, Killian slows the motion of his hips, the way he likes to, so he can feel my every throb and twitch. Panting, he puts his hand around my throat and his mouth to my ear. His voice is raw with emotion.

"I want you to lie to me. Just this one lie. Just this once."

I moan, not understanding.

He raises his head and looks at me with burning eyes. "Tell me you're mine."

My heart clenches to a fist. Nose to nose, we stare at each other. He thrusts slowly in and out.

It's a lie. A small, simple lie. There can't be any harm since we both know it.

I draw a ragged breath. "I...I'm yours."

His lids flutter. Thrusting harder, he moistens his lips. He wants more. And god help me, I want to give it to him.

"I belong to you. Only you."

His moan is soft but his eyes are softer. Inside my chest, something delicate begins to tear apart.

"I'll always be yours," I whisper, my voice breaking. "No matter what. Body and soul. Heart and mind. All of me will belong to you forever."

He kisses me suddenly, his mouth devouring. His thrusts turn fast and desperate. He makes a sound deep in his chest, a purely masculine sound that could either be pain or pleasure.

Biting my lips, he fucks me until he breaks away with a garbled groan.

I sink to my knees on the flour dusted floor, wrap my hands around his engorged cock, and open my mouth over the crown.

He fists his hands into my hair and comes, staring down at me.

I have to close my eyes as I swallow so I can't see the look in his.

The look that tells me the lie he asked me to tell is going to turn out to be anything but small and simple.

23

JULES

*a*fter that night, we're inseparable.

He eats meals with me, wanders the town and marina with me, sleeps beside me in my small motel bed. At least I assume he sleeps. He must. Every time I wake, however, he's already up, with coffee and pastries waiting.

I never hear him come and go. A part of me thinks he can turn to smoke and slink silently in and out of rooms through cracks in windowpanes or under doors, like Dracula.

Honestly, it wouldn't surprise me.

Over dinner in the evenings, he asks me questions, dozens of them. They grow more and more personal each day. He asks me about Fin and Max. About my favorite movies and TV shows. About my favorite foods and books. He asks what I wanted to be when I was growing up, what I remember about my mother, what it was like being an only child.

If I've ever been in love.

I answer everything honestly. I ask no questions in return.

If he wonders why, he doesn't mention it. Perhaps he knows it's the only way I can protect myself. I'm afraid that the more I discover of that poet's heart that beats beneath his powerful, dangerous exterior, the more unable I'll be to walk away when it's time.

He takes me dancing. He takes me to the movies. He rents a sailboat and captains it himself. We visit art galleries and museums, we listen to a jazz trio at a bar overlooking the ocean, we stuff ourselves on lobster and crab. We do all the silly tourist things any normal couple would do on vacation.

And, everywhere, we make love.

On a dock at night. On a merry-go-round in a park. In the motel jacuzzi. Down a dimly lit, secluded back hallway of a restaurant. In a high school auditorium we snuck into after dark.

It's always frantic and almost always wordless. We'll be walking hand in hand down the street or standing at a beachside railing watching the sea birds circle overhead, and suddenly we'll look at each other and be overcome.

That's the only way I can describe it: overcome. Overwhelmed by heat and hunger.

Overpowered by need.

When I wonder if this is how my mother felt when she met my father, I feel deeply afraid. And more certain that my moratorium on this affair is wise.

Not wise enough, though.

I didn't know it then, but I'd already lost my heart.

The guy who approaches me is about thirty, well-built and nicely dressed, and smiling. He's got a man bun and a tattoo of a katana on his forearm. He's Caucasian, so getting a traditional Japanese cultural symbol inked onto a visible body part means he's either a devout student of martial arts, or a douche.

"Hi," he says, and takes the stool next to mine at the bar.

Killian's in the restroom. Behind the bar, Harley looks at the new arrival with an expression like he's just taken his life into his own hands by occupying Killian's seat.

When Harley looks over at me, brows raised, I shrug. If this guy wants to get his face rearranged, so be it.

Harley pours Man Bun a shot of tequila and sets it in front of him.

Surprised, Man Bun says, "Oh. No thanks, bro. I'll take a strawberry daiquiri."

"Of course you will," deadpans Harley. "Do you need a tampon for that mangina of yours, too?"

Man Bun is insulted, puffing up his chest. "*Excuse* me?"

Harley looks him up and down then snorts. "Oh, don't get your panties in a bunch, sweetheart. You'll be dead within five minutes. Enjoy yourself while you can. And try going out with some dignity." He looks at Man Bun's hair and grimaces. "You've embarrassed yourself enough."

He walks off to serve another customer. Man Bun looks after him in astonishment, then at me.

I smile. "Colorful, isn't he?"

Disgruntled, he says, "Uh, yeah. I guess you could call it that."

I sip my wine and wait for him to introduce himself. When he does, I nearly spit the wine out of my mouth.

"I'm Tripp. With two Ps."

I swallow with difficulty, then reclaim my smile from where it fell onto the floor in shock. "Hi, Tripp with two Ps. I'm Juliet."

His brows shoot up. "Really? Juliet? Like from Shakespeare?"

Oh, the irony of having my name met with surprise by a guy named after what happens when you're too clumsy to walk a straight line without stumbling.

"Yes, like from Shakespeare."

"Huh." He grins. "I guess you need a Romeo, then."

Or a Taser.

I see Killian approaching from behind Tripp, his long legs eating up the distance between the men's room and the bar with alarming speed, and think for a frantic moment that I should probably warn Tripp off before he gets hurt.

Until he leans closer to me and says, "I'm up for the job, if you're looking." He waggles his eyebrows up and down.

Your fate is sealed, Man Bun.

But Killian surprises me by maintaining his cool. He walks up beside me, kisses the top of my head, and turns to Man Bun with a friendly smile. "Hullo, mate. I see you've met my woman. Knockout, isn't she?"

He looks Killian up and down, swallowing. A shade of color fades from his face. "Uh…"

"Nice ink," says Killian, looking at Man Bun's sword tattoo. "*Shinogi-Zukuri* was originally produced after the Heian period. I prefer *Kissaki-Moroha-Zukuri* myself. Unlike *Shinogi-Zukuri*, the blade is double-edged. I like to have both edges of my swords sharp. Much more cutting power that way."

He grins at Man Bun's deer-in-the-headlights look. "Are you into firearms, too, by any chance? I'd love to show you my collection."

Grinning, Harley sets down a strawberry daiquiri in front of Man Bun. He drops a paper umbrella into it and dodders away, cackling.

Man Bun stands, grabs his daiquiri, and smiles stiffly at us. "Nice meeting you."

Watching him run away, Killian chuckles. "I guess I'm paying for his drink."

I say, "What's it like, going through life the way you do?"

"Which way is that?"

"King of the jungle. Lord of the manor. Master of all you survey."

Killian slides onto the stool Man Bun just deserted and

smiles at me. "Gratifying. Convenient." His smile falters. His voice drops. "Lonely."

It kills me when he's vulnerable. I glance down at my glass of wine.

Switching back to a normal tone, he says, "What's it like being so attractive random strangers try to pick you up in bars?"

I snort, looking over at a trio of women sitting at a nearby table, gawking our way. "You should know, stud."

He follows my gaze. "Maybe we should give them something to take back to their husbands."

"What do you mean?"

Instead of answering, he shows me.

He leans over, takes my face in his hands, looks deeply into my eyes, then kisses me.

It's a passionate kiss, but it's also searingly tender. My head tilted back, I sink into him, fisting my hands into the front of his shirt and breathing his scent into my nose.

When he breaks the kiss, it's to whisper another line from *Romeo and Juliet* into my ear.

"'But, soft! what light through yonder window breaks? It is the east, and Juliet is the sun.'"

My voice strangled, I whisper back, "I will stab you in the heart with a cocktail fork."

He pulls away, still cradling my face in his hands. His smile is achingly beautiful and sad.

"You've already stabbed me in the heart, thief. Now it's just a matter of seeing how long it will take for me to bleed to death."

We gaze at each other, all thoughts of the three staring women vanished. He sweeps his thumb gently over my cheekbone, then back and forth over my lips.

I blurt, "You wrote in your note that I make you want to live a different kind of life. Was that true?"

"Aye."

"And..." My heart pounds so hard I have to take a breath.

"And what if I asked you to do that? To give up the life you have? Would you do that for me?"

He answers without hesitation, his voice husky. "I would if you said you trusted me. I would if you gave me your whole heart. If you stopped holding back."

His throat works. He moistens his lips. His voice drops to a whisper. "If it meant I could have you for good, I'd light my whole life on fire and walk away from the ashes."

It sits there between us, crackling dangerously like a live wire.

He waits, tense and silent, staring at me. His hands tremble on the sides of my face. He murmurs my name, his voice so raw it guts me.

I almost say it.

I almost blurt, "Yes, I trust you, yes, I'm crazy for you, yes, let's be together and tell the whole world to go take a flying fuck."

But at that moment, the music changes.

"Let It Be" by the Beatles comes on.

An icy chill runs through me, raising the hair on the back of my neck and the skin on my arms in gooseflesh. It feels like my mother is reaching out to me from beyond the grave with a warning. I can almost hear her ghostly voice hissing in my ear.

Don't do what I did. Don't fall in love with a bad man, or you'll wind up dead like me.

And just like that, the spell is broken.

I lean away from Killian, taking my face from his hands and facing forward in the stool to stare blankly ahead. My hands shaking, I reach for my wine. I drink it, trembling all over, stunned by how close I came to the edge of the cliff.

Stunned by how much I wanted to fling myself off it.

Beside me, he blows out a hard breath. His laugh is low and brittle. "Harley."

The bartender snaps to attention when Killian calls his name. "What can I get you, boss?"

"Glenlivet. Three fingers. No ice."

"You got it."

We sit in tense silence, side by side, watching Harley get a glass and pour the liquor. As soon as he sets it down, Killian grabs it and shoots it down. He exhales, sets the glass back on the bar with a sharp *thunk*, and turns to me.

His voice is sandpaper rough. "Let's not drag this out. I'll leave tonight instead of tomorrow morning."

I smother the little voice inside me screaming *No! No! No!* and try to keep my voice calm. "It's not that I don't want to trust you. It's that I can't."

His laugh is bitter. "You can. You just choose not to."

"Can you honestly blame me?"

He curls his hand around my upper arm and turns me to face him. His jaw is hard, his eyes are blazing with fury, and he's never looked more handsome.

He snaps, "Aye, I can fucking blame you, because you know how good this is, but you're too scared to give it a go."

"*Scared?*" I repeat, my voice climbing. "More like smart. More like sensible!"

He leans in and pins me with his burning stare. He growls, "Bullshit."

I blink at the vehemence in his tone. "Excuse me?"

"That's total bullshit, and you know it. It's an excuse."

My voice rises even higher. "You're a criminal."

"So are you."

"You're a *gangster*!"

"And you're a thief."

I cry, "I do what I do to *help* people!"

He stares at me, all the tendons in his neck standing out and his nostrils flared. After a bristling moment of silence, he says, "Me, too, thief. *Me fucking too.*"

Then he jolts to his feet and stalks away through the crowd, hands clenched and shoulders stiff, turning heads as he goes.

Harley says gently, "Don't worry about the drinks, sweetheart. This round's on the house."

He walks away, leaving me alone with the oddest sensation that I've just made a terrible mistake, only I can't figure out why.

When I get back to the motel, Killian is already there, waiting for me.

24

KILLIAN

I meant to head back to Boston straight from the restaurant, but as soon as I got into the car, I realized I couldn't.

I still have one night left.

I'm taking it.

Juliet unlocks the door to her motel room, pausing when she sees me standing beside the bed. She exhales a quiet breath, then shuts the door behind her. She doesn't bother to ask how I got in.

When she turns back to me, her eyes are shining with emotion. "You can't expect me to throw away my whole life for you."

"Yet you expect it of me," I say gruffly.

Biting her lip, she looks down at her shoes. She's wearing another one of those gauzy sleeveless summer dresses that look so good on her. That look so goddamn good as I tear them off.

"I…" She stops, takes a breath, and starts again, still looking at her feet. "I'm not trying to be argumentative. Or mean. Or unfair." She glances up at me, her brows drawn together. "But there's so much about you that doesn't make sense."

I take a step toward her, because I can't stand not to touch her for one second more. My hands are itching to feel her skin. "I said I'd tell you everything."

That makes her eyes flash. "But I have to trust you first."

"Aye."

She's getting angrier. I can see her trying not to, but she can't help it. The blood is already rising in her cheeks.

"Why do I have to go first? Why can't *you* trust *me* and tell me everything?"

"Because there are too many lives at stake to take that risk."

That stops her short. But not for long. She steps toward me, insisting, "What does that mean?"

I shake my head sharply. It pisses her off.

She steps closer. "Your delivery boy, Diego. He said something that's been bothering me."

Damn Diego and his big mouth.

"He said what you were doing was important work," she goes on when I don't say anything. "I thought it was ridiculous at the time, that he was just misguided, looking up to the biggest bad guy he knows like some kind of father figure. Like something to aspire to be. The worst of the worst. King of criminals.

"But then on the walk back here I remembered how you said you erased my FBI file. That *you* erased it, not someone else. Which means you have access to the FBI's database. Which— taken with your ability to manipulate government satellites, and find people like they're needles in a haystack, and run the kind of background checks that can tell you how I like my fucking eggs, is very, very interesting, to say the least."

She walks closer and closer until she stops in front of me and stares up into my face. Her voice drops. Her eyes burn like she's on fire.

"And then you said you were helping people, too. '*Me fucking, too,*' you said, all angry and proud, like I'd insulted you.

Which, of course, makes no sense. How can the head of the Irish mafia possibly be *helping* people when it's in the job description to lie, cheat, and kill?"

She waits for an answer. I have to curl my hands to fists at my side not to reach for her. Not to crush my mouth to hers and rip off her dress and bury myself inside her.

Not to force her to be mine.

She has to offer that willingly.

"And then there's the matter of your name," she whispers, staring into my eyes. "Killian. A name, as far as I can tell, that no one else knows you by but me. To the whole world, you're Liam Black, ruthless gangster extraordinaire, but you asked me to call you Killian. You said it was your real name. Strangely enough, I believe you."

She's so close I can smell her skin. Feel her body heat. See the pulse pounding in the hollow of her throat.

We stare at each other in superheated silence, only inches apart, until she demands, "Tell me what the big mystery is, gangster."

I fire back, "Tell me you're in love with me."

Her cheeks turn scarlet. She grinds her back teeth together. "Tell me how you found out who my father is. Who *I* am."

"Tell me you're mine and mean it."

She's looking at me like she wants so badly to smash in my skull with a blunt object. "Tell me what you meant by there are too many lives at stake for you to trust me first."

"Tell me that lie I made you tell in the supply closet wasn't a lie at all, and I'll tell you whatever you want to know."

She examines my face in tense silence. Then she exhales, throwing her hands in the air. "You know what? Just go. I'm done playing this game with you."

She turns away. I grab her arm, spin her around, and pull her against my chest. I clasp her jaw in my hand, forcing her to look at me.

"I'm not a boy," I say gruffly. "I'm a man. I don't play games. I know who I am, what I want, and what I'm willing to do to get it. And I'm willing to do anything to have you."

Breathing hard, she stares at me with thinned lips and distrustful eyes.

I lower my voice. "But you have to make the same level of commitment, lass. You have to be mine. In every way. In all ways. You have to take a leap of faith—"

"Faith! Ha!"

"—and let this thing between us be what it is. Stop fighting it. *Let it be.*"

She blinks. Her lips part. The distrustful look in her eyes vanishes and is replaced by one of deep confusion. Maybe even fear.

She glances away, swallowing. When she looks back at me, she seems lost.

She says quietly, "I'm afraid."

"I know."

"I do want you. I do…" She looks away again. Her voice drops to a whisper. "I do have feelings for you."

Christ. My fucking heart.

I almost groan out loud. I almost crush my mouth to hers. Instead, I stay still and silent, waiting. Giving her time.

It's probably the most difficult thing I've ever done.

When she looks back at me, she's chewing her lip. "But I just have, like, zero frame of reference for how to deal with this. I want to trust you, but I don't even trust myself. I can't figure any of this out. It's so *wrong* that you're you, and I'm me, and we're even standing here, having this conversation."

Stroking my thumb over her satin cheek, I murmur, "I know."

"And you know what would happen if my father found out we were together, right? You know that would start a war. You know people would die. A *lot* of people, on both sides. It would be a bloodbath."

"Aye."

Her voice rises. She's starting to look panicked. "And maybe innocent people, too. I can't be responsible for that. I don't want blood on my hands. I don't want—"

I say firmly, "Listen to me."

She falls silent, staring wide-eyed up into my face.

"I'll handle your father."

Her brows lift. "Is 'handle' code for kill?"

"No."

"So, what? You'll go talk to him? You'll work it all out?" Her laugh sounds slightly hysterical.

"Aye," I say softly, gazing into her eyes. "I'll go talk to him. I'll ask him permission to marry you, and we'll work it all out."

She gapes at me in blank astonishment for a long moment. Then she pushes me away with both hands flat on my chest and shouts, "*Are you crazy?*"

All things considered, that's not a bad reaction. I expected to be bleeding by now.

I say calmly, "No."

"Are you—are you joking? Are you *toying* with me?"

"No."

She starts to pace back and forth, wild-eyed and shaking, her arms clasped around her chest. "You're a mental patient. That's it, isn't it? That's the mystery. You're an escapee from a psychiatric ward who's impersonating an infamous criminal. Or no—wait!" She throws her head back, laughing. "I'm starring in a new reality show where the main character doesn't know she's being filmed. Like what was that movie where the guy's whole life was televised but he didn't know it?"

"*The Truman Show.*"

"Yes! That one! I'm Truman!"

"You're not Truman."

She spins around and paces the other direction. "Or maybe this is all a hallucination. Maybe I was involved in a serious car accident, and I'm in a hospital somewhere right now, dreaming this all up. Maybe—"

I grab her by both arms and pull her against my chest again, because this is getting out of hand. I growl, "Does this feel like a dream to you?"

Then I fit my mouth over hers and give her the kiss she doesn't think she needs, but absolutely does.

She instantly melts against me the way she always melts when I kiss her. The way she'd deny to the death that she melts. She winds her arms around my waist and falls against me, moaning a little, giving me her weight. I sink my hands into her hair, cradle her head, and kiss her until we're both breathless.

I break away and demand, "Tell me you're in love with me."

Her lids drift open. Her eyes look like she's drugged. She says slowly, "I'm in deep, conflicted, weirdly, ambivalently *something* with you. That's for damn sure."

"Not good enough." I kiss her again, harder.

This time she breaks away first, groaning. "No! I'm not in love with you! That would be the stupidest thing *ever!*"

Stubborn wench. I kiss her again, walking her backward toward the bed.

I push her down to the mattress, sink to my knees on the floor, and push her dress up her thighs. Bending down, I take a big mouthful of her flesh, the tender, succulent flesh a few inches to the left of her panties. I suck, then gently bite down.

She moans. Sinks shaking hands into my hair. Curses me.

I rub my thumb up and down the warm center of her panties. "Where else do you want me to suck, baby?"

"I hate you. You know where."

"You don't hate me. Unless you're substituting one four-letter word for another."

I inhale deeply against her panties. Fuck, I love that scent. Warm, earthy, and utterly female. Utterly her.

Already hard, my cock twitches. It twitches again when I pull her panties aside and expose her beautiful pink pussy, wet and ready to eat.

I blow softly over the plump little nub of her clit, and she whimpers.

"Is that a please, baby?"

Her head moves restlessly back and forth. She rocks her hips.

That's a definite fucking *please*.

Very gently, I swirl my tongue over her clit. She gasps, her body bowing against the mattress.

"Do you like that?"

"I love it."

"What else do you love?"

I swirl my tongue around and around, then gently suck. I slide my finger inside her. My reward is a long, low moan of pleasure.

Then she says through gritted teeth, "Aardvark."

Challenge accepted.

I suck more firmly on her clit, flicking my tongue back and forth when she shudders. My dick throbs, aching to plunge into all that sweet, wet heat, but I control the urge to sink it into her and start pounding and simply lick and suck and press my finger in and out until she's writhing against my face and pulling at my hair.

I love how she responds to me. How she never holds anything back in bed.

If only I could get her to do the same with her feelings, I'd be a very happy fucking man.

Still licking her pussy, I open the fly on my jeans and release my cock from my briefs. It pops out like it's spring-loaded, rock hard and eager in my hand.

I rise to my knees, my dick in one hand and her clit pinched between two fingers of the other hand, and stare down at her. My heart pounds.

I growl, "Show me those beautiful tits."

Her eyes hazy and her cheeks flushed, she fumbles with the buttons on the bodice of her dress. She gets them all open and bares her chest to me, thrusting her breasts up like a dare.

She's not wearing a bra. Her nipples are hard, pink, and impossible to resist.

I lean over and take one into my mouth, sucking.

She gasps. Arches. Sinks her fingers into the muscles of my shoulders. I rub the head of my cock back and forth through her wet folds until she's moaning and panting, begging me for more.

Then I rise to my feet, kick off my shoes, rip off the rest of my clothes, and peel her out of her dress. I sit on the edge of the mattress, drag her onto my lap so her thighs are spread around my hips, and kiss her, guiding my cock inside her slick heat.

She tightens her arms around my shoulders and moans into my mouth.

Then she rides me, hard and fast, bucking her hips.

I pull her hair. Her head falls back. I kiss her throat, driving into her as she bounces up and down on my cock. Her breasts are smashed against my chest. She makes these small, feminine sounds of pleasure that make me feel like some sort of wild animal.

When she sobs my name, her thighs and arms clenching around my body, I lose myself.

I roll her to her back and come inside her, biting her neck, seeing stars.

Her pussy convulses around my dick in hard, rhythmic contractions. She shudders and cries out beneath me.

I keep coming. In wave after wave, I spill myself inside her, mindless and grunting. My skin is drenched in sweat. Every muscle in my body is clenched.

Then we're kissing again. Deep, delicious kisses mixed with

soft moans as our orgasms fade and our limbs begin to relax around each other.

When I finally open my eyes and look at her, she's lying underneath me with a blissed-out expression, her eyes closed and a small, satisfied smile on her flushed face.

The smile lasts for about two seconds.

Then her eyes fly open, and her whole body stiffens. She stares at me in horror, sucking in a breath.

Fuck.

I say, "Before you start to hurl insults at me, let me defend myself by saying that wasn't on purpose. I simply got carried away."

It's true, but she doesn't believe me. I can tell by the look on her face that she thinks I laid a trap for her and fucked her right into it.

"Is this a bad time to remind you that you got carried away, too?"

She says, "This is a bad time for you to be saying *anything*, gangster. Especially that."

She pushes at my chest, trying to get out from underneath me. I ignore that and stay firmly seated inside her. "Look at me."

She stares at me with eyes like razor blades. I stare right back. "When was your last period?"

She scoffs. "Oh, are you a gynecologist now, too?"

"One more smart remark and I'll spank your ass until it's red and my hand is stinging. Answer the question."

She wants to kill me. God, how much she wants to put a hole in my brain. If her eyes were loaded guns, I'd be riddled with bullets.

She says, "Just over three weeks ago."

"Thank you."

"You're welcome."

"And are your periods regular?"

She closes her eyes and mutters, "Jesus Christ."

"Just answer the goddamn question."

With a sigh, she says, "Yes, doctor. My periods are regular."

I kiss her gently on the lips. "Then you're in the luteal phase."

"I've never heard that term in my life. What the hell are you saying?"

"I'm saying you probably won't get pregnant."

"Probably isn't definitely."

"No, it isn't." We stare at each other. I say, "What do you think of twins?"

Her face drains of color.

"Because they run in my family."

She stares at me, horrified.

"I'm just saying. Don't look so nauseated."

She sputters, "Y-you can't—you can't be *okay* with…with…"

"What? You carrying my child?"

"Yes!"

I kiss her again. "The only problem I can foresee is what will happen to your temper with pregnancy hormones. It could get ugly. I'll have to take out extra life insurance. Hire a few more bodyguards."

She's dismayed. "This isn't funny!"

"No, lass, it isn't funny. It's life. Messy, complicated, and, occasionally, fucking beautiful. If you're pregnant, we'll figure it out."

"*We?*"

I freeze. My heart skips a beat. I hadn't considered the other alternatives.

Seeing the look on my face, she says softly, "I can't believe I'm going to say this out loud, but thank you for being offended by that."

My voice thick, I say, "More like appalled. That felt like a knife through my heart."

"I'm sorry. I wasn't suggesting that you wouldn't be involved…" She trails off, then sighs. "Okay, maybe I was suggesting that." She thinks for a moment. "Actually, it would never in a million years occur to me that you'd even want to be involved. You, with a baby?"

Then she groans and puts a hand over her eyes. "Oh god. This is a disaster."

I whisper, "Or it could be a miracle."

She takes her hand away from her eyes and glares at me in outrage.

I say solemnly, "You're right. Disaster it is. Should I fly into a rage and throw things around the room now, or would you prefer tears? I haven't cried since I was thirteen years old, though, so I should warn you it might take a while for me to work them up."

This time when she shoves against my chest, I let her push me away. As soon as I roll off her, she pops up and starts to dress, her shaking hands fumbling with her clothes.

I sit on the edge of the mattress with my elbows on my knees and watch her.

Running away again. Always running away.

Maybe she's right. Maybe this is a disaster. She's an iceberg, and I'm the Titanic, its captain too arrogant to bother to correct course, leading to the deaths of hundreds of innocent people.

A number that could match how many would die in a war started by a mafia king who fell in love with his enemy's daughter.

Liam's words come back to haunt me. *"You're the most controlling arsehole who's ever lived."*

And where has all that control gotten me?

Sitting on the edge of a bed in a rented motel room, watching the only woman I've ever wanted to take my last name freak out at the idea of carrying my child.

I realize with a sick feeling in the pit of my stomach that this is all there is for me. All there ever has been or ever will be. All that a man like me can expect:

Nothing.

I drag a hand through my hair, exhale a slow breath, and reach for my clothing.

JULES

We dress in silence. When we're done, Killian looks at me with distant eyes, his whole demeanor cool and withdrawn. His voice is cool, too, when he says, "If you need me, you know how to find me."

Then he walks out the door.

I sink into the nearest chair and press my hand over my pounding heart, too stunned to think straight.

I sit there like that for a long time, until finally my bubble of shock breaks.

I burst into tears.

I cry as I gather my things, cry as I call for a taxi, cry all the way home in the back of the cab. I don't know exactly why I'm so upset, except that everything is wrong, wrong, wrong. The way he left, the way I feel, how badly my heart is aching.

I wanted this to be over.

Now it is.

Except maybe it isn't. Because maybe baby.

Because maybe I am the stupidest person who has ever lived.

When I open the door to my apartment, it's almost ten p.m.

Fin and Max are sitting at the kitchen table in their underwear, drinking wine and playing poker.

Max shouts, "You're fucking cheating!"

Fin laughs. "Just because you have no idea how to play this game doesn't mean I'm cheating."

I drop my handbag onto the floor in the foyer. They look over at me. Their eyes widen.

Max says, "Oh shit."

Fin says, "Hun. What happened? Are you okay?"

I burst into tears again, because that's just how my day is going.

"Okay, wait. Rewind. *Luteal phase*? What man on earth knows what the heck the luteal phase is? I didn't even know, and I own a pair of ovaries!"

Max holds up her phone. She's just queried Siri, who affirmed the definition for us all.

Fin says, "Maybe the study of women's reproductive cycles is one of his hobbies."

Max shoots me a loaded glance. "Or he's been in this situation before."

I groan. "Oh god. He could already have kids for all I know. Hell, he could have a wife! I don't really know anything about him!"

Fin shakes her head. "He doesn't have a wife."

"How can you be sure?"

"Married men are neutered. You can see it in the way they walk. That 'I've-surrendered-my-free-will' slouchy, shuffling walk. They've lost the desire to live. Your Mr. Black walks like a peacock. Like a lion. Very unneutered. Very unmarried. His balls are very much intact."

Max crinkles her nose. "Since when are you such an expert on married men and their balls? Or men at all, for that matter?"

"I'm not in the straight fishbowl. You people can't see each other clearly, but I'm looking in from the outside, an impartial observer. There's a married man walk, an unmarried man walk, and a cheating married man walk. That one is super distinctive. Cocky but also furtive, like a fox slinking away from a henhouse with a dead bird between its teeth."

It's nearly two o'clock in the morning. We've been sitting at the kitchen table for hours, going over everything that's happened since I left. The two of them are drinking wine, but I'm drinking water, trying to pretend that's a completely normal thing for me to do on a Saturday night.

We've already asked Siri how soon a pregnancy test can confirm if a woman is, in fact, pregnant. To my great dismay, it seems that even the most sensitive tests need about eight days from conception to let you know for certain if Hot Gangster, Jr. will be arriving in nine months.

Max looks at me. When she takes my hands across the table and gently squeezes them, I know it's going to be bad.

She says carefully, "Okay. We've never talked about this before, so I don't know how you feel about it, but I'm just going to float the possibility that you do have other options besides keeping the baby. You could have an—"

"No."

Fin and Max are surprised by the vehemence of my answer. I look down at my hands, spread flat on the table, and blow out a breath.

"My mother had this thing about becoming a grandmother. Somebody asked her when she was a little girl what she wanted to be when she grew up, and she said she wanted to be a grandmother. That it seemed like the most wonderful thing to be in the world."

I have to take another breath before I go on. "She always

talked about the day I'd have my own baby. How happy she'd be. How she hoped it was a girl. If I ever do have a girl, I'll name her after my mother."

After a moment, Fin says gently, "This is about what *you* want, though. What's good for *you*."

My laugh is dry. "If it turns out that I'm pregnant, it's not about me anymore at all."

Max squeezes my hand and sits back in her chair, smiling at me. "Damn. I never thought I'd be a godmother so young."

Fin scoffs. "Excuse me, but *I'm* going to be the baby's godmother. You can barely tie your own shoes."

I say loudly, "You'll be co-godmothers of the maybe-not-even-actual baby. Now can you please give me a break?"

Max is quiet for a moment, then gasps. "Oh, jeez."

"What?"

She looks at me with big eyes. "Who'll be the god*father*?"

I groan and collapse facedown onto the table.

Fin pats my back reassuringly. "We're getting ahead of ourselves. You're probably going to be fine. In all likelihood, this is just a false alarm."

Max says brightly, "At least we know where to get diapers if we end up needing them."

I groan again, more pathetically.

They put me to bed and tuck me in, cooing and clucking over me like a couple of mother hens. Like I'm a sick child. Like I'm some kind of basket case, a totally lost cause.

Which I suppose I am.

When I wake up in the morning, there's a brief, lovely moment where I don't remember where I am or where I've been or what's happening.

Then I spot the stuffed unicorn pony staring accusingly at me from my dresser across the room, and it all comes flooding back.

I pull the covers over my head and stay in bed for the rest of the day.

~

Like a funeral, Monday arrives.

I go to work. Hank takes one look at my face and laughs. "You look exactly like my sister at about five o'clock every afternoon."

"Your sister with the half-dozen evil Viking banshee children who's forty-two but looks one hundred and two?"

"She's the one."

"Thank you for that."

He leans his forearms over the top of my cubicle and sends me a sympathetic look. "Guess the vacation didn't take, huh?"

I chuckle darkly. "Oh, it took all right. It planted itself right in and took root."

Now Hank looks perturbed. "Not sure how to respond to that, kiddo."

I wave him off. "Forget about it. I've traumatized you enough with my personal life. Anything exciting happen while I was gone?"

He shrugs. "George broke the copy machine again. Sandy and Donna got into a screaming match about *The Real Housewives of Beverly Hills*. At the weekly staff meeting, Rudy launched into an epic rant about Tom Brady leaving the Patriots and joining that obscure Florida team. Whatever their name is."

"The Buccaneers."

"That's the one. Orange jerseys that make 'em look like Creamsicles. Rudy's beside himself. Thinks the whole thing was set up by some anarchist shadow group to sow discontent among the masses and overthrow the government. Oh, and there's a new FedEx delivery guy all the girls are salivating over. If I hear the term 'sex on a stick' one more time, I'm quitting in protest."

"So it was business as usual."

"Yup." He studies me for a moment. "You need to talk?"

"I need a time machine so I can go back to before I was a dumbass."

He gazes at me, laughter shining in his eyes. "So many jokes."

"I know. You're showing amazing restraint. Now please go away so I can try to work."

"'Try' being the operative word." He raps his knuckles on the top of the cubicle. "I'm here if you need me."

I swallow around the lump forming in my throat. "Thanks, Hank."

"Anytime, kiddo."

He turns and walks into his office, leaving me with a searing mental image of Killian's face when I thanked him for saving my life. He said the same thing Hank just did. *"Anytime."*

I know it's first thing Monday morning, but I could really use a drink.

It hits me that if I actually am pregnant, I'm not going to be able to have a drink for nine months. I almost burst into tears again, but manage to control myself.

Barely.

A week goes by. I don't hear from Killian. I don't call him, either. The big black SUVs are still parked in front of the apartment, changing every few hours in shifts, but he isn't one of the men who arrives to sit and watch over us.

I buy six pregnancy tests and take three, knowing it's too early but unable to stop myself.

They're all negative. That does nothing for my peace of mind.

I go to the bank, take out the safety deposit box, and stare at the diamond necklace. I run my fingers over the coldly glittering stones, wondering if they used to belong to someone my maybe-baby daddy killed.

I develop a nasty case of insomnia.

Then, the following Tuesday, something crosses my desk that stops me cold.

It's an article in the digital edition of the newspaper. A small article, three pages deep, about an elderly man living in obscurity in a small town in Arizona who went to the grocery store one morning and wound up in jail a few days later, charged with multiple crimes committed many years ago.

According to the prosecutor, the man was a former mafia member who'd vanished without a trace thirty years prior. His family and associates thought him dead, the victim of a contract killing. But he'd been living out West all these years under an assumed name, quietly going about his business.

It wasn't so much the man himself that got my attention, but the way he was caught.

An informant identified him.

Another former mafia member, now on the police payroll and working undercover, happened to be in that particular grocery store on that particular morning, buying cigarettes. He was on a driving trip from New York to California to visit his only grand-child, his crippling fear of flying keeping him off a plane.

Former mafioso number two saw former mafioso number one at the checkout, and the rest, as they say, was history.

I stare at the article with my heart racing like mad in my chest, reading it over and over. One word keeps jumping out at me.

Informant.

I grab a yellow legal pad from the top drawer of my desk and hastily scribble a list.

- Secrets
- Mafia
- Different name
- Access to FBI database
- Access to air force satellite
- Scary good background checks
- No personal artifacts in residence
- Geo-location device in business cards
- Arrested on multiple felony charges but quickly let go
- "He's doing important work."
- "There are too many lives at stake to take that risk."

I add *Shakespeare buff* and *annoyingly arrogant*, but cross them out because they don't matter.

Then I sit back in my chair, stunned.

It blows over me like nuclear fallout. An atomic mushroom cloud, raining toxic ash.

Killian Black is working with the federal government.

He made a deal with the FBI to keep himself out of prison. He's an informant on the mafia.

My maybe-baby daddy is a snitch.

"Holy shit," I say aloud, causing a girl walking past my cubicle to look at me strangely.

I don't care. I'm in the middle of something too big to give a damn what anyone thinks about me right now.

And I have to admit, my idea makes total sense.

He was arrested on multiple felony charges but let go the same day. He says cryptic things about how he's helping people, and that there are too many lives at stake to trust me first. He has access to all kinds of technology that regular people don't—I mean, who puts a biometric fingerprint scanner on their friggin' computer?

Someone who's working for the government, that's who.

All the puzzle pieces finally come together, so I see the whole picture at last.

I'm so stunned, I'm numb. I can't feel a thing. I don't know if I'm happy, sad, or crushingly disappointed. I've got an abandoned Western town of tumble weeds and rutted mud roads inside me, with empty buildings and no signs of life except for the vultures picking over bleached bones.

My desk phone rings. I answer with something that could be, "Huh?" but I'm not sure because my brain isn't working.

"Hullo, lass."

His voice is low, but it's enough to make every cell in my body wake up from their comas.

I hunch over my desk, clutching the phone to my ear, my heart pounding like mad. "*You.*"

There's a pause, then Killian says, "Aye. Me. Who were you expecting?"

Though he can't see me, I wave my hand frantically in the air to dismiss the small talk. Speaking in a combination of a whisper and a hiss, I say, "I figured it out!"

His voice sharpens. "Figured what out?"

I open my mouth to answer, but realize with a cold snap of fear that it might not be in my best interests to let him know what I know. In fact, this call might even be being recorded. The FBI could be listening in on all his communications.

Then something else—something far worse—occurs to me.

What if this hot pursuit of his hasn't been about me at all?

What if the romantic gestures and Shakespeare quotes and aching vulnerability have all been part of an act, part of a much bigger web designed to catch a much bigger spider than me?

A spider, for instance, like my father.

"I'll handle your father. I'll ask him permission to marry you, and we'll work it all out."

Those were his exact words. His exact insane, ridiculous words.

All his insistence that I trust him, that we tell each other nothing but the truth, that I give in to our intense chemistry and "let it be," *that I tell him I belong to him*…all of it could be with the ultimate goal of getting closer to me so he could get closer to Antonio Moretti.

Because how better to bring down the head of the New York mafia than by using his own daughter to get to him?

I see it all in horrifying, crystal clear Technicolor, like a movie playing on a screen inside my head.

He gets me to fall in love with him. He gets me pregnant. He insists on arranging a reunion with my father, insists that we should patch things up…then he slithers in like a snake into the heart of my family and hands us all to the government on a platter.

Bugs. Surveillance. Tracking devices. He'd deploy all his specialties to catch my father and his associates in his trap.

And I'm just collateral. A means to an end.

A tool to be used and discarded like a dirty Kleenex.

A strangled noise rises from my throat. I think I'm going to be sick all over my desk.

Killian says, "Juliet?"

I slam down the receiver, disconnecting the call, and sit there staring at it, shaking.

The baby. Oh my god. What if I'm pregnant?

What have I done?

I think back to the first time I saw him in the bar at La Fiesta the night we stole the truckload of diapers from him. I remember the look on his face.

That smug, self-satisfied look.

How he and his FBI buddies must have laughed at my

stupidity. After all, it was me who started the ball rolling. I broke into his warehouse. What a gift that was to them! What a fantastic turn of events! They'd probably been trying to find a way to bring down my father for years, and there I came, waltzing in like an oblivious idiot, the perfect solution to their problem.

I remember every time Killian looked deep into my eyes as he made love to me, and an animal sound of anguish breaks from my chest.

I barely make it down the hall and into a stall in the restroom before I throw up.

26

JULES

I manage to get through the rest of the day at work. My desk phone rings intermittently, but I always let it go to voicemail. No one ever leaves a message, but I know who it is.

I throw my cell phone into the trash chute at the office, smashing the SIM card before I do. On the drive home, I pick up another at a kiosk inside the mall, along with a pre-paid card for minutes.

Back at the apartment, Max is home but Fin is still out. I put my finger to my lips and point at the ceiling, making a circular motion in the air with a finger. She nods, goes into her room, and returns with an electronic device that sweeps the place for bugs.

When the sweep comes up clean, she looks at me. "You know I do this twice a week already, right?"

"Make it twice a day from now on. I'm not taking any chances."

She examines my face. "You okay?"

"No, but I don't want to talk about it. Just assume for the time being that we're under heavy surveillance. Get a new

229

phone, new email address, new everything. Wipe your hard drive. Burn anything incriminating. We're going full dark."

"We've been on full dark since you started dating GQ Gangster," she says gently.

"Oh. Really?"

She nods. "If anyone's on the cops' radar, it's him. So yeah, really. If they decide to take a look inside this apartment, we're squeaky clean."

I heave a sigh of relief. At least one of us has her head screwed on straight. "Okay, great. Thank you."

I give her a hug, then head downstairs to go have a talk with the driver of one of the black SUVs.

When I knock on the window, it's the handsome one named Declan who rolls it down.

"Well, isn't this a nice surprise," he says, smirking. "Good to see you, Your Royal Highness."

I decide to skip the pleasantries, because I hate his boss. "I'm gonna need you guys to clear out. Right now."

Declan raises his dark brows and looks me up and down, his baby blue eyes sparkling with amusement. "I'm sorry, were you operating under the mistaken impression that you're in charge here?"

I anticipated that. Gangsters aren't generally known for being accommodating.

"If you're not gone in two minutes, I'll call Channel 5 News and tell them that Killian Black has some SUVs filled with mobsters parked on Mount Vernon street and give them the license plate numbers. Maybe they'd like to ask you a few questions about your boss's unusual and abrupt release from federal custody last year."

Declan's smile vanishes. I think he's angry about the threat, but then he says with quiet astonishment, "He told you his real name."

"He told me *a* name. I have no idea if it's the real one or not."

"Oh, it's the real one, lass," says Declan, gazing at me with furrowed brows. He doesn't look as if he approves of this development.

"If you're worried I'll tell anyone, don't be. I don't care if he wants to call himself Jabba the Hutt. I don't care about anything to do with him at all. I just want you guys to leave. And stay gone."

Declan cocks his head and narrows his eyes at me. From his jacket pocket, he produces a pack of cigarettes. He shakes one out, sticks it between his lips, puts the cigarettes back into his pocket, and fishes a Zippo out of another pocket.

Then he lights his smoke, all the while staring at me like I'm an interesting but untrustworthy riddle.

"You're upset."

"And you're a genius. Now leave."

"What did he do?"

When I sigh heavily, rolling my eyes, Declan says, "Because if anyone knows how he can be, it's me."

I say drily, "That's a fascinating tidbit of information. Bye now."

I turn to walk away, but Declan calls out, "I've never seen him like this before, lass. He's crazy about you."

I stop in my tracks, my face heating instantly. I whirl around and send Declan a murderous glare. "Tell your boss I'm not as dumb as he thinks I am. And that he can go to hell." I laugh darkly. "And that I got my period. That should pop his scheming little bubble."

I walk up the apartment steps with my head held high and my heart breaking.

When I get back inside, I head to my room and close the door. I stand by the window, looking out at the street, until both SUVs pull away. I'm a little surprised, but if Declan told Killian what I said, maybe he'll leave me alone now. Maybe he'll find some other girl to seduce and lie to.

Hopefully, she's smarter than me and will take pruning shears to his balls.

I get another pregnancy test from the bag in the top drawer of my dresser, then go into the bathroom and pee onto the little white stick.

I sit on the toilet for two minutes that feel like two hours, staring at the damn thing.

I release the breath I'd been holding when the results are negative.

But I still haven't had my period, and it was due yesterday.

Nine days after I had unprotected sex.

One day after the earliest the test could possibly detect pregnancy hormones.

I go to bed early with a bad feeling the rest of the week is going to be a nightmare.

I wake up in the middle of the night with the distinct sense that someone else is in the room with me.

I don't move or give any indication I'm awake. I just lie on my side, facing the wall, listening hard over the drumbeat of my pulse. The room is dark and silent. *Where did I leave my knife?*

"If you're looking for your knife, it's on the bathroom sink. Next to the pregnancy test wrapper."

The voice is low, calm, and unmistakable. My blood turns to fire in my veins.

I sit up abruptly, turn on the light on the nightstand, and stare at Killian sitting with one leg casually crossed over the other in an armchair across the room.

He's in his Armani power suit. The one he wears like a suit

of armor. The one that makes him look elegant and dangerous, a hungry tiger dressed in a gentleman's clothes.

His eyes are dark and glittering. Not even a hint of warmth softens the hard angles of his face.

I say, "Get out."

"No."

We stare at each other. My hands begin to shake. My mouth goes bone dry. "What do you want?"

"You. But you already know that."

He's deadly serious. Feeling vulnerable, I pull the sheets over my chest. I'm wearing a short cotton nightgown and nothing else.

Watching every minute change of expression on my face, he says, "So we're not pregnant."

We. I could kill him. "No, *I'm* not pregnant."

Gazing steadily at me, he drums his fingers slowly on the arm of the chair. A muscle slides in his jaw. I sense his frustration and disappointment, but I don't know if it's directed at me or at what I've just told him.

"If you don't believe me, go look at the test yourself. It's in the trashcan in the bathroom."

"I know where it is."

The stare-off continues. The room feels as if it's too hot. Too close. I'm starting to sweat. I'm definitely starting to get claustrophobic.

"I want you to leave. I don't have anything to say to you."

A faint, dangerous smile curves the corners of his mouth. He says softly, "Don't you?"

I curl the sheets in my hands to try to control their shaking. "No, I don't. And I'm not interested in your games. So whatever this is—"

"I don't like it when you lie to me. I want to know why you're doing it now."

My skin feels like it's on fire. At any moment, my nightgown and the sheets and the bed itself are going to burst into flames. "I don't care what you like or don't like. And I don't owe you any explanations. About anything."

His voice drops. His eyes burn. The slow, steady drum of his fingers on the arm of the chair continues. "You owe me the truth, thief. If nothing else, you promised me that."

"You're the one who walked out of that motel room, not me."

His eyes flare. For a brief moment, his fingers fall still. Then he exhales and resumes the slow, steady drumming.

I know that if I were a man, I'd be shitting myself in fright right now. It's obvious he's controlling his temper by sheer force of will.

But I'm not afraid of him. This is my house. He can go back to whatever rock he crawled out from under.

"Get out."

"We've already been over that. I'm not going anywhere until you tell me why you're lying to me." He narrows his eyes. "And what you meant when you said 'I figured it out.' And also what you meant when you told Declan you're smarter than I think you are."

"Exactly that."

When I don't offer more, he stands. He stares down at me with half-lowered lids and slowly unbuttons his suit jacket.

I remember how he told me he'd take me over his knee if I lied to him again, and my heart explodes in panic.

"Don't you dare," I whisper, scooching closer to the wall.

"Why, little thief. You look frightened. Whatever is it you think I'm going to do?"

He's mocking me, the son of a bitch. Stepping toward the bed like he's got all the time in the world, his smile small and his movements leisurely.

Anger gives me wings.

I leap to my feet on the mattress, throw down the sheets, and holler, "Get the hell out of my house, you arrogant bastard!"

His small smile turns to a dangerous grin. "There's my hell-cat," he says in a pleased, husky voice, still advancing. "I wondered how long it would take for the claws to come out."

He whips off his jacket and tosses it to the floor.

He lunges for me.

I yelp and jump to one side, but he's too fast. He catches me easily, grabbing me in the steel vise of his arms, and takes us down to the mattress.

He lands on top of me, pins my arms over my head, and gives me his full weight, trapping me.

I don't bother trying to struggle. I'd probably just dislocate something, and it wouldn't work anyway. He's far too strong for me to escape. So I simply lie underneath him, breathing hard and glaring up into his smug, handsome face.

Looking down at me, he says, "You are, by far, the most beautiful goddamn woman I've ever seen in my life."

"And you are, by far, the worst liar I've ever met. You should get a trophy. Biggest Bullshitter Alive."

"So *angry*," he breathes, moistening his lips.

Crap. I'm turning him on. What's worse is that his scent is in my nose and his big hard body is all over me, pinning me down, reminding me exactly how good it feels to have him inside me.

"What have I done now to incur your wrath? Aside from honoring your request to leave you alone, that is."

"Oh, look, he's talking like a dictionary again."

He puts his mouth next to my ear. "Would you prefer I tell you how much I want to shove my cock deep into that sweet cunt of yours and fuck you until you forget how much you hate me?"

I growl at him through gritted teeth, but it only makes him chuckle.

"I didn't think so. You probably don't want me to tell you how this past week has been a living hell for me, either." He chuckles again, inhaling against my neck. "Or maybe you do.

Maybe you'd love to know how I haven't been able to eat. Or sleep. Or do anything but think about you."

His voice drops to a whisper. "Tell me you missed me, too. It almost killed me not seeing you."

"What doesn't kill you, disappoints me."

"Tell me you thought about me."

"I did. It reminded me to take out the garbage."

He laughs. It's a deep, satisfied, masculine laugh that really makes me want to gouge his eyes out.

"Okay, thief. Now tell me the truth: what did you mean on the phone when you said you figured it out?"

I turn my head, refusing to look at him.

When he presses a gentle kiss to the sensitive spot underneath my earlobe, I close my eyes. "That's not going to work."

He murmurs, "I'll have to do better, then."

He brushes his lips slowly up and down the length of my neck, trailing the tip of his tongue over my skin as lightly as possible.

I force myself to suppress a shudder.

"No? Hmm. How about this?"

He gently sucks on my throat. It sends a starburst of pleasure zinging through me, but I lie still and silent, hating that he can make me feel so much when all I want him to do is drop dead.

Against my pelvis, his erection throbs. He presses his hips into mine, gently sucking my earlobe. I have to bite my lip to keep silent.

When he moves down from my throat to my chest and nuzzles his nose against my nipple, I can't help the gasp that slips from my lips.

He whispers, "Your nipples are hard, thief."

"It's cold in here. Get off me."

"Tell me the truth, and I will."

He gently kisses my nipple, then sucks on it through the cotton, drawing it into the wet heat of his mouth. I don't tell him to stop, because it feels too good, but also because emotion is fighting its way up my throat, silencing me.

He's using me. I know it, but I'm a fool because it all feels so real.

When I drag in a hitching breath, he raises his head. His hands are big enough that they can trap both my wrists. He keeps me pinned down with one hand but takes my jaw in the other and turns my face toward his.

"Open your eyes."

"No."

Very gently, he kisses me. "Baby. Open your eyes for me."

My voice comes out hoarse. "If you call me baby again, I will make it my mission in life to destroy you."

He's still for a moment. I can tell he's searching my face, but I refuse to look at him. Then, in one swift, surprising movement, he rolls onto his back and takes me with him.

He clasps his arms around my body and holds me against him, cupping a hand around the back of my head. We're chest to chest, belly to belly, thighs on top of thighs, our bodies in alignment. I know he won't let me go, so I simply hide my face in his neck and lie on top of him, struggling to regulate my breathing.

He exhales a heavy breath. "Whatever it is you think you figured out, you're wrong."

"Of course you'd say that."

"Try me. What's this theory of yours?"

"I'm not telling you anything."

He squeezes me, pressing a kiss to my hair, then exhales again. "All right."

I don't know what to say to that. I lie in silence, wondering what new tactic this is and hating myself for liking what a comfortable mattress he makes, until he says softly, "For the record, I think you'll make an amazing mother someday."

I choke back a sob and pound a fist onto his big, stupid chest.

He whispers, "Violent, but amazing."

"Stop talking. Please stop talking. My heart can't take much more of this."

He gives me another squeeze and mercifully shuts up.

He holds me like that, cradling my head and rubbing slow circles over my back, until I can breathe easily again. Under my ear, his heart beats a slow, steady thump.

I whisper, "This isn't right, what you're doing. I'm a person, not a Kleenex."

His hand on my back falls still. "I'm aware that you're not a Kleenex. What the hell does that even mean?"

"It means that I have feelings. I'm not…" I suppress a sob. "I'm not something to be used and thrown away."

His body is completely frozen for a few seconds. Except for his heart, which has started pounding, every part of him is still.

Then he rolls me onto my back, rises up on an elbow, and takes my face in his hand. His eyes blaze with emotion. His voice is urgent and rough.

"I swear to you, I'm *not* using you. What would possibly make you think that?"

My god. The man is an exquisite liar. Oh, now I remember: he said acting didn't come until after he turned to a life of crime.

He should win a damn Oscar for this performance.

When I don't answer him, he says, "Everything I've done and said til now, every single word I've spoken to you has been the truth."

I groan, closing my eyes.

He grips my face more tightly, leans closer to my ear. "*Every fucking word*, Juliet. Goddammit. Where is this coming from?"

"Just go," I whisper, miserable. "Please just try to find one tiny bit of decency inside you and leave me alone. Forever."

He's breathing hard, holding my face like he's never going to release it. "I'm not going anywhere until you tell me what the hell this is about."

"No. Go!"

"Look at me."

"No."

He roars, "Stop fucking hiding!"

That does it. All my sad self-pity evaporates like two fingers snapping and is instantly replaced with thermonuclear rage.

I open my eyes and let him see every ounce of my fury.

But somehow my voice stays eerily, coldly calm.

"*You're* the one who's hiding, Killian Black. Liam Black. Whoever you are. *You're* the one with secrets. *You're* the one with an agenda here, not me."

"What agenda?" he says angrily. "What are you *talking* about?"

I'm so frustrated by this farce that it just comes out. I shout it right into his face.

"I know you're a narc, so you can cut the shit now, okay?"

He blinks. His brows draw together. Cocking his head, he stares at me in what looks like sincere confusion. "You think I'm a narcotics agent?"

"No! A narc, like a police informant! You made a deal to stay out of prison and now you're on the cops' payroll!"

After a beat of astonished silence, he starts to laugh.

He rolls off me and lies on his back, gripping his stomach and laughing heartily up at the ceiling like I've just told him the funniest joke in the world.

I jump off the bed and stand staring at him, my arms folded over my chest. "Admit it. You're using me to get to my father."

He laughs harder. His face is turning red.

I go into my closet, pick up the nearest shoe, then go back into the bedroom and throw it at him. It hits his tree trunk of a thigh. He ignores it. He's too busy laughing.

I have to shout to make sure he can hear me over all the noise. "Keep it up and I'll use your fat head for target practice, you jerk!"

He finally gets control of himself, sighing in pleasure and

wiping his eyes. Then he rises from the bed, picks up his suit jacket from the floor, and slings it over his broad shoulders.

Smiling warmly at me, he says, "Thank you for that. I haven't laughed like that in…" He pauses, thinking. "Ever."

He crosses to me and kisses my forehead. With a finger crooked under my chin, he tilts my head up and looks into my angry eyes. His own are warm and soft.

"My offer still stands, lass: tell me you're mine and mean it, and I'll tell you everything. Until then, keep guessing. I can use the laughs."

He turns around and walks out my bedroom door.

27

JULES

*W*hen I get up in the morning to use the toilet, the water in the bowl is red.

My period has arrived.

My initial reaction isn't what I expected. I assumed I'd feel a huge wave of relief, like a weight had been lifted. That does come, but first there's an uncertain pang of melancholy, a faint sense that I lost something important I wasn't sure I wanted in the first place.

When I relay that to Fin, she looks at me in surprise. "That's called ambivalence, hun."

"Ambivalence." A word that could be used to sum up my entire relationship with Killian Black.

That or "insanity."

I go to work in a fog of confusion. I almost liked it better when I was so sure Killian was using me. At least that felt definite. Painful, but definite. But now I'm back where I started, wandering blindly in a maze.

I suppose he could've been putting me on, but boy, that laughter felt real. It *was* real. He thought my idea that he was an informant for the police was hysterical.

When I get home from work that evening, the big black SUVs are parked back out front. Seeing me in the apartment window, Declan sends me a jaunty salute. I answer with the royal wave like the Queen of England does, all stiff wrist and superiority. He laughs, shaking his head.

Who are these jolly, laughing gangsters? In what upside-down universe am I living?

More importantly, what am I supposed to do now?

Two weeks go by. Nothing out of the ordinary happens. I don't hear from Killian, but I don't attempt to contact him, either. Once, a police cruiser pulls alongside one of the SUVs on the street outside. It lingers for less than thirty seconds, then drives away, never to be seen again.

I figure Mrs. Lieberman downstairs finally called the cops. They arrived, discovered who they were dealing with, then immediately left.

Not who they were dealing with…what.

But *what*? WHAT?

I become obsessed with finding out what Killian's hiding. Every day at work, I spend hours crawling the internet for clues. Any story that mentions Killian or Liam Black. Any photographs. Any anything. But there's nothing to be found.

Even the reports of his arrest last year have vanished. As have all of his corporations listed in the Massachusetts Secretary of State database.

It's like he doesn't exist.

Like he's a ghost, arriving to haunt me then disappearing without a trace.

Needless to say, I'm deeply unsettled by all this. At one point, I'm so desperate for an explanation I even consider that he might be a time-traveler or an alien sent on a fact-finding mission from outer space.

It's good that I'm not pregnant. Considering the amount of wine that I'm consuming, my poor fetus would be pickled.

~

"So when are we gonna start planning our next job? I'm ready for some excitement."

I snort at Max's question. "Right. Because our last one went so well."

Fin says, "It did go well. Just because you slipped and fell onto a gangster's magical dick right after doesn't mean it didn't go well."

We're at the kitchen table on a weekday night, eating the lasagna I made to distract myself from hurling my body onto the hood of Declan's black SUV and screaming at him to tell me where Killian is.

I could call the man himself to find out, but that would require admitting that I want to know.

Max says, "What about a politician? There are a lot of sleazy politicians we could hit."

Fin says, "They don't have the right assets."

"They've got lots of assets. Stocks, bonds, yachts. You name it."

"Are we going to steal a yacht and park it in front of an orphanage? I don't think so."

I say, "I'm not in the right head space yet to plan another job."

They glance at each other, then look at me. Fin says, "Head space. Right."

"Oh, for god's sake, don't take a tone with me."

"Tone?" she says innocently, looking around as if for support from an invisible crowd of onlookers. "I didn't take a tone."

"You totally took a tone."

"Max, did I take a tone?"

Max makes a face at her. "Your tones are about as subtle as a sledgehammer. You took a big, fat tone, and you know it."

I say, "Thank you."

Fin shrugs and swallows a bite of food. "So I took a tone. Sue me."

"My point, if anyone's interested, is that I don't have the concentration right now that it would take to plan a job. I can't think about anything but…"

Max smiles. "The gangster's magical dick. By the way, you never did spill the tea about that. How big is it?"

I say with a straight face, "Two, maybe three inches."

"Bitch. It's a total fatty, isn't it? C'mon, don't be stingy. Give us all the details. Cut? Uncut? Shaved balls? Pierced head? There's a reason he's got such mad swagger, and it's his giant eggplant, right?"

"Max, I can't believe I have to say this to you, but you really need to get laid."

She waves a hand around dismissively. "Stop trying to change the subject."

Fin sighs. "I'm eating here, people. I don't want to hear anything about anybody's dick. I'm liable to gag on my lasagna."

"You're the one who brought the subject up in the first place."

"And now I'm closing the subject. The end."

We eat in silence for a while, until I say quietly, "Huge. *Huge.*"

Everyone freezes. I look at Fin. "Sorry."

Max hoots. "I knew it! You came home from your little vacay walking like you'd just spent two weeks on a dude ranch breaking in stallions. Ha!" She slaps the table. "Good for you, girl!"

Fin curls her lip in distaste. "Ugh. Just the thought of a veiny, purple, engorged cock bobbing in my face makes me want to barf."

I start laughing so hard I almost choke.

Max says sourly, "Thanks for that. Next time I see a dick up close, I'll be thinking of you."

Fin says sweetly, "Why, Max. How nice. Next time I see a B movie where everyone dresses like rodeo clowns, I'll be thinking of *you*."

"Oh, you think you're such a stunner, huh? You look like something I drew with my left hand."

I say, "Girls." They ignore me.

Max says, "Bite me."

"I would, but I don't want to have to get a tetanus shot."

I say brightly, "Okay. That was fun. Is everyone ready to go back into their cages now?"

Max sticks out her tongue at Fin, who looks at the ceiling, shaking her head.

I say, "Between the three of us, I figure we've got half a brain. So I need your help figuring out something."

They look at me. I lean my elbows on the table and prop my chin in my hands. "What do these things add up to? Secrets. Charisma. Surveillance skills. Computer skills. Undetectable access into buildings and locked rooms."

Max says, "Me."

Fin says, "Me."

I roll my eyes. "Let me finish. Advanced technology. A loyal army of soldiers. A mythical reputation but no verifiable evidence of existence on paper."

Max says, "Batman."

Fin says, "Lisbeth Salander."

"Both of those are loners. They don't have armies of loyal soldiers. Pay attention."

Max raises her hand. "I have a question."

"Of course you do. What is it?"

"Is there gonna be a test at the end? Because I missed some of the first part."

Sighing, I continue. "Ruthlessness. Intelligence. Sophistication. Vast sums of money. A gigantic ego. Excellent skills with firearms. A complete lack of fear. Incredible style. Magnificent hair."

Fin snaps her fingers. "A supervillain."

Max chuckles. "Or a psychopath."

"Maybe both. But seriously, if you put all those characteristics together in one person…what do you get?"

They think for a moment, until Fin says, "A real person? Like, not a comic book superhero?"

"Yeah."

She lifts a shoulder. "The head of the CIA."

"No," says Max instantly. "That guy looks like a dentist. He has orthopedic shoes and an overbite. No style, charisma, or magnificent hair."

"Let's hear your idea, then."

"I don't have one. I'm just pointing out that yours sucks."

They bicker back and forth, but I've already stopped listening. I rise and go stand at the windows, looking down onto the street.

Looking down onto the big SUVs with the shiny rims and blacked-out windows, filled with armed men in suits.

"The head of the CIA." Fin's words echo over and over inside my skull.

Maybe I had it backward when I thought Killian worked for the police.

Maybe they're working for him.

Maybe *everyone's* working for him.

Maybe he's much more powerful than I thought.

Or maybe I should get drunk and have a séance with the ghost of Pippi Longstocking, my beloved childhood cat, because I'm already hallucinating anyway.

The next day at work, I Google "Head of the CIA."

Clicking on a link, I'm taken to a Wikipedia page where I learn that the Director of the Central Intelligence Agency is a petite brunette woman named Gina who looks like a middle school teacher.

She doesn't appear ruthless, sophisticated, or as if she possesses any skills with firearms. She does, however, look like she can crochet a rather excellent throw pillow and has perfected a recipe for tender and flavorful meatloaf.

I'm filled with disappointment.

I decide to abandon my shiny new conspiracy theory that Killian is Secret Boss of Everything. If he were in any way related to government work, he wouldn't own so many Armani suits. Not to mention, he wouldn't be a bazillionaire who lives in a skyscraper. He'd probably have a 401(k) and a great dental plan, but that's about it.

So I'm back to square one. All I have to go on is that he's sexy, rich, arrogant, mysterious, and a champ at performing oral sex.

I give serious consideration to the idea that his whole cloak-and-dagger, not-who-but-what, I'm-helping-people-too routine is a bag of baloney, and he's just getting his kicks by messing with my head. That he's nothing more than a mobster with delusions of grandeur.

It's the simplest explanation. Especially considering that gargantuan ego of his.

But somehow it doesn't fit.

What's with the accents?

What's with the Shakespeare?

What's with hacking a satellite? I mean, *who the fuck knows how to hack a satellite?*

This whole thing is exhausting.

On the way home from work, I decide to treat myself to dinner. I'm not in the mood to play referee between Fin and Max again, so I stop at a little Italian place that makes lasagna almost as good as mine.

I sit down and order a glass of red wine and a plate of spaghetti Bolognese from the elderly Italian waiter. Then I settle into my chair and look around at the charming décor.

Just as I'm lifting my glass to take a sip of the wine, I happen to look out the front window.

And there, on the street outside, is Killian.

With a woman.

A very pregnant woman.

She's in his arms. He's tenderly kissing her.

One hand cradles her face, the other caresses her swollen belly.

I turn to stone. Every muscle in my body clenches. I'm unable to breathe or move or even blink as I stare at them out on the sidewalk.

She's young and pretty, about my age. Brunette like me, too. She gazes up at him with stars in her eyes. He stares down at her, smiling.

God, how it hurts. How it *burns*.

I don't recall ever feeling pain like this. It's like acid eating down through my flesh to dissolve my bones. I'm breathless with it. I'm about to explode from it. I'm dying, one agonized heartbeat at a time.

In a moment, they move off, walking arm in arm down the street until they pass out of my line of vision. But I remain frozen, my wine glass clenched in my hand, hot tears pooling in the corners of my eyes.

He swore he wasn't using me. He looked deep into my eyes and said every word he'd ever told me had been the truth.

He told me he thought I'd make an amazing mother.

When the waiter arrives at the table with my entrée, it breaks the spell I'm under. I set the glass down carefully, my hands shaking hard. I take money from my purse and leave it on the table, then I rise and walk blindly to my car.

My heart pounds. My skin turns clammy. My stomach is in knots. I know I'm hyperventilating, but I can't help it. The world looks fuzzy around the edges, as if I might be about to pass out.

Pregnant. She's pregnant with his baby. Like I almost was.

I feel like such a fool. Like such a stupid, naïve child. I feel like I could get sick and never stop throwing up, as if my body wants to purge all my organs.

Especially my dumb heart.

Because if I'd been able to delude myself until now, seeing him with her—his wife? Mistress? Another blind idiot like me? —has proven with sickening clarity just how much I actually care for him.

Though I tried not to, though I resisted with all my might, I fell for him.

I fell for him hard.

A sob breaks from my chest. I slap a hand over my mouth to smother it. I drive too fast through the city streets, blind and shaking, with no idea where I am or where I'm going, until I screech to a stop in front of a liquor store.

I run inside, panting and wild-eyed, knowing I look like a lunatic but not caring.

"I'll ask your father for permission to marry you."

"You idiot," I whisper, stumbling down an aisle. "You knew he was bad. A liar. You knew it. And look at you now."

I grab a big bottle of tequila off a shelf and turn around, heading for the exit.

"You let him seduce you. You let him fuck you. *You let him in.*"

I shove open the glass door and stumble outside, the bottle of tequila clutched against my chest like a lifejacket. I can't think of anything else I want to do more than get shitfaced. I need to block it all out, all this pain and shame, this horrible rage.

This jealousy.

I've never felt anything like this jealousy. It feels like I'm being stabbed in the heart, over and over, from the inside.

His hand gently cradling her swollen belly...I'll never forget that image for the rest of my life.

I yank open my car door. I'm about to jump in, but someone pulls me away, shouting.

"What?" I spin around, disoriented.

A man is shouting at me. In Korean, so I have no idea what he's saying. But he's shouting angrily at me and pulling at my arm, jerking at it, and like a slap on the face I realize what's happening.

I left the store without paying for the tequila.

"Oh. Sorry! I'm so sorry, I didn't mean—wait, my purse—I'll get money—"

Then I realize I must have left my purse at the restaurant, because it isn't inside the car.

The Korean shop owner is still screaming at me. A small crowd has gathered on the sidewalk, looking at me with various expressions ranging from curiosity to disdain. I try to back away, to explain that it's all a mistake and I'll pay for the bottle, of course I'll pay for it, but now the Korean guy is shouting, "Thief! Thief!" and things are starting to get ugly.

A few spectators have their cell phones out. They're videoing.

A big guy says loudly, "Call the cops."

Another guy says, "She's trying to get away!"

"No! I'm not! This is all a misunderstanding!" But I'm backing away, trying to yank my arm out of the shopkeeper's hard grip, and I know exactly how it looks.

Then someone grabs me from behind, the crowd starts hollering, and everything goes to shit.

28

JULES

*T*he cop who books me smells like soup.

Not a good kind of soup, but something with a funky, sour note, like feet. I get fingerprinted, have my mug shot taken, am frisked and asked about gang affiliations and communicable diseases, then I'm brought to a holding cell and told to stay put.

"When can I make my phone call?" I ask the cop.

"Soon as I work up the energy to give a shit." He ambles off.

I'm alone in the cell. I sit on the hard metal bench against the cement wall and try to ignore the dark yellow stain on the floor in the corner.

An hour goes by. Then two. By the third hour, I'm beginning to wonder if there's a police strike happening, because no one has come to see me. For a small crime like petty theft, I should be able to post bail and get out right away. They don't have reason to keep me indefinitely.

But hour after hour goes by and no one comes.

Finally, about four o'clock in the morning, a new cop unlocks my cell. He's big, with a shaved head and scary eyes. I decide not to take him to task for the delay and quietly follow him out of the cell and down the hallway.

He turns to an unmarked door and ushers me into a small room. The only furniture in the room is two metal chairs and a dented metal desk with nothing on it. He points at one of the chairs.

"Sit."

I look around, baffled. The room looks exactly like one of those interrogation rooms from the movies. It's stark white with bare cement walls, except for the one with dark reflective glass that people are definitely lurking behind.

"What's going on?"

He says, "*Sit.*" It sounds like, "Ask me one more question and I'll rip off your eyebrows."

I sit.

He leaves, slamming the door behind him. A camera up in the corner near the ceiling stares at me with a red, unblinking eye.

After a few minutes, I turn to the dark glass wall. "Seriously? It was a bottle of tequila. Off brand. Are you guys having a slow night or what?"

Nothing happens. More time passes. No one comes.

Just as I'm about to start pounding on the glass and screaming about my rights as an American citizen, the door to the room opens. A woman walks in.

A pregnant woman.

That woman.

She's dressed in a chic black suit that manages to make her belly look less like there's a baby inside it and more like she ate a big dinner. She's carrying a briefcase in one hand and a cup of coffee in the other. She smiles warmly at me.

"Hi, Juliet. I'm Truvy. You can call me Tru. It's so nice to meet y'all."

Her Texas twang is soft and lovely, and I am going to tear her eyes right out of her skull.

Blood throbbing in my cheeks, I say stiffly, "What. The. *Fuck*."

"I can see we'll get along just fine." She laughs. It's a charming laugh. Soft, feminine, and charming. The witch.

She sits in the chair on the opposite side of the desk, sets her briefcase on the floor, pushes the cup of coffee toward me, folds her hands together in her lap, and takes me in.

I mean she really *looks* at me.

And I look at her enormous ruby and diamond ring.

My voice choked, I say, "You're married."

"I am."

I close my eyes, draw in a deep breath, and curse the day I decided to raid that fucking diaper warehouse.

She says, "I'm also your attorney, in case you're wondering."

My eyelids fly open. I stare at her. I never truly understood the word "flabbergasted" until right now.

She knits her brows together. Her eyes are a stunning shade of pale green, like sea glass. She says, "Don't look so surprised. Just because I'm from a tiny shithole town in Texas doesn't mean I can't argue the law. I'll have you know I passed the bar on my first try."

I want to burst out laughing. I also want a flamethrower. "How long have you been married?"

She beams, twisting her wedding ring with her thumb. "Seven months now. We went to the Civil Registry Office the same day we found out we were pregnant."

"So we're not pregnant." I remember Killian's disappointed tone that night he broke into my bedroom and want to retch.

Tru glances up at me. Her eyes are as soft as her voice. "We're having a girl. We're going to name her Maribel, after my mama."

I almost break down and cry then. Almost. I feel the pressure behind my eyes, the sting and the pressure. But I refuse to make more of a fool out of myself than I already have, so I jump to my feet and start pacing.

After a few turns back and forth, I stop and glare at her accusingly. "So, what? He's a bigamist in addition to being a huge asshole and a gigantic liar?"

She blinks.

I press my advantage. "Are you part of a cult? Some nutjob religious group that brainwashes women into becoming sister wives, some bullshit like that?"

She looks to her left, then her right, like she has no idea what's happening and hopes someone will burst in and save her from the crazy woman. "Um…"

I scoff. "Don't play coy with me. He sent you in here. You know exactly who I am."

"Yes," she says carefully. "And I've heard such nice things about you."

I throw my hands in the air and shout, "And you're *okay* with it? *Jesus!*"

"I'm sorry…okay with what?"

My laugh is dark and scarier than the eyes of the cop who put me in here. "Oh, you're screwed up, lady. You need *help*."

She frowns at me, sits up straight in her chair, and snaps, "Actually, *you're* the one who needs help. And I'm here to give it. At four o'clock in the morning, no less. And I do *not* appreciate the snark, or the attitude, or whatever the heck it is you're trying to insinuate."

Instead of tearing all her hair out of her head like I want to, I fold my arms over my chest and stare at her, breathing hard. "I bet he tells you that you're the most beautiful woman he's ever seen, right?"

She says through a tight jaw, "As a matter of fact, he does."

Bastard. If I ever see him again, I'll pluck out all his pubic hair one by one with tweezers, then stuff it up his nose and light it on fire.

"And I bet he gives you lavish gifts. Ridiculously expensive gifts. Jewelry you can't even wear in public because you'd get mugged in ten seconds flat."

She stares at me. Her sea glass eyes are as hard as flint.

I say sarcastically, "Yeah. He's great that way. Sooo generous. Sooo romantic. And what about Shakespeare? I bet he blows that Shakespeare smoke right up your ass, too, doesn't he?"

She cocks her head.

"No? Oh, am I the only special one?" I laugh. I sound unhinged, like I've been mainlining cocaine.

She says, "Hold on a second—"

"And how about those accents, huh?" I cackle. "Oh, god! The Chris Hemsworth is totally my favorite! I mean, James Bond is a close second, but sweet baby Jesus, that Australian accent is the *bomb*, right? I bet he used that one on you the night he got you pregnant."

All my hysterical laughter dies in my throat. I suck in a breath. It comes out as a broken sob.

Tru rises to her feet, pressing a hand over her chest. She says gently, "Oh, sweetie. Oh lord. You think I'm married to Killian, don't you?"

I thunder, "*You just told me you were married to him!*"

She shakes her head. Clucks her tongue. Looks at me with sympathy. She rounds the desk between us and puts her hands on my shoulders. She gazes deep into my eyes.

She says softly, "I'm not married to Killian, sweetie. I'm married to his brother."

It feels like she just punched me in the gut. "But…but I saw you. I *saw* you two, on the street outside the restaurant last night!"

She thinks for a moment, then her eyes widen. "He didn't tell you, did he?" She sighs. "For heaven's sake, that impossible man."

I almost explode when I yell, "*Tell me what?*"

She waits a moment for her hair to settle around her face. "Killian and Liam are identical twins."

Liam.

Killian.

Twins.

All the air is sucked out of the room. My heartbeat flatlines.

Tru smiles at the look on my face and pats my shoulders. "I know. I had exactly that same expression when I found out." She crinkles her nose. "And that's only the tip of the iceberg, I'm afraid."

The sound I make is the same one a cat makes when it's trying to expel a hairball.

"Maybe you should sit back down."

She guides me to the chair then sits across from me again. We stare at each other. I think she's waiting for me to go first.

I say weakly, "Um."

"Liam said he knew the night Killian called to tell him about you that you were the one. He went on and on about how it felt like he was dying from cancer. Or something like that. It probably sounded better when he said it. Anyway, Liam had never heard his brother talk like that about a woman. He's not exactly the settling down type, if you know what I mean. He's never been serious about a woman before. Can you imagine? At his age? Personally, I think it's incredibly romantic. I'm telling you, when the Black boys fall, they fall *hard*."

She laughs her feminine, delightful laugh. "For such alpha wolves, they're just marshmallows when it comes to their women. Oh, I can't wait to get to know you better! I've got three sisters already, but I'd love to have a fourth. What fun we'll have! Y'all will have to come visit us in Argentina as soon as you can."

"Argentina. Um. Uh-huh."

"You poor thing. I've crossed all the wires in your brain, haven't I?" Her voice goes from sympathetic to brisk. "Well, Killian's gonna get an earful from me, I'll tell you what. Here, drink your coffee."

She pushes the cup of coffee closer to me. I pick it up, but can't find the brain power to remember how to drink. I just sit there and stare at her like a big dummy.

"Twins."

Tru nods. "Identical. Nobody can tell them apart except me."

I remember something Killian said to me one night when we were standing in his kitchen. I made a smart comment about his décor, the acres of black marble, and his answer sounded loaded, like there was much more to it beneath the surface.

"It was like this when I moved in."

Then, during the same conversation, he asked me to call him Killian. Not Liam, the name everyone else knew him by. When I asked for an explanation, he said he couldn't tell me.

Not that he didn't want to, but that he couldn't.

And now I find out he and his brother are identical twins.

I say carefully, "Tru?"

"Yes?"

"What does Liam do for work?"

"Oh, he's retired." She smiles mysteriously.

If I thought Killian had secrets in his eyes, this steel magnolia has got him beat by miles.

I drink the coffee in one long gulp, setting the cup on the table when I finish. Unsurprisingly, my hand is shaking.

Tru rests her hand on top of mine. She says softly, "It's Killian's story to tell, not mine. So I'll let him tell it. But I can say this: I was sitting right where you are once. Well, not exactly *right* there. I've never been arrested for stealing cheap tequila—"

I say loudly, "I got it."

"My point is that I know how confused you are, but you can trust him. With anything. With your life."

I whisper, "But he's a gangster."

She leans back in her chair and gives me the secretive eyes thing again. "He's a gangster like you're a thief."

"What does that mean?"

"I told you: it's Killian's story to tell. But, sweetie, if you've been giving him a hard time about his line of work...be prepared to do some apologizing."

"Seriously? Does anyone in your family *not* talk in riddles?"

She laughs. "If you're lucky, pretty soon you'll be talking in riddles, too."

My voice climbs. "*Lucky?*"

She picks up her briefcase and stands, smiling. "C'mon. Let's get you home. I'm sure you can use some sleep. When Killian gets back from Prague tomorrow, he can tell you everything."

"Prague?"

She looks at me with raised brows. "You didn't think he'd send anyone else if he were in the country, did you?"

"I didn't think anything. Because I am no longer capable of comprehensible thought. Because...Killian."

She says drily, "Trust me, I understand."

I rise, blinking, utterly confused. "Didn't you just tell me you lived in Argentina? Or am I hallucinating that, too?"

"We wanted to visit before the baby was born. We arrived last week. And I can't tell you how many times your name has come up in conversation. Killian keeps pestering me for examples of what drives women crazy."

I'm momentarily horrified. "What, like in *bed?*"

"Ha! No. If he's anything like his brother, he's got that covered, I'm sure. He asks about what kinds of things will make a woman want to push a man into traffic."

Relieved, I mutter, "He's got that covered, too."

"I think he's trying to annoy you less."

"I don't think that's humanly possible."

We leave the room and walk down the corridor. I feel like I'm in a dream. A strange, nonsensical dream, featuring car chases, pregnancy scares, gang shootouts, and unicorn ponies.

Tru's already posted my bond, so I just have to complete some paperwork before I'm released. Then I'm following her down the front steps of the police station toward the waiting SUV, still in a fog.

Which is why it takes me longer than it usually would to react when the men step out of the shadows around the side of the building.

They grab me.

I open my mouth to scream, but the chemical-smelling cloth is already smashed over my nose and mouth.

As my legs turn to Jell-O and the world fades to black, one of the men says something to the other in a language I don't recognize.

But I don't have to recognize it to guess that it's Serbian.

29

JULES

When I regain consciousness, I'm lying on my side in the trunk of a moving vehicle. My hands and feet are bound with something, maybe rope. A rough black cloth hood covers my head. I'm barefoot. Except for a splitting headache and some mild soreness on my biceps where the men grabbed me, I'm unharmed.

My first instinct is to scream.

I fight it, concentrating instead on remaining as calm as possible. I breathe in squares to control my panic, as I was trained to do as a child.

Inhale for four counts. Hold it for four counts. Exhale for four counts. Hold it for four counts. Start over again.

There's nothing to be done yet but try to keep track of time. If I can estimate how far the men drive before stopping at the final location they'll hold me, it will help the police search for me later. If I can somehow get that information to the police.

If the men don't kill me first.

Inhale for four counts. Hold it for four counts. Exhale for four counts. Hold it for four counts. Start over again.

I tell myself that it's likely I won't be killed. If the men who took me are with the same Serbian gang that Killian said were looking for collateral in a war with my father, I have value. As long as I'm alive, they can negotiate terms. And to negotiate terms, they'll have to provide proof of life to my father.

He won't just take their word that they have me. Pictures won't do it, either, because they could have been taken any time. Years ago, even.

They're going to have to film me.

Or, worse, put me on the phone with him.

Once they've agreed to terms, my captors will have to produce me—still breathing and in mostly one piece—in order to get what they want.

Unless Daddy Dearest doesn't want me back. Unless he tells them that I'm dead to him already and they can do to me whatever they want.

Inhale for four counts. Hold it for four counts. Exhale for four counts. Hold it for four counts. Start over again.

He'll want me back. It would dishonor the family if he allowed his enemies to harm his only child. It would weaken his reputation. He'll pay what they ask, if only to save face.

Then…oh god.

Then *he'll* have me.

And there's no way in hell he'll ever let me go again.

I'll be locked up. Locked down. Forced to live as a captive. He might even send me away to Italy. To live with the Sicilian side of the family, far out of reach of his enemies in New York.

I'll be married off to one of my brutal, hairy cousins. I'll be forced to have sex with him. Have his children. Cook his meals. Scrub his toilet.

Inhale for four counts. Hold it for four counts. Exhale for four counts. Hold it for four counts. Start over again.

I can't let myself despair. I have to remain positive. Remain calm. Take things one minute at a time. Stay alert and non-combative. Stay alive.

And, no matter what, I can't let myself think about Killian.

I can't think about his beautiful dark eyes and his heart-breaking smile. I can't think about how his voice grows husky when he wants me. I can't think about how he touches me, or how he kisses me, or his incredibly intoxicating combination of masculinity and tenderness. How gentle he is when we make love. How passionately he fucks me.

How he has an identical twin brother.

I definitely can't think about that, even if I wanted to, because my brain keeps bouncing off the possibilities. The *im*possibilities.

The total insanity of what *two* of them could mean.

What they could do.

Who they could really be.

Or what.

The car pulls to a stop. Doors open and slam closed. Heavy footsteps crunch on gravel. The trunk lid opens, and a rush of cool night air blows in. A male voice addresses me in a heavy Eastern European accent.

"Rule number one: be good or I cut something off."

His tone is businesslike. Almost bored. This is the kind of threat he makes regularly. Makes and follows through on.

My heart palpitating, I say, "I'll be good."

I hate myself that it comes out in a whisper.

He grunts his approval. Grabbing me by the upper arm, he hauls me to a sitting position, then roughly up and over the lip of the trunk. My ankles are tied, so I almost fall forward onto my face when my feet hit the ground, but he yanks me upright and steadies me. Sharp, icy gravel cuts into the soles of my bare feet.

He picks me up and throws me over his shoulder.

Though I can't see him through the hood, I can tell he's big. Strong, too. This is no mastermind. No strategist. This is the guy the higher-ups send when they need serious muscle. His arm around my thighs is as hard as steel. He's got an easy, loping walk, like my weight on his shoulder is completely insubstantial.

He's probably used to carrying weight like this a lot.

Dead weight.

Inhale for four counts. Hold it for four counts. Exhale for four counts. Hold it for four counts. Start over again.

We go up steps. His boots make a different sound on wood than they do on gravel. A heavy, hollow sound. He stops for a moment. I hear a metallic clang, then the complaining creak of unoiled hinges. Then it sounds like a large door is being pulled open—no, rolled open from one side.

The pungent, distinct scent of horses and damp hay hits my nose, followed by the fainter scent of fresh water.

We must be in the country. There are no sounds other than the gentle chirping of crickets and tree leaves rustling in the cool breeze. I probably have been unconscious for a long time. I'm far away from the city.

If anyone's looking, they'll never find me.

Inhale for four counts. Hold it for four counts. Exhale for four counts. Hold it for four counts. Start over again.

My captor starts walking again. He changes directions a few times, disorienting me. The building we're in must be large because we walk for quite a while until we stop.

We abruptly begin to descend.

When the elevator lurches downward with a loud creak, I suck in a startled breath.

"Rule number two: be silent unless you're told to speak."

I bite my lower lip and swallow the scream clawing its way up my throat.

When the elevator stops, the air is warm and stale. I smell cigarette smoke and the low drone of a radio tuned to a talk channel. There's a burst of electronic noise, then a voice crackles over a ham radio.

The voice doesn't speak in English, so I can't understand what it says.

I'm flipped upright and deposited onto a hard metal chair. The hood vanishes. I blink into blinding white lights directly in front of me. Beneath my feet, the floor is dirt.

From beyond the lights, a man says in English, "State your name for the camera."

We're doing this already? They're not wasting any time.

I moisten my dry lips. Breathe slowly. Sit up straighter in the chair. "Juliet Moretti."

"Louder."

"Juliet Moretti."

"State your date of birth and birthplace."

He's totally dispassionate. Emotionless. This is only a job for him. I'm nothing more than a means to an end. He probably doesn't even see me as human.

Behind my back, my hands shake so badly I can't curl them to fists.

"January twenty-eighth, nineteen-ninety-five. New York Presbyterian Hospital, Manhattan."

"State your mother's maiden name and the name of your favorite childhood pet."

I have to use the toilet. My bladder is so full it feels like it will burst. "Elizabeth Bushnell. Pippi Longstocking."

The blinding white lights shift to reveal the shadow of a man behind the video camera. The camera is on a tripod. Three more men stand to one side, silently observing. I can't see their faces, but I feel their eyes on me. I feel their focus.

One of them has a short leather whip in his hand.

I start to hyperventilate. Breathing in squares does nothing to help.

Killian. I'm so sorry. I was an idiot. I was a fool.

If I could see him right now, I'd tell him that none of it

matters. His secrets, his past, his whole life—I don't care. All I care about is how I feel when he looks into my eyes.

All I care about is him.

No matter who. No matter what.

Just him.

"Say hello to your father, Juliet."

My eyes are full of water. I blink rapidly to clear them. My pulse is like the roar of the ocean in my ears. I whisper hoarsely, "*Addio, papa.*"

Addio is the formal way in Italian of saying goodbye to someone you believe you'll never see again. It's what I was trained to say in this situation if I felt that the odds of my survival weren't good. A code to let my rescuers know they needed to hurry.

It's what I said to my mother's closed casket the day they lowered her into the ground.

All the little pieces of her they could scrape together.

The man behind the camera steps forward. His head is shaved. He's wearing all black. A skull tattoo covers his Adam's apple.

He puts a hand on my shoulder and shoves.

I crash backward. My head hits the floor with a horrible dull *thud.* I gasp in pain, instinctively rolling to my side, but the man grabs my tied ankles and whips a plastic cable tie around them, binding my feet to one leg of the chair.

I lie on my back with my feet in the air staring up into darkness, panting, convinced I'm about to die.

But death isn't what they've got planned for me. At least not yet.

For now, it's a little light torture.

I hear the *zizz* of the whip cutting through the air a split second before it hits my flesh. The tender, unprotected flesh of the sole of my right foot, between the ball and the heel.

The pain is worse than fire. Worse than a hot metal brand

pressed against my skin. It's searing. Stabbing. It goes through me like a spear. I jerk violently, but I don't scream. Not then. Then I still have hope that it might be over quickly.

The man with the whip extinguishes that hope with ruthless efficiency.

As the camera rolls, he lashes the soles of both of my feet over and over again, until my flesh is shredded and bloody and my screams are so loud, they drown out the sound of his laughter.

Sometime later, when I swim up into consciousness through a throbbing red sea of misery, I find myself in a room. A cramped room dug out of the earth with no windows and no doors, and only an empty metal pot for—I assume—a toilet. The ceiling is an iron grate, about twelve feet above me.

Okay, it's not a room. Technically, it's a hole in the ground.

It's a dungeon.

I look around, fighting panic.

On the plus side, there will be no chance of developing a pesky case of Stockholm Syndrome, because unless one of my captors jumps down here with me for a chat and some brain-washing, it looks like I'm going to be in solitary confinement for the foreseeable future.

On the downside…it's a dungeon.

I sit up, surprised to find my hands and ankles unbound. I've still got my clothes on, which is another plus. But judging by the state of my feet, I won't be able to walk for a while, much less run away.

Not that it matters in any case, because there's no way out of here unless someone lowers a ladder.

I peer up at the bars of the grate, wondering if they've sent the video to my father yet.

Then I decide I have to pee.

I discover quickly that being unable to walk is a big hindrance to going to the bathroom. Or using a pee pot, as it were.

When I'm done rolling around in the dirt and cursing, I spend several horrified minutes wondering what the hell I'm going to do when I have to go number two. I can't crouch, and there's no toilet paper. Things are going to get ugly, fast.

I get distracted by the sound of shuffling from above.

"Head's up."

It's the one who whipped me.

I sit silently against the wall with my legs folded to one side, staring up at him. I'm careful to keep my expression neutral and not glare. I don't want a follow-up performance of his whipping technique.

He lifts a small square in the grate and lowers a red plastic bucket attached to a rope.

When it comes in contact with the dirt floor of the cell, he jiggles the rope, releasing the bucket. He retracts the rope, closes the grate, and leaves without another word.

I crawl over to the bucket. In it, I find two bottles of water, aspirin, a protein bar, a banana, and a thin wool blanket folded into a square. There's also a pack of baby wipes, a tube of antibiotic ointment, and a pair of white athletic socks.

I'm not stupid or stubborn enough to refuse these gifts. I know I need to keep up my energy, so I scarf down the power bar and the banana. I pop four aspirin and guzzle a bottle of water. Wincing and gritting my teeth, I clean the bottoms of my lacerated feet with the baby wipes, then apply the ointment.

Then I put on the socks and sit back against the wall.

If I thought jail was good for serious thinking, a hole in the ground is a thousand times better. And it all keeps coming back to Killian.

The possibility that I might never see him again is far more agonizing than my feet.

I must fall asleep, because I wake up with a jerk in total darkness. For a moment of sheer, blinding panic, I think I'm dead. But then I smell cigarette smoke and look up.

Someone sits smoking in darkness above me.

I stay silent. He told me not to speak unless spoken to: this could be a test.

After what seems an eternity, he says, "You did good. No crying. No begging. They always cry and beg. Even the men."

It's pitch black, so I feel safe flipping him the bird with both hands while baring my teeth. But I keep my tone mild when I answer.

"Thank you."

His voice drops an octave. "I like the way you scream."

Inhale for four counts. Hold it for four counts. Exhale for four counts. Hold it for four counts. Start over again.

After another long pause, he says, "Your father's a hard man to get a hold of."

Oh shit. My mind goes a million miles an hour, scrambling for anything to offer him. He's clearly telling me they haven't been able to make contact with my father yet. He hasn't seen the video yet.

They don't have their money yet, or whatever it is they're after.

And the longer they can't contact him, the longer I rot in this hole.

"It's August. He's probably on his yacht."

Silence. He smokes, waiting.

"He takes three weeks every August to sail around the islands of Croatia. The name of the yacht is *Penetrator*."

He snorts in derision.

I agree. My father is many things, but he's not a romantic.

I hear a creak above me, like my captor is leaning forward in his chair. If he's even in a chair. Maybe those are the bolts in his neck making the noise.

"Okay. We find this yacht of daddy's, you can come up out of the hole. We find out you told me a lie, we fill up the hole with dirt."

He leaves me alone with only darkness and my own growing fear for company.

For the longest time, I hear nothing. No one comes to tell me anything. I'm so hungry my stomach starts nibbling at itself around the edges. I've finished the other bottle of water, and there's nothing left to eat.

They still don't come. For hours and hours. Maybe days. I have no idea how long I've been in this dark hole, only that no training I had as a child prepared me for this.

For the possibility that I'd be left so utterly alone.

I'll die down here. I'll starve to death. No—first I'll die of dehydration.

And no one will ever find my body. Nobody knows where I am.

Killian. I would give anything to see your face one last time.

That thought is what finally makes me break down and cry.

I lean against the dirt wall with the thin blanket wrapped around my shoulders, shivering like a dog, tears streaming down my face, and let myself sob. I let it all out. All the pain and confusion, all the regret and despair, all the dashed hopes and lost dreams.

I cry for Max and Fin, who'll never know what happened to me. I cry for the life I could've lived, for all the warm summer nights and glorious winter sunrises and dinners with friends I'll miss. For all the years I had ahead of me.

Years I might have spent with a man. Raising a family. Being in love.

Being loved.

I cry until I'm empty. Until I'm as hollow as a shell.

Then I wipe my face on the blanket, blow out a hard breath, and stand. On my heels, because that's the only way I can do it without collapsing from pain. I take one of the empty plastic water bottles and use the uncapped end to start digging footholds into the dirt wall.

Because of all the things I am, a fucking quitter isn't one of them.

I've only been digging for maybe five minutes when an explosion nearby knocks me onto my ass.

There's an abrupt change in the air pressure, followed by a shower of dirt clods raining down onto my head. That explosion is followed quickly by several smaller ones. Then I hear bursts of automatic gunfire and the sound of men screaming. There's more gunfire, closer, then an enraged, unearthly roar, like nothing I've ever heard. It comes again, raising all the hair on my arms.

It's a scream of fury. Of vengeance. The scream of a demon thirsty for blood, its frenzied bellows echoing down the tunnels.

But it's not a demon. It's a man.

It's *my* man, and somehow, he found me. He came for me.

And from the sound of it, he's kicking some serious ass.

My heart takes off like a rocket. I scramble to my knees, craning my neck up toward the grate, toward the flickering orange light and the billowing smoke.

At the top of my lungs, I scream, "*Killian! I'm here!*"

Footsteps pound on dirt. Closer and closer they come, until a figure appears to one side of the grate and skids to a stop, looking down at me.

He looks like something out of a doomsday movie. He's a soldier after the apocalypse, combing the ashes of the world for his lost love.

Clad in a military-style camouflage combat uniform, he's wearing night vision goggles, heavy boots, kneepads, and a black helmet that Darth Vader would approve of. It covers his entire head and face. On his back is a tactical rucksack. The belt around his waist carries a huge knife in a sheath and several sidearms in holders. His chest is covered by a vest that has Velcro pockets stuffed with ammunition cartridges and grenades. Gripped in his gloved hands is an enormous black rifle with an infrared scope on the end.

I can't even see his face because of the helmet, but I know it's him.

I'd know that man anywhere.

I gaze up at him, my heart expanding inside my chest. With a hitch in my voice, I say, "Hi, honey. What took you so long?"

JULES

*K*illian lowers a metal ladder, slides down it like a fireman on a pole, grabs me, throws me over his shoulder, and climbs out of the dungeon with swift, silent efficiency. He doesn't even jostle me on the way up.

I get the feeling he's done this sort of thing before.

When we reach the top, he flips me over into his arms. He carries me through the wreckage of a building, navigating easily around smoking piles of rubble, stepping over bodies like they're planks of wood.

The bald guy with the skull tattoo on his Adam's apple lies on his back with his eyes wide open, a gaping wound in the side of his head where his brains were blown out.

I bury my face in Killian's tactical vest and close my eyes.

He carefully loads me into the back of an SUV and throws a heavy blanket over me. We drive in silence broken only by the sound of the tires spitting gravel when he takes a curve in the country road too fast.

We park in a deserted field. Then there's a helicopter ride.

Killian is the pilot, because of course he would be.

I'm behind the pilot's chair strapped onto a stretcher, wondering how soon is too soon to ask for a shot of tequila.

We land on the roof of a hospital. A team of doctors and nurses sprint out to the helipad to greet us. I'm loaded onto another stretcher and whisked inside.

No one pays any attention to my insistence that I'm fine with the exception of my feet, which might need a Band-Aid or two and a few squirts of Bactine.

Killian runs alongside my stretcher. He's removed the Darth Vader helmet, but is still loaded with weapons. He scares the shit out of everyone we pass in the halls. I gaze up at him, deeply impressed.

And crazier about him than ever.

We burst through the swinging doors of a room so brightly lit my eyes water. A doctor starts shouting instructions at people in scrubs. They scurry around, turning on machines. I'm parked near a wall bristling with medical instruments.

In full badass mode, Killian stands to one side of the doors with his arms folded over his broad chest and his tree trunk legs braced apart, watching all the activity with laser focus.

His jaw is tight. His nostrils are flared. His eyes threaten murder on anyone who so much as glances at him and takes their attention away from me.

"Hey. Gangster."

He turns his mutant laser beam eyes to me.

"Is this a bad time to tell you that I'm in love with you?"

Someone is sticking a needle into my arm, but I'm barely aware of it.

Killian's gaze has turned to fire. It scorches straight through me, the same way it has since the moment we met.

I say, "Because I am. I mean, I have been, but I only realized it recently."

Nurses run back and forth around the bed, hooking me up to various machines and talking to each other in medical shorthand.

I know this is all because of him. All the frenzy of activity and attention. I'm not just another patient.

I'm a patient brought in by the mysterious and powerful Mr. Black.

Obviously, everyone else is as impressed with him as I am.

Actually, the nurses seem impressed, but the doctor looks downright terrified.

I say, "I'm sorry I didn't trust you. You were right: I was scared. I'm not anymore, though. And I promise I'll make it up to you. Just as soon as all these people quit poking me with needles."

Killian unfolds his arms, takes two steps forward, and booms, "Everybody out."

His command rolls through the room like thunder. All the activity comes to a screeching halt.

When he shoots the doctor a threatening look like, *Don't make me have to say it again,* the guy waves his arm in the air, saying briskly, "You heard the man. Everybody out."

He ushers his staff out, letting the doors swing shut behind them.

Then it's only me and my superhero gangster, staring at each other across the cold hospital emergency suite. My heartbeat monitor sounds like a malfunctioning smoke alarm.

I say, "I'm not dying. Just thirsty. I could use a burger, too. Maybe some fries."

He takes a step toward me, his gaze darting all over my body and face. He's searching me for injuries.

"Thank you for arranging all this, but I think I'd rather just go to your bat cave to recuperate, if that's okay with you."

His voice is a low rasp. "You're hurt."

"Nothing that can't be easily fixed."

"You need medical attention."

"I need you."

He takes another hesitant step forward, like he wants to keep away but can't help himself. I can tell by the look in his eyes that he wants nothing more than to rush over and crush his mouth to mine, to throw himself on top of me and kiss me until we're both breathless, but he thinks he'll injure me. He thinks I'm too fragile for that right now.

He doesn't know that the only thing hurting me is the distance between us.

I say crossly, "I'm dehydrated and hungry. The soles of my feet have seen better days. But otherwise I'm fine, and I'm perfectly lucid, and I really, really need to have you touch me right now, before I lose my freaking mind. Like *right* now. So step on it."

It must be the sass that does it. The man can't resist my sass.

He reaches me in a few quick, long strides, leans down, and takes me into his arms.

He holds me so tightly against his chest I have a hard time breathing.

I turn my face to his neck and inhale deeply, sucking in his scent and clinging to him. Or, rather, to something that feels like it could be a grenade.

His voices comes near my ear as a harsh whisper. "I'll never forgive myself."

For not preventing my kidnapping, he means. For being in Prague when he should have been with me. Or maybe for not finding me sooner. Or all of the above.

"Don't be silly, honey. You saved my life. Again. Also, I think you kind of glossed over the more important development since we last saw each other."

He pulls away slightly, staring into my face with dark, burning eyes. I gaze at him, feeling better than I have in years.

He says gruffly, "You're in love with me."

"Completely."

He closes his eyes, draws a breath, licks his lips. When he

275

opens his eyes again, they blaze with so much emotion it takes my breath away.

"And you trust me."

"Implicitly."

"All of which means..." He draws another ragged breath. "You're mine."

I smile. "God help you, but yes. I'm yours. I don't care what you do for a living, what secrets you keep, or anything else. The thing I've been most afraid of my whole life finally happened, and it wasn't half as bad as the thought that I'd never see you again. All I care about is you." I pause, smiling up into his face. "Your sister-in-law is pretty great, too."

He crushes me against his chest again. The hand that cradles my head is trembling.

How I adore it that this big, studly, arrogant badass is such a softie for me.

Then I think of something that hasn't occurred to me yet, and my mind goes blank with terror. "Oh god!"

He breaks away, frantic. "What? What is it?"

"Truvy! Is she okay? She was with me at the police station! The men didn't take her, too—"

"No," he interrupts softly, exhaling in relief. "She's fine."

"One minute I was walking right behind her, the next..."

"I know, lass. I know everything that's happened from then til now."

I study his face. "How do you know?"

"I'm me."

He says it without a trace of sarcasm. Then he's kissing me, tenderly holding my face between his huge, rough hands. Breathing erratically, he kisses my cheeks and my neck and my mouth, every press of his lips possessive and loving.

I laugh softly, closing my eyes, falling deeper into him with every beat of my heart.

~

Before he reluctantly agrees to take me home, Killian insists I allow the doctor to examine me.

He does, looking like he thinks he'll be executed by firing squad if he makes a mistake.

I feel a little bad for him, but then we're leaving, and I can think of nothing else but getting into a hot bath and getting into bed.

Killian's bed. Where, if I get my way, I will never leave.

The doctor cleaned and bandaged my feet so they're in much better shape than they were, but Killian insists on carrying me out of the hospital himself. Apparently, a wheelchair is out of the question.

He doesn't let me sit in front of the SUV with him, either. He bundles me across the back seat, tucking a blanket all around me with fierce concentration.

I don't mention that it's probably safer for me up front, what with the seat belts and all, because I sense he's holding onto his calm by a thread.

We drive in the middle of a caravan of what seems like a hundred black SUVs until we reach the skyscraper he calls his home. When we pull in front of the elevators in the parking garage, there must be fifty armed men lined up along either side. He leaves the car running, runs around to my side, and gently picks me up again.

On the ride up to the penthouse, he's silent. I don't know what's brewing in his head, and I don't ask. I sense a deep, simmering rage inside him.

I get the feeling those bodies he left behind when he rescued me aren't going to be nearly enough to slake his fury.

I don't think he'll stop taking retribution until the corpses are piled so high they block out the sun.

The first thing he does when we get inside the penthouse is

head straight for the bedroom. He sets me carefully on the bed, props my head up on pillows, and tells me he'll be right back. He returns quickly with a big bottle of water and a plate of food.

Fruit, potato chips, and a tuna fish sandwich.

Seeing that tuna fish sandwich makes me tear up.

While I stuff my face, he disappears into the master bathroom. I hear the sound of running water. I think he's taking a shower, but he returns fully dressed.

"Bath?"

I groan in anticipation. "Yes, please."

He nods and drags a hand through his hair. I watch in fascination as he removes his tactical vest, knee pads, boots, socks, and the utility belt of death. He pulls the long-sleeve camouflage shirt over his head and discards it. Beneath it is a bulletproof vest strapped over an olive drab T-shirt, both of which he removes as well.

Then he's standing bare chested in front of me wearing only a pair of camouflage tactical pants. The kind with all the pockets for stashing knives, radios, scalps, and whatnot.

In a low voice, he says, "I can't talk about it yet. Not just yet. I'm too…" He shakes his head, looking away and swallowing. "But you have my word I'll tell you everything. No more secrets."

Who he is, he means.

What he is.

I say softly, "Okay. Whenever you're ready. I trust you."

He cuts his eyes back to me, and now they're burning. He growls, "I could hear you tell me that every day for the rest of my life."

My heart is doing something strange. Some kind of weird tango, swinging wildly around underneath my ribcage. But I try to keep the mood light. We've had enough drama to last us a while.

"If you play your cards right, gangster, you just might."

For the first time since he pulled me out of that hole, a flicker of light shines in his eyes. A corner of his mouth tugs up, but fails to convince the rest of his mouth to smile.

He carries me into the bathroom, sits me on the closed toilet lid, and helps me undress. Then he lowers me carefully into the hot water, gently scolding me to keep my bandaged feet up on the edge of the tub so they stay dry.

I just smile at him.

I smile as he washes my skin and my hair, smile as he concentrates on rinsing all the suds off me, smile as he lifts me to the edge of the tub and dries me off with a big, fluffy towel.

For a change of pace, I yawn as he carries me back to bed.

He pulls the covers over me and kisses my forehead. "Do you need anything?"

"Not right now. But when I wake up, watch out. You should probably start stretching." I yawn again, fatigue starting to over-whelm me. I'm tired down to the marrow of my bones.

"Promises, promises," he whispers, brushing his lips over my temple.

He sits on the edge of the bed, caressing my hair, until I'm drifting fast into the arms of sleep. Just as I'm about to tumble over a cliff into darkness, he lies down beside me, pulls me back against his chest, kisses the nape of my neck, and sighs.

I mumble, "You okay?"

"Just thinking about your father."

"While you're spooning me? That's vaguely disturbing."

"I'll have to go see him soon."

"Why?"

"To ask him permission to marry you."

"Ha. Good one."

I smile and burrow into the pillow, knowing I'm already deep asleep and dreaming.

KILLIAN

"What's past is prologue."

It's a famous quote from *The Tempest* by Shakespeare. People often incorrectly think it means the past predicts the future, that what's to come has already been decided. But the full quote says the opposite: "Whereof what's past is prologue; what to come, in yours and my discharge."

In other words, we write our own destinies. The past is simply what comes before the first act.

Watching Juliet sleep, I realize that my entire life leading up to this moment has been prologue.

I've been waiting for the first act to begin.

I had to find her before I could really start living.

Careful not to disturb her, I rise from the bed and go into the kitchen. I pour myself three fingers of scotch. Then I call Liam.

He answers after only one ring, his voice tense with worry. "Brother. Talk to me."

"It's done. She's safe."

His exhalation is heavy and filled with relief. "Injuries?"

A fleeting smile crosses my lips. "Nothing that stopped her from bossing me around the minute she laid eyes on me."

He scoffs. "Because you would never do such a thing."

One of the many reasons we're a perfect match.

I drink more of my scotch. We sit for a moment in silence until he speaks again, his voice low. "I owe you an apology."

"I know what you're about to say. Don't say it."

"No, it has to be said. I was the one who let them get away."

"You sank thirty rounds into that car."

"I should've gone inside with Tru."

"You had no reason to. It was a police station, for fuck's sake. It doesn't get much safer than that. It shows how desperate they were that they decided to take her there."

After a short pause, he says miserably, "I feel responsible."

"Your first responsibility was ensuring your wife's safety. Your *pregnant* wife's safety. Which you did. You put her into the SUV and locked her in. Then you emptied three clips into a car speeding away from you, without a single bullet penetrating the trunk." I pause for effect. "Where Juliet was."

When he doesn't say anything, I add, "My woman, my responsibility. If I hadn't been in Prague—"

"Hundreds of people would be dead. Who else would've stopped Alfassi from setting off that bomb in the mosque?"

I swallow the scotch, enjoying the burn as it works its way down my throat. Then I pour myself another three fingers, because I need it. "I've been meaning to ask you: how's retirement?"

He chuckles. "Getting tired of heading an international criminal empire *and* being an international superspy, are you? Feeling a tad overbooked?"

I say drily, "It does have its challenges."

"So quit."

"You say that like it's a possibility."

"You can't save the entire world, brother. Especially now."

Because of Juliet, he means. Because my priorities have shifted.

When I remain silent, he suggests, "Or pick one. Ditch the gangster gig."

"Right. As if there's a succession plan if I retire from your former job."

"You know what they say: nature abhors a vacuum. Someone would be there to step in. What about Declan? He'd do a credible job. We could kill you off in some kind of fantastic fiery explosion and let him take the reins."

"Declan's strictly back office. He hates the spotlight."

"How about Diego? You said he was doing well for you. And he's ambitious enough, I'd guess."

"You're suggesting the Irish mafia be run by a Latino kid? How confusing for the competition."

"He's not a kid, brother. You're just old."

"I'm only older than you by two minutes. So If I'm old, that means you are, too."

He ignores that bit of logic. "And the Irish have always been more inclusive than the Italians. It's not so much about pure blood as it is about getting results. By the way, I still can't believe you bought his mother a house."

"I had to bribe him somehow into keeping his mouth shut that there are two of us."

Liam pauses. "Or you thought it was hilarious how he kept trying to kill you because he thought you were me."

"I admit it was highly entertaining. He still asks about your wife, by the way."

Liam makes a sound like a bear's growl. "Will you please find him a girlfriend so he can bury that torch?"

"I'm sure he does just fine with the ladies on his own. He's got the Latin lover thing down pat. Oh, I've been meaning to ask you—whose genius idea was it to spell your name backward in the Secretary of State's listings of your corporations?"

"Mine. Why?"

"Because it's not exactly an uncrackable code, that's why.

You should really invest in more sophisticated identity obfuscation protocols. Your name should never appear anywhere."

"Oh, please. Who'd ever put that together?"

"Juliet did."

Into his astonished pause, I say, "She did her research before breaking into my diaper warehouse. Sorry—*our* diaper warehouse."

He sounds impressed. "Clever girl."

I smile. "You have no idea. But don't worry, I took care of it. Mail Kcalb no longer exists."

"Thank you." He pauses. "Have you told her yet?"

I exhale slowly, drink more of my scotch. "Not yet."

"Why not?"

"She's sleeping at the moment."

He knows me better than I think he does, because he sees right through that and laughs.

Dropping my voice, I say, "How exactly do you tell the woman you love that you've been a spy since you were recruited out of the military and into MI-6 when you were twenty years old?"

"Exactly like that, idiot."

"Right. Except that's only the beginning, isn't it? That's only scratching the surface. How do I find the right words to explain how I hated working for the government so I went freelance? How I've spent the past two decades killing bad guys all over the world in an attempt to avenge the murders of our entire family and prevent the same thing from happening to others?"

I'm starting to get worked up. Saying this out loud makes it all the more impossible to imagine actually doing.

"How can I tell her that I formed an independent group of a dozen like-minded associates who specialize in espionage, intelligence, geopolitics, guerilla warfare, and advanced spycraft to thwart global terrorism? And that we call ourselves the Thirteen because we couldn't agree on a better name, so now we sound like a boy band?

"How do I tell her all of us are working undercover in some capacity, masquerading as mob kings and corrupt politicians and shady business tycoons, because we know the best way to kill a rat is from inside its own nest? How I've killed hundreds of men alone?"

My voice rises. My heart pounds. Heat crawls up my neck. "And how do I tell her that all this carnage started because a lifetime ago I put a bullet in my own father's brain?"

Liam's tone turns sharply reprimanding. "That was mercy. He was hanging from a tree, hamstrung, and on fire. In agony. *Dying.* He was beyond saving, but you saved him more misery in his final moments. Then you saved me. Used for target practice, shot five times and left for dead, you still somehow crawled into a burning house and saved your brother. I owe you my life.

"Don't get it twisted around, Killian. Eoin McGrath and his gang murdered our family. The only thing we could do was sweep up the ashes."

When I gulp the dregs of the scotch, my hand shakes. My laugh, when it comes, is cold and dry. "Aye. And now I'm standing here twenty-seven years and three thousand miles later, faced with confessing my bloody history to a woman who thought merely being a mafioso was bad. Christ. She'll run away screaming. And no one would blame her."

We sit in silence for a long time, both of us lost in dark memories. Finally, Liam sighs.

"If she's really the one, brother, she won't run away. She'll love you all the more for what you've been through."

I promised her I'd tell her everything, so I suppose we'll just have to see.

After a beat, he says brightly, "I have an idea."

"Oh no."

"Write her a letter."

"I know you can't see it, but I'm making a face."

"Women love getting letters. It's a thing for them. It's even better than flowers or jewelry."

He sounds very sure, but I hesitate. "Really?"

"Aye. Really."

"Would Ryan Reynolds write a woman a letter?"

"Absolutely."

"Then I'm definitely not fucking doing it."

He sighs. "Christ, you're such an arse."

"On that note, I'm hanging up. I've got an important phone call to make."

He sounds insulted. "Who's more important than your brother?"

"My future father-in-law."

I really wish we were on a video call so I could get the full effect of his astonishment, because I can almost hear his eyes popping out of his skull.

"Mr. Black. To what do I owe this unexpected honor?"

The voice on the other end of the line sounds exactly like DeNiro in *GoodFellas*. The head of the New York mafia has a Brooklyn accent thicker than stew. The sarcasm is that thick, too.

I cut through the bullshit and get right to it. "Your daughter, Juliet."

Silence.

Then, in an apoplectic roar: "You motherfucking cocksucking son of a ten-dollar whore! It was *you* who was behind her abduction? I'll cut off every fucking thing on your fucking body that can be cut off and choke you to death with my bare hands, you worthless Limey bastard!"

Apparently, the kidnappers made contact with him before I made contact with them.

"I didn't kidnap her. Miro Petrovic did. He's dead now. I killed him."

More silence. Then he says in a low, deadly voice, "What the fuck kind of game are you playing?"

"No games. They demanded to renegotiate narcotrafficking routes that were in conflict with yours, correct?" I don't bother waiting for an answer. He sounds too busy swallowing his tongue in rage, anyway. "You don't have to worry about that conflict anymore. Their organization is in tatters. It'll be a long time before they can recover. All the top brass are dead, in addition to the best of their foot soldiers."

"Oh yeah? How am I supposed to know that? How am I supposed to know this isn't some fucking joke you're trying to play on me?"

"I'm sending you their heads on ice. You'll have them in the morning."

After an astonished pause, he laughs a short, hard laugh. "Put 'em in the mail, did you? They're gonna show up on my doorstep first thing?"

"No. I sent them via a private courier who specializes in this sort of transaction. And they're going to show up on the aft deck of the *Penetrator* at six o'clock your local time. You're ten nautical miles off the coast of Krapanj at the moment, if I'm not mistaken. Which I'm not. I never am. That was just a figure of speech."

When he doesn't say anything, I add, "I'll give you the courier's information. I highly recommend them. I'm sure you'll find they come in quite handy from time to time."

There follows another blistering string of curses. It's long and colorful and revolves primarily around separating my genitals from my body and subjecting them to various unpleasantries.

When he runs out of steam, I say, "The reason I'm calling is that I'm in love with your daughter."

A strange sound comes over the line. A gagging or choking sound. It's very severe. He could be having a heart attack.

"Sorry—back up. I neglected to mention that I was the one who saved her from the Serbians. They had her in a hole in the ground underneath an abandoned barn in the middle of the Massachusetts countryside. But obviously I wasn't going to let that stand, considering she's going to be my wife."

He sputters, "Y-you…you f-fucking…"

"I know. But if Russia and the United States can make it through the cold war, you and I should be able to work something out."

To someone in the background, he shouts, "This fucking guy! Can you believe this fucking guy?"

He comes back on the line, seething. "Listen, numbnuts. I don't like crank calls, I don't put up with assholes, and I sure as hell don't allow the head of the Irish mafia to disrespect my family with this garbage you're talking. *Consider yourself dead!*"

"That would be inconvenient, since I was hoping we could meet face-to-face sometime in the next few days. I want to do you the respect of asking for your daughter's hand in person."

More silence. More strange sounds. Plus some gasping.

I don't think I'm particularly good for his health.

"Not that she needs your permission, obviously, but I'm old-fashioned. And perhaps we can also come to some agreement about what kind of contact you'll have with your grandchildren. To be honest, it doesn't sound like Juliet wants anything to do with you, but maybe I could convince her to let me send along a picture of our kids every once in a while. I can't promise anything, though, so don't hold me to it."

A loud *thud* comes over the line, followed by a wheeze.

"How does Tuesday at ten in the morning sound? I'll come alone." I chuckle. "I'll have to, considering I'll be parachuting onto the deck of your megayacht."

I hear a weak gurgling and take that as an affirmation. "Great. See you then."

Just to twist the knife a little deeper, I add solemnly, "Dad."

I hang up, feeling pleased with myself. I think that went rather well.

Then, after wrestling with my conscience for a while, I sit down to write a letter.

JULIET

*J*wake up from a dream where I'm riding a unicorn through billowy rainbow clouds to find a folded letter on the pillow beside me.

I'm alone in the room. It's morning. Beyond the penthouse windows, Boston sparkles like a gem.

I sit up, swing my legs over the edge of the mattress, and gingerly place my feet onto the floor. I try my weight on them, supporting myself with a hand on the bed, and discover that the pain is manageable.

The doctor at the hospital probably worked some kind of voodoo magic, knowing Killian would rip off his head on the spot if he didn't.

I stand, hobble into the bathroom, use the toilet, and brush my teeth. With my own purple toothbrush, which has somehow magically appeared in a tumbler by the sink. When I happen to glance into the giant closet in passing, I discover all my clothes are in there, too, hanging alongside miles of identical black Armani suits and crisp white dress shirts.

Apparently, Killian has been busy while I've been asleep. It looks like I've officially moved in. I'd give him a hard time about not asking me if I wanted to or not, but he'd know I was only bluffing.

But if I have any say in the matter, we're redecorating. The Batman didn't have a wife, but if he did, he'd never have gotten away with having the bat cave be so depressing. The place needs some colorful throw pillows and scented candles, at the very least.

I remove one of the white dress shirts from its hanger and put it on. The hem hangs down to my knees. I have to fold the sleeves up over and over just to get them past my wrists. This thing could double as a dress for me.

Then I head back to the bed, sit on the edge of the mattress, and pick up the letter. I unfold it and start to read.

Twenty minutes later, I've reread the letter half a dozen times. I'm sitting in the same spot with tears streaming down my cheeks, sobbing.

Which is how Killian finds me.

He stops short in the bedroom doorway. He's barefoot, dressed in faded jeans and a white T-shirt. His dark hair is unkempt. His eyes are bloodshot. It looks like he hasn't slept in weeks.

But the man is still so gorgeous it takes my breath away.

He shoves his hands into the front pockets of his jeans and looks at his feet. His voice is low and uncharacteristically hesitant. "So. You read it."

Sniffling, I nod. It's about all I can manage.

He glances up at me, examines my expression in silence, then looks down again, drawing a deep breath. "I'm sorry. I know it's…a lot. I wasn't sure…Liam suggested…" He trails off, muttering a curse under his breath. "If you want to leave, I'll understand."

"Leave? Are you kidding me?"

He jerks his head up and stares at me without blinking. It could be hope I see in his eyes, or it could be terror, considering

the combo sob-wail that just left my mouth. It sounded frighten-
ing, even to me.

I try to compose myself a little, but fail. More sob-wails are
forthcoming.

"Killian. My god. This letter." I wave it hysterically around
in the air. "This letter ripped my heart out. It burned my soul
down. It tore me to pieces!"

His dark brows draw slowly together. He waits, looking
confused.

I can barely speak, so I just fling open my arms and keep
sobbing.

He's on me in a flash, taking me into his arms and pressing
me back onto the mattress, giving me his full, delicious weight.
Then he's kissing me all over my wet face.

I throw my arms around his big shoulders and cry into his
neck.

His chuckle is low and husky. "Does this mean you're okay
with being in love with a spy?"

"Yes. Are you okay with being in love with a thief?"

He raises his head and looks at me with warm, shining eyes,
framing my face in his big hands. He says softly, "Aye, lass.
More than okay. It's better than I could've dreamed."

The way he's looking at me makes me burst into a fresh
round of tears.

He rolls over to his back, taking me with him, and holds me
tightly against his body. He rubs a hand slowly up and down my
spine until the wails taper off and I'm only gulping breaths
instead of impersonating a banshee.

Against his shoulder, I whisper, "I can't believe it. All these
years…all the danger…how did you survive?"

"I'm me."

I hear the shrug in his voice and want to pound a fist on his
arrogant chest. Instead, I start weakly laughing.

"That's better." He kisses the top of my head. "For a minute there, I thought I'd have to call my friend at the psych ward at Boston Medical and tell him to bring over a straightjacket."

"I mean, can you blame me?"

His chest expands with his slowly drawn breath. "No. But…"

I lift my head and stare down at him, horrified. "But what? Oh god. What else could you possibly have to tell me?"

"I spoke to your father." He winces at my expression. "That's not the worst part."

I say slowly, "What's the worst part?"

"I might have told him I'd send him pictures of our kids. You know. When we have them."

I can feel myself blinking like an owl, but I can't stop it. Maybe we're going to need that straightjacket after all.

Killian says quickly, "Or I could just send him photos I cut out of a magazine. He won't know the difference." He pauses. "Sorry, are you going to say anything soon?"

"I'm still processing the kids part."

He gently brushes the hair off my face. "I'd like a big family," he murmurs. "But if you don't want kids, that's okay, too. I want you more than I want children. I want you more than anything."

I feel a sob working its way up my throat. I have to swallow several times to choke it down. I drop my head onto his chest and listen to the slow, steady beat of his beautiful heart.

He says, "I'm meeting with him Tuesday at ten o'clock."

I squeeze my eyes shut, not sure if I should laugh or start crying again. "This just keeps getting better and better."

"I'm telling you because I don't want there to be any lies between us. By omission or otherwise."

"I feel like a white lie or two would be okay. Like if I say, 'Does my ass look fat in these jeans?' you should say, 'No. Your ass always looks amazing.' Even if my ass looks like an elephant's backside."

"Your ass *would* look amazing, even if it was the size of an elephant's backside."

"You're only saying that because you're afraid I'm about to poke out your eyeballs for meeting with my father."

When he chuckles, I lift my head and stare at him. "It's not necessary. Plus, it's dangerous. He'll try to put a bullet in your chest the second he sets eyes on you."

"Aye. No doubt of that. But I've got a few things on the agenda besides asking for your hand in marriage."

When I lift my brows, he says, "Like how he shouldn't try to expand his operations into Boston when I retire, or I'll give my contacts at the FBI enough evidence of his smuggling, racketeering, and drug trafficking activities to send him to prison for life."

I shove myself up onto my palms and lock my elbows, staring down at him in shock. He misinterprets my expression.

"I know. I'm conflicted about it. He really should be behind bars, but he's going to be family. It feels weird that I'd be the one to put him away. How can we tell the kids that dad ratted out grandpa?"

This entire conversation is making my head spin. "That's not what I'm freaking out about."

"What are you freaking out about?"

I say deliberately, *"Retire?"*

"From the gangster business," he says, nodding. "I don't think I'll have time for it anymore, considering I'm taking on some new responsibilities. Looking after you is a full-time job." He gives me a squeeze, smiling. "You do have a tendency to get into trouble."

I give up.

I collapse onto his chest. He rolls me to my back, throws a leg over both of mine, and kisses me deeply, his hand around my throat so he can feel my pulse go haywire.

When we come up for air, I whisper, "You're impossible."

"If 'impossible' is code for 'amazing,' I agree."

"It's not code for amazing. Please kiss me again before you say something that pisses me off."

He chuckles. "I see a lot of kissing in my future."

I pull his head down, laughing softly against his lips. "One can only hope."

We kiss again, this time even more deeply. When I start to squirm impatiently beneath him, he knows what I want. He murmurs, "You're hurt, love."

Love. I will never, ever get tired of hearing him call me that.

But I can't tell him that, because his head is far too big already.

Tugging at the hem of his T-shirt, I grouse, "I'm not the only one about to be hurt here. If you're not naked in five seconds, I'm liable to do something drastic."

He pretends to be shocked. "You? Drastic? Never."

"C'mon. Off with all of it. Hurry."

He fights himself for about two seconds, then gives in with a grin. He rises to his knees, pulls his T-shirt over his head and tosses it away, and yanks open the fly on his jeans.

Gazing at his beautiful tattooed bare chest and abs, I sigh happily. I'm sure I've got little sparkly red hearts for eyes.

He says in a husky voice, "Ah, lass. You're so goddamn beautiful."

"You're only saying that because I'm ogling your muscles."

"Aye." He chuckles again. "It's honestly one of my favorite things."

Staring into my eyes, he slides his palms up my thighs, bunching his white dress shirt up until it's crumpled around my waist. He looks down at me, exposed underneath him, and licks his lips.

"All right then, little thief. What's it to be first? My tongue or my cock?"

Lord. Dear lord. Chris Hemsworth is staring with naked lust at my body.

I whisper, "Either. But no accent. I just want you, honey. Only you. Forever."

Killian's gaze flashes back up to mine. His eyes are dark and heated. He executes some kind of Ninja moves to get out of his jeans and briefs with lightning-fast speed, rips open the buttons on the dress shirt so my breasts are exposed, then lowers himself between my spread thighs.

When I laugh, he says, "What?"

"You're going to need to buy me a sewing machine with all the buttons that get torn off around here."

"Anything you want," he says softly, pushing between my legs. He slides deep inside me as I arch, gasping. He whispers, "Anything you ever want, all you have to do is tell me."

He fits his mouth to mine and starts to thrust into me. I wrap my legs around his waist and rock my hips, matching his pace. It's slow and steady, building, just like the pressure building inside my chest.

No one ever told me it could be like this. No one ever says that falling is the wrong word for what happens when you're in love.

I'm not falling. I'm flying. I'm soaring. I'm up in the rainbow clouds on the back of my unicorn pony, shooting far into the brilliant blue sky.

When Killian groans, shuddering, I whisper, "Is this a bad time to tell you that just because you're retiring doesn't mean I want to? There are so many more bad guys on our list. Fin and Max would be really disappointed if I wanted to break up the band, if you know what I mean."

He stares down at me in disbelief. "Aye, it's a bad time!"

I make a zipper motion over my lips. "Got it. Sorry. Proceed."

He stares at me for a moment longer, then dissolves into laughter, dropping his forehead to my chest. His whole body shakes.

After a moment, I grumble, "It's not *that* funny."

He rolls over, keeping his hands on my hips and his hard cock buried deep inside me. Smiling his signature hot, smug smile, he presses his thumb to my clit.

"Be quiet, woman," he commands. "And ride me."

I smile down at him, for once grateful that he's so bossy.

My beautiful, bossy, dominant gangster, who turned out to be something so much more.

Not who but what, indeed.

EPILOGUE

*wo months later*

"Come away from the window. You've been standing there for almost an hour."

"I want to see them as soon as they drive up."

Chuckling, Killian wraps his arms around my waist and kisses the side of my neck. "You just can't wait to meet that baby, can you?"

Peering out the big living room window of *Estancia Los Dos Hermanos*, Liam and Tru's ranch in the countryside near Buenos Aires, I'm all nervous excitement. I don't know exactly why, because I'm not one of those girls who go gaga over babies. Maybe I'm getting soft in my old age.

Or maybe it's because Tru and Liam gave little Maribel the middle name Elizabeth. The first name after Tru's mother, the middle name after mine.

When Tru told me that's what they wanted to do and asked if it was okay with me, I ugly cried. I can't think of anything sweeter or more thoughtful than that. But that's Tru in a nutshell: sweet and thoughtful.

When she's not being feisty, that is. She comes off as reserved and ladylike at first, but she can give me a run for my money in the sass department, that's for sure.

A black limo crests the hill of the long gravel driveway and drives toward the house.

"Oh! Here they come!" I jump a little, clapping.

Killian gives me a squeeze. "C'mon. Let's meet them on the porch."

He takes me by the hand and leads me to the front door. When I run out onto the porch in front of him, he laughs. I stand on the top step, waving madly at the approaching limo. He stands beside me, slings an arm around my shoulders, and kisses me on top of my head.

He loves it that Tru and I have grown so close. In the three weeks we've been staying with them, Tru and I have been inseparable. She's the only pregnant girlfriend I've ever had. I bombarded her with questions as her due date grew nearer.

Not that I'm ready for my own babies yet. I've still got sticky fingers. As soon as Killian and I get back to Boston, the girls and I are going to start planning our next job.

With the help of Mr. Superspy, maybe we'll even have a backup plan for if something goes wrong.

When something goes wrong. Let's be realistic.

The limo pulls to a stop. Liam bounds out one of the back doors, grinning like a lunatic. He rounds the trunk and pulls open the other back door. Leaning inside, he gathers Tru into his arms and walks toward us.

He's carrying her, and she's carrying the baby. A tiny bundle of pink blankets with a pink knitted hat and a pink face scrunched into a fierce scowl.

Killian snorts. "Looks like little Maribel takes after her daddy."

I whisper, "Oh, stop! She was recently squeezed out of an opening that's normally the size of a dime. She probably has a headache, the poor thing."

Then they're on the porch with us and everyone's smiling. Not the baby, though. She looks like she thinks this is a bunch of shit.

"You guys, she's so beautiful!"

Tru smiles at me. She looks tired, but happy. Very, very happy. "Isn't she, though? I know I'm partial, but I think she's the prettiest thing I've ever seen."

Gazing down at his wife, Liam says softly, "Next to her mother."

Killian pounds Liam on the back. "Congratulations, brother."

"Thank you." They grin at each other. I jump a little and clap again, because if there's any time to be ridiculous, it's now.

The sound of my clapping makes Maribel open her eyes. She looks right at me, her focus startling for such a tiny little thing. The color of her eyes is startling, too. It's a pale, clear shade of sea glass green, just like Tru's.

She has Tru's rosebud lips, also. And they've pursed into a small, disapproving pink pucker as she stares at me. I can almost hear her telling me that if I make that noise again, I'll get a smack.

I put my hand over my mouth and start laughing.

"What?" says Liam.

"This is a terrible thing to say, but I think Maribel wants to clobber me."

"Oh, for sure," says Tru, nodding. "You should've seen her at the hospital. She came out swinging. She absolutely terrorized the doctor. I think she gave him a black eye."

Liam says, "Two days old and she hasn't cried at all yet, but she definitely lets you know when she's unhappy." Looking proudly down at his daughter, he smiles. "She could melt paint right off the walls with nothing more than a glance."

299

Tru says innocently, "Gee, I wonder where she gets that from?"

I glance at Killian. "It's a family trait, I think."

He grabs me around the waist, grinning, and we all go inside.

"So are you and Killian staying in Boston permanently?"

Tru and I are sitting in the living room having tea. The boys disappeared a few minutes ago into the kitchen, probably for a scotch and some guy talk. The countryside beyond the windows is turning bronze and gold as the sun sets over the distant hills.

"I don't know. He said he was going to retire from the gangster gig, but not when." I shrug, trusting that he'll let me know when he's out. "He might be wrapping up loose ends. I'm sure it's complicated."

"I ask because we'd love it if you moved down here with us."

When I look at her, startled, she smiles. "There's a reason it's called Two Brothers' Ranch. It's just as much Killian's as it is Liam's. They bought it together."

"But this is *your* place. You've been living here. Wouldn't you feel…you know. Crowded?"

She laughs softly, rocking in her chair. Maribel is asleep in her arms. "I grew up with seven sisters and brothers in a house with one bathroom. Four adults and a baby in a ten-thousand square foot hacienda would *not* be crowded."

I think about it. The ranch itself is spectacular. And spacious, like she said.

But I think I'm a city girl at heart.

"We'll see. Thank you for the offer."

Tru smiles. "That's a no. But you have to promise you'll come visit a lot."

Making a small disgruntled noise, Maribel shifts in her arms.

Tru leans closer to her and whispers, "Hush, little bee. Mommy and Auntie Juliet are talking."

Maribel makes a face like she just took a big poop in her diaper.

I drop my face into my hands and laugh, careful to do it silently so the baby doesn't wake up and kick my ass.

Liam strolls into the room, leans down, and kisses Tru on the forehead. He glances at me, smiling. "Your man's asking for you in the kitchen."

"Oh? Does he need help loading the dishwasher? Because he recently tried to tell me how I was doing it all wrong and demonstrate the proper technique, and I almost broke a plate over his head."

Shaking his head, Liam presses his lips together to hold in a laugh.

I rise and head to the kitchen, where I find Killian standing at the sink with a newspaper in his hands. He glances up when I enter and looks at me with guarded eyes, his expression somber.

"What's wrong?" I ask, instantly worried.

Setting the paper on the counter, he holds out an arm. I tuck myself under it and against his big body, wrapping my arms around his waist and staring up into his face.

"Nothing," he murmurs, cupping my jaw in his hand. He sweeps his thumb over my cheekbone. "Everything is about as right as it could be."

"Then why do you have a face like someone died?"

"Someone did die."

My heart skips a beat. "Who?"

"Me."

I blink an unnecessary amount of times. "Is that code for something?"

He turns to the newspaper and slides it across the counter with one finger until it's in front of me. It's the Sunday edition of *The New York Times*.

The headline reads: *"Is This the New Face of the Mafia?"*

Below it is a picture of a handsome young dark-haired man. It's taken from the side as he's getting into a big black SUV. He's looking into the distance with a secretive smile, buttoning his black Armani suit jacket.

"Wait," I say, looking closer. "Is that…?"

"Diego," Killian says, nodding.

"He was the one who brought the roses and necklace to me at work. Your delivery boy."

Killian chuckles. "Not any longer. Read the article."

My heart beating faster, I snatch up the paper and start to read.

Made infamous by movies that glamorized their violent lifestyle, the gangsters of yesteryear are all but extinct. From crackdowns at the federal level to dissent within their ranks leading to a string of murders that wiped out the main bosses, the mafia in America has lost much of its power.

But not all.

The Sicilian mafia, La Cosa Nostra, still operates within the shadows, as does the Irish mob, its main rival in the United States. According to reliable sources, the two fractured groups have recently reached an agreement to join forces to reclaim what they've lost.

And a twenty-seven-year-old Latino man is their new leader.

I read on until the article ends, then look up at Killian. He's watching every nuance of expression that crosses my face.

"It says that the assumed head of the Irish mafia, Liam Black, is rumored to be dead."

"Aye."

"Killed by the assumed head of the Italian mafia, Antonio Moretti."

"Aye."

"Who is also rumored to have died of his injuries during the same gun battle that killed Liam Black."

"Aye."

"So...you and my father killed each other in a shootout. Allegedly."

"Aye. It had to be rumor and conjecture, otherwise there would have to be bodies to identify."

After a moment, I say, "Does my father know he's supposed to be dead?"

"He's the one who suggested it."

After another moment, I say, "I feel like I'm missing some important information here."

"Well, you remember that I said I met with him."

"Yes. You said it was cordial. That he only tried to shoot you three times."

"And that I asked him permission to marry you."

"And he told you to go take a flying leap off the nearest tall building."

"And that I showed him all the evidence I had of his criminal activities and told him I'd give him a choice of going directly to prison or stepping down from his position as capo and retiring from the mobster life."

I wrinkle my forehead. "Step down? No. You left that part out."

"Did I? Hmm."

I push at his chest. "That was on purpose!"

He grins. "I wanted it to be a surprise. Your father said the only way he'd agree to retirement is if he got to kill me. I said I'd be happy to let him shoot me. On paper, you know, not literally. Then we negotiated some more, and we decided the only real way it would work is if we were *both* dead."

"The only way *what* would work?"

"Diego taking over the entire operation. Both his and mine."

I stare at him in disbelief. "And he *agreed* to that?"

When he hesitates, I demand, "What?"

When he makes a face, I groan. "Oh god. Oh no. What did you promise him?"

"That he could call you on your birthday."

"*What?*"

"He misses you. He wants to apologize. He said he has many regrets."

I stare at him. My eyes couldn't blink, even if they wanted to.

"And I mean, if the cost of replacing the head of the New York mafia with someone who's going to be subverting the entire organization is one short yearly phone call—"

"*Yearly?*"

He studies my face. "Is this going well? I can't tell."

I'm about to search for something to smash over his skull, but he sidetracks me by saying, "Because if not, maybe this will help."

He takes the paper from me, flips it a few pages forward, folds it in half, and holds it out.

I snatch it from his hands and look at the headline of the article he gestures to.

"An Anonymous Donor Gifted the Red Cross One Hundred Million Dollars."

My heart stops. Then a line in the article jumps out at me and my heart starts to pound.

An unsigned note included with the donation contained four lines from Romeo and Juliet *by William Shakespeare:*

My bounty is as boundless as the sea,
My love as deep; the more I give to thee
The more I have, for both are infinite.

Killian murmurs, "I know you said one million, but I wanted your engagement gift to be special."

He holds out his hand. In his palm sits a ring.

It's an eternity band composed entirely of diamonds.

The newspaper flutters to the floor. I clap my hands over my mouth. Tears instantly spring into my eyes and begin to slide down my cheeks.

His voice husky, he says, "Since I'm dead, we won't be able to live in Boston anymore. I'm thinking Paris. You and your merry band of thieves can take your operation international."

I sob, looking up at him. His eyes burn with a dark, beautiful fire.

The most beautiful fire I've ever seen.

ACKNOWLEDGMENTS

First off: I swear I don't have anything against man buns. It's only fiction. I like a good top knot just as much as the next girl.

I hope you read the first book in this series, Beautifully Cruel, before picking up this one, because otherwise you were probably confused much of the time. If you'd like more of Killian, you can get it in the Dangerous Beauty series. (That series takes place before this one in time, but isn't related to this one. He's more of a mysterious side character than the main event. Still kicking ass and incinerating panties, though.)

Crossover characters from the Dangerous Beauty series are also in the Bad Habit and Wicked Games series. My reader group on Facebook, Geissinger's Gang, will have strong opinions on the proper reading order of these books. Come join us.

Thank you to all my readers who showed such amazing enthusiasm for Beautifully Cruel and demanded I give Killian his own book. I wasn't going to, but you forced me. I love you for it.

Thank you to Letita Hasser, Social Butterfly PR, and Jenn Watson.

Thank you to my writing buddy, Zoe the rescue cat.

Thank you to Jay for everything. If you'd stop telling me how to properly load the dishwasher, that would be great.

And thank *you*, dear reader. I love you. Take care of yourself, and be kind to others. We're all in this shit show together.

ABOUT THE AUTHOR

J.T. Geissinger is a #1 international and Top Ten Amazon bestselling author of emotionally charged romance and women's fiction. Ranging from funny, feisty romcoms to intense, edgy suspense, her books have sold over seven million copies and been translated into more than twenty languages.

She is a three-time finalist in both contemporary and paranormal romance for the RITA® Award, the highest distinction in romance fiction from the Romance Writers of America®. She is also a recipient of the Prism Award for Best First Book and the Golden Quill Award for Best Paranormal/Urban Fantasy.

She hates selfies, adores cocktail hour, and passionately believes in true love.

Join her reader group, Geissinger's Gang, for sneak peeks at works in progress and access to exclusive giveaways.

Find her on the web at www.jtgeissinger.com

ALSO BY J.T. GEISSINGER

For a full bibliography, visit www.jtgeissinger.com

Queens & Monsters Series

Ruthless Creatures

Carnal Urges

Savage Hearts

Brutal Vows

Dangerous Beauty Series

Dangerous Beauty

Dangerous Desires

Dangerous Games

Slow Burn Series

Burn for You

Melt for You

Ache for You

Bad Habit Series

Sweet As Sin

Make Me Sin

Sin With Me

Hot As Sin

Wicked Games Series

Wicked Beautiful

Wicked Sexy

Wicked Intentions

Printed in Great Britain
by Amazon